I0847564

SANDOR

ROYAL PROTECTORS BOOK 1

KAT MIZERA

Copyright © 2020 by Kat Mizera

All rights reserved.

No part of this book may be reproduced in any form or by any electronic or mechanical means, including information storage and retrieval systems, without written permission from the author, except for the use of brief quotations in a book review.

Editing: Tera Cuskaden, Ashley Martin

Cover Design: Dar Albert, Wicked Smart Designs

Cover Photo: Wander Aguiar

Cover Model: Josh Mario John

❀ Created with Vellum

ALSO BY KAT MIZERA

Las Vegas Sidewinders Series:

Dominic

Cody's Christmas Surprise

Drake

Karl

Anatoli

Zakk

Toli & Tessa

Brock

Vladimir

Royce

Nate

Sidewinders: Ever After

Jared

Dmitri's Christmas Angel

Ian

Inferno Series:

Salvation's Inferno

Temptation's Inferno

Redemption's Inferno

Tropical Inferno (formerly "Tropical Ice")

Romancing Europe Series:

Adonis in Athens

Smitten in Santorini

Lucky in Lugano

Alaska Blizzard Series:

Defending Dani

Holding Hailey

Winning Whitney

Losing Laurel

Saving Sara

Chasing Charli (2020)

The Nowhere Trilogy:

Nowhere Left to Fall

Nowhere Left to Run

Nowhere Left to Hide

Royal Protectors:

Sandor

Xander (2020)

Other Books:

Special Forces: Operation Alpha: Protecting Bobbi (Susan Stoker's Special Forces World)

Special Forces: Operation Alpha: Protecting Delilah (Susan Stoker's Special Forces World)

Brotherhood Protectors: Catching Lana (Elle James's Brotherhood Protectors World)

ACKNOWLEDGMENTS

Special thanks to Amy Briggs, for helping me make Lennox a badass!

1

____

S *andor*

I GLANCED down at my watch for what was probably the hundredth time. We'd been in the General Assembly Room of Parliament for nearly eleven hours and weren't getting anywhere. We should have been on a plane heading to the U.S. hours ago, but we weren't. I hated politics, and though I loved the strides we were making in my country, this wasn't my life. I was a bodyguard, no matter what the royal blood running through my veins said, and having to sit through these sessions was torture.

My phone buzzed and I looked down, trying to hide my amusement at the text from my cousin, the king, who was across the table from me.

Erik: If your distaste was any more visible, you'd have a sign on your forehead.

Sandor: Fuck you. We've been battling the same issue for six hours. Enough already.

Erik: You know, you're right. Please hold.

To my surprise and delight, Erik cleared his throat and raised a hand to get everyone's attention. "Gentlemen—" He paused and looked at the only woman in the room, my sister, who grinned at him. "And Elen. As you know, my wife is nine-months pregnant and about to give birth in the U.S. Her due date was yesterday. I was to be at her side already, yet here we are, arguing the same points we've been arguing for three damn months. We have two options: Continue to argue a point that's holding up everything else, or find a compromise and move on. Education isn't optional, it's not a luxury. The bill isn't for gold-plated desks and a professional baseball stadium. It's for teacher salaries and school buses for the rural areas. It's for digital textbooks, which are efficient for both the environment and our pockets since there are no printing costs. It's for modernizing buildings with heat so our children are safe and warm in the winter. We have—"

"Your Majesty!" Xander Holt came running into the room. He was the head of Erik's personal security team as well as former U.S. Special Forces. "We need to move everyone. Right. Now." He met my gaze and gave me a meaningful nod.

Without hesitation, I leaped over the table, grabbed Erik by the arm, and pulled him toward a back exit. This was something we'd practiced a dozen times in the event of another attack on Parliament.

"Everyone, listen up!" Xander yelled. "Get to the bomb shelter immediately!"

People began to run, and I glanced over my shoulder for Elen, though I didn't stop moving. Xander seemed to be arguing with her and the last thing I saw as I rounded the corner was him throwing her over his shoulder. She was going to be pissed, but I didn't have time to worry about that.

"I'm getting really fucking tired of this," Erik grunted as I typed a code into the security panel and threw open the reinforced steel door that led to a secret tunnel. It wasn't finished and it didn't go very far yet, but if someone set off a bomb, it would protect the king.

"Put me down!" Elen was swatting at Xander, who finally placed her on her feet.

"Then stop fighting me," Xander snapped. "I have a job to do. If you're going to be difficult, talk to the king, but I follow his orders, not yours."

"Fuck you." Elen glared at him and then moved past him to fall into step beside me. "Why does he have to manhandle me?"

"Because he asked you to do something in an emergency and you obviously didn't do it," I replied with a shrug.

"I'm not a child and—"

"Stop it." Erik swung around to look at her, frowning. "Xander's job in an emergency is to protect me. If Sandor is here, like today, then Xander's job is to protect *you*. So knock it off."

Elen looked pissed but she knew this was neither the time nor the place to get into something like this.

We trudged down a set of concrete steps and into the tunnel.

"How far has it extended since we began construction?" Daniil, who'd followed us, asked.

"Only about two thousand feet," I replied. "This is it." We stopped walking and I went to another panel on the wall. Punching in yet another code, I released the latch and opened a compartment containing an arsenal of firearms.

"This is why you're in charge of security," Erik said, grinning at me.

I grinned back, but I was anything but jovial. This was a clusterfuck of epic proportions. Erik had only been in power six months and this was the second attempt on his life. Granted, we didn't know who or what was going on this time, but Xander wouldn't have ushered us down here if there hadn't been a viable threat.

"We need to establish—" I instinctively ducked as an explosion shook us. We all braced for some kind of impact, but the tunnel had been well-built and other than a little shaking, nothing happened.

"Fuck." Erik and I exchanged worried glances.

"Is there a way out of here?" Elen asked after a moment.

I nodded. "Yes, but there hasn't been time to do a test run on the exit."

"So what's the alternative? Sit here and wait for them to find us?"

"For now, I'm going to try to make contact with someone on the outside." I flipped a switch on another panel, this one inside the compartment, and then typed in another code. I pulled out my phone and breathed a sigh of relief when the Wi-Fi came online. I quickly tapped out a text to someone I trusted.

Sandor: Explosion at Parliament. Lion is safe for now. Need exit strategy.

I was gratified to see a response come back within seconds.

Ace: Give me a few minutes to put a plan in motion.

"Okay, I've got a man on the outside looking into things. Let's just hang out until I hear back from him."

"What happened?" Erik turned to Xander.

"I found two guards by the back stairway, dead, shot at point-blank range, and I knew something had to be going down. After the last attack, I wasn't going to wait around to find out what."

"Fuck." I shook my head. "This is the second attack, Erik. Someone on the inside has to be working against you."

"It comes with the territory," he said, leaning against the wall. "There will always be threats against me."

"The people voted for you, and Parliament didn't just vote you in as king, they voted for you to be President of Parliament as well. You have a ninety-three percent approval rating. That's unheard of with a leader of any democratic country."

"The people spent eleven years ruled by a theocratic dictator masquerading as their king," he reminded me needlessly. "They'd be happy with a leprechaun as long as they have food and heat again. I reopened the ports, we've had a modicum of tourism so far this summer, and the farmers are selling to the cities again. It's a start but not enough, so no matter what I do, I'm always going to have enemies."

"Yes, but most monarchs don't have assassination attempts twice in six months," I responded.

"He's right." My brother, Daniil, who had a temporary seat in Parliament and had been with us today, spoke quietly. "I've been busy rebuilding the military but it takes time. The young men aren't anxious to serve, and numbers are small. The troops don't trust the government yet, and when I should be building relationships with other countries, I spend most of my time placating the generals and giving speeches to boost morale at our military bases."

"Where's Jesper?" Erik asked suddenly, looking around. Jesper was a close confidante as well as the newly appointed Minister of Commerce, and he'd been lost in the shuffle when we'd left the General Assembly Room.

"He would have made sure everyone else was safe before worrying about himself," Daniil said quietly.

"Not acceptable." Erik turned to Xander. "I need those closest to me to be a priority."

Xander help up his hands. "I'm not making excuses, sir, but there's only one of me, and you told me Elen was my priority. Jesper was on the other side of the room and I had to make a choice."

Erik let out a huff of frustration and turned to me. "This is why I need you here. We don't have enough people we trust."

I opted not to spar with him about this in front of the others. We went back and forth about where he needed me most, and most recently he'd asked me to take a place in Parliament. It was temporary and had a very specific purpose, but it was a nuisance nonetheless. Especially at times like this when I itched to be in charge of security. Not that Xander had done anything wrong, but as he'd pointed out, he was still just a single person and there was too much going on; it wasn't a job for just one man.

Another explosion jolted us, this one stronger than the last, and I reached for my phone, texting our CIA friend, Ace Ross, again.

Sandor: We've been hit again. Any idea what's going on?

Ace: Get out of the tunnel. I have a ride waiting for you. Old black pickup truck, you're going to have to pile in. Code word is Loco.

"Let's move," I said to Xander. "Ace has a ride waiting."

We moved to another hidden panel and I put in yet another code. Two electronic doors opened and revealed a ladder.

"I'll go first," Xander said. "Is there a pass code for the top?"

I shook my head. "At that point, if we need to use the exit, we need to get out and not worry about codes."

Xander climbed up about twenty-five feet and pushed open the hatch that led to the street. It was strategically placed in an abandoned alley, between two buildings that no longer had any businesses or tenants.

"There's no one here," Xander called back down. He crawled out and since I was already halfway up the ladder, I followed.

"Erik, you come out last. If you don't get the go-ahead from me, you don't come out. You understand?"

He didn't answer, but I knew he would do what I told him to do. As I crawled out after Xander, I looked around in frustration. There wasn't a vehicle anywhere in sight. We were in downtown Hiskale, the capital of Limaj, but in a rundown part of town. We weren't far from Parliament House, but with the state of the country right now, much of the city was still in disarray.

I yanked out my phone and called Ace.

"They had to abort," Ace said as he answered. "They picked up a tail. Hang on, I'm on it."

"We're in the middle of an alley," I said as Daniil joined us on the street and reached out a hand to help Elen. "Do I call for Erik or not?"

"We haven't tested the tunnel to see if it can withstand multiple explosions. Get him out of there. The majority of the people love him; he's safer on the street than underground."

"Shit." I disconnected and called down to Erik. "Come on up."

"I don't like this." Xander looked around worriedly.

"There's a café," I said. "It's still in business. We've known the owners for years. It used to be my father's favorite place. I think they'll hide us if necessary."

Erik came out of the tunnel and glanced at me. "Casey's going to kill me if I don't get there in time."

He wasn't kidding. His wife was going to be pissed if he missed the birth of their child. Unfortunately, there was no help for that now.

2

L*ennox*

IN THE FIVE years I'd been working for Westfield Security, I'd never had a client as high-profile as Casey Hart. Not only was she one of the biggest rock stars in the world, she'd married the king of an eastern European country and was now a queen. She was also nine-months pregnant and extremely irritated that her husband hadn't responded to any of her calls or texts so far today. She was a great lady, but her pacing was wearing me out, and I wasn't even the one who was pregnant.

"Casey, relax already, would you?" My boss, Joe Westfield, gave her a fond smile. "He's probably on his way and going to surprise you by walking in the door any minute now."

She shook her head. "I've got a bad feeling. I can't describe it, but something's wrong."

"Let me get Sandor on..." His voice faded as he looked down at his phone. "Shit. Can we turn on the TV?"

"What's going on?" Casey reached for the remote and turned on the massive television hanging on the wall of the family room in her spacious mansion.

"Put on the BBC station," he told her.

"What the hell..." Her face paled as we watched a building on fire.

"Is that…" My voice trailed off because I knew what we were looking at, and that was where her husband was supposed to be today.

"There have been two explosions at Parliament House," Joe said, typing on his laptop and not looking up.

"Did Erik get out?" Casey asked immediately.

"I don't know, hon. Give me a minute."

"Sonofabitch." She closed her eyes and appeared to be counting to ten.

I didn't know what to do. Usually when I was on security duty for famous people, they kept to themselves and I focused solely on their safety. Casey had invited me into the house and made me feel at home the last few days, but this was supposed to be a temporary thing, until Sandor Gustaffson got back. I'd never met the guy, but he typically ran security for the royal family, both here and in Limaj. He'd been on a special assignment as some kind of Minister of Parliament over there, and Joe had thought adding a woman to the team here in Las Vegas would be a good idea. Especially in the event that Casey went into labor before Sandor got back. He thought it would be easier having a female bodyguard in the room with her, which was fine with me, but nothing appeared to be going according to plan.

Frankly, this household was a little chaotic for my liking. The younger three kids were constantly on the go, there was an adult daughter who didn't have a schedule of any kind, and friends and family were in and out constantly. We had a state-of-the-art alarm system, a security team that guarded the property twenty-four seven, and Joe oversaw everything, but there were so many things that could go wrong in a family like this.

"Two bombs were set off at Parliament House," Joe said quietly. "But Erik got out. Ace just sent me an encrypted message."

"Thank god." Casey sank onto the couch, her face a little pale as she stared up at the TV.

"The tunnel," Joe sighed. "I'm so fucking glad we didn't wait to get it started."

"Construction was a nightmare because it had to be done surreptitiously," Casey said, "but I told Erik it wasn't optional."

"Sandor pressed for it, too," Joe said. "They should be on their way—"

Casey's phone rang and she jumped up. "It's Erik! Babe?" She answered and then quickly left the room.

"This isn't good," I told Joe. "Two attempts on his life in such a short time?"

"I know." He drummed his fingers on his lap. "We don't have a big enough security team for this shit."

"What do you need from me?"

"Exactly what you're doing. Stick close to Casey. Chains is with Luke at his other dad's house, Sasha, Leni, and the twins are here, and everything is quiet for now."

"If things are escalating in Limaj, they could be coming after Casey or the kids next."

"I know." He didn't look happy, but there wasn't much we could do about it right now. "And once Erik comes to town, the danger will be exponentially higher until she gives birth."

"We've got this." I spoke with conviction but glanced back at the TV worriedly. I didn't like what I saw at all.

I'D JUST WOKEN up for the day when I heard a sound in the hallway and then a light tapping on the door of the guest room where I slept.

"Lennox, I think it's time." Casey stood in the doorway in shorts and a T-shirt and didn't look like she'd gotten any sleep.

"Has your water broken?"

"Just now."

"Okay, give me three minutes." I swung my legs over the side of the bed and quickly got dressed. I washed my face, brushed my teeth and pulled my hair back in a ponytail. I put my shoulder holster on under my lightweight blazer, made sure my gun was loaded and that there were an extra couple of clips in the pockets of my pants, and slid my feet into my boots. They were hot as hell to wear this time of year in Vegas, but they gave me the best support if I needed to run, jump or fight.

I found Casey in the kitchen a few minutes later, drinking a cup of coffee.

"Are you supposed to eat when you're in labor?"

She shrugged. "Every doctor, every hospital, every delivery is different. I've had two fairly easy deliveries and my doctor is pretty chill, so I'm going to go with what my body's telling me. Right now, the contractions aren't too bad and not that close together."

"How far apart are they?" I asked.

"About ten minutes."

"Have you talked to your husband?"

"The plane's an hour out and then it'll be at least half an hour before he gets to the hospital from the airport. Maybe longer. Hopefully, I can hang on until then."

"Do you want to call anyone?"

She shook her head. "Sandor was with me both of the other times I gave birth, along with my ex-husbands, so hopefully Erik will get here in time."

"Are you ready to go?"

"I'm going to wake up Sasha, tell her it's time, and then we can go."

"I'll let Joe know what's going on."

She nodded and left the room, and I went to tell Joe we were heading to the hospital. He would stay here with the kids, and the other bodyguard that worked closely with us, Darryl "Chains" Carruthers, would meet us there. Chains didn't actually work for Joe anymore, but he had a relationship with Casey from about a decade ago when he ran security on tour with her, so he helped out whenever the family needed extra security here in Las Vegas.

I'd been in Atlanta the last few months, protecting a movie star shooting a film, so when that job was done, I'd been happy to come home to Vegas to help Joe with protecting Casey and her family. He'd hinted that it might turn into something long-term, which I wasn't sure about, but Joe had been good to me after I'd left the Marines, and I'd do anything for him.

Joe had just gotten out of the shower—we were both early risers—and he looked up when I walked into his room. "Is it time?"

I nodded. "She's ready to go."

"You're good with the route and—"

"Not my first rodeo, Westfield." I gave him a grin and he smiled back. "The plane with the king and the rest of the crew is about an hour out so I'm assuming they'll go right to the hospital?"

"Most likely, yes. I'll check in with Sandor now."

"Okay. I sent Chains a text, and he's leaving for the hospital now."

"All right. Keep in touch."

3

———————

S *andor*

ERIK'S private jet touched down at McCarran International Airport at seven in the morning and we were off the plane within a handful of minutes. He went through a private security checkpoint, utilizing his status as a foreign head of state to get us in and out in just a few minutes, immediately heading for the limousine sent for us by our friend Nick Kingsley, who owned the Charleston Hotel here in Las Vegas. He was also Casey's ex-husband and Erik's current brother-in-law, since Nick was now married to Erik's sister, Skye. We trusted him implicitly, and he'd been gracious enough to send a limo since we needed everyone we trusted either with Casey or the kids.

Joe's name flashed on the screen of my phone and I answered quickly. "We're heading out to the limo now."

"Okay, good. Casey's settled in the birthing suite, and Lennox says everything is quiet for now."

"Lennox?" I asked, frowning. "Chains is supposed to be with Casey."

"We needed more help and I thought a woman would be easier in the delivery room with her. When her last assignment ended and she became available, I got her on board."

"I thought she was one of the people that was going to be working overnights on the perimeter of the house? Dammit, Joe, you know I need to personally vet everyone who gets close to the family."

"Do you not trust me all of a sudden?" he asked. "You tasked me with keeping the family safe while you were gone and that's what I've done. Don't panic because she's in labor. Everything is okay."

I blew out a breath. There was absolutely not supposed to be someone I didn't know with Casey during the delivery, and definitely not a woman. No matter how good she was, she couldn't take on the men Erik's enemies could potentially send.

"You're freaking out and you're not even the one having a kid," Erik said, eyeing me with a smirk once I'd disconnected.

I gave him a look. "You've had two attempts on your life in six months—I think freaking out is warranted. With Casey in labor, she'll be completely vulnerable, and Joe has someone I don't know with her. I don't like it."

"I know Lennox," Xander said quietly. "We served together. She's good people and she's badass. Trust me, Casey's in good hands."

I grunted in response, folding my arms across my chest. When it came to Erik, Casey, and the kids, I didn't trust many people.

"You'll check her out thoroughly now that you're here," Erik said. "Don't worry so much."

"How can you not worry?" I countered.

"Because if I allowed myself to worry, I'd worry all the time, about everything. It's bad enough that my wife and children are in danger now, simply because they're my family, but allowing it to rule my life would be counterproductive."

And this was why he was king and not me. Technically, I'd been next in line after the death of the last king, our uncle, and all of his heirs, but that had never been what I'd wanted. As an official Bodyguard to the Royal Family, a role I'd willingly taken on more than twenty years ago, I'd been tasked with the lifelong protection of my best friend, first cousin, and now king—King Erik Benjamin al-Hassani. My duties had veered way off course twelve years ago when he'd faked his death to protect the woman he loved and their unborn child. Erik hadn't been a king then, and we'd both gone into hiding with new identities, him completely off the grid and me doing exactly what he'd asked of me—protecting his woman and the son no one but a select few of us knew about.

Fast forward twelve years and Erik was now King of Limaj, married to Casey, and about to have their second child together. Erik had given me my choice of duties and I'd chosen to continue to protect Luke, his firstborn, but it was complicated right now. Casey had wanted to give birth here in her hometown of Las Vegas, which was also where we'd lived until she and Erik had reunited last year. Now she split her time between Las Vegas and the eastern European country Erik and I came from, Limaj. Casey had wanted to use the same doctor she'd used for the deliveries of her other children, though, so we'd been here for several months in preparation for that.

The last two times Casey had given birth had been fairly quick, all things considered, but she was thirty-five now, and this was her third pregnancy, so I was trying to be prepared for anything. Well, except for Joe hiring a bodyguard I knew nothing about and a woman to boot, which annoyed me because Joe should have known I wouldn't be okay with it. That's probably why I hadn't been told he'd reassigned her.

DURING MY YEARS living under an assumed name, Joe had trained me as a security agent, which went well with my military and private training as Bodyguard to the Royal Family. Westfield Security had provided me with a new identity and a paycheck, even though I had plenty of my own money, and had given me legitimacy during a tumultuous time in my life. He'd been an indispensable ally to both myself and the royal family, and the handful of guys he'd sent to help protect us over the years, including Xander, had all been stellar human beings as well as kickass bodyguards. I wasn't sure what had come over me and I'd make sure to apologize next time I saw him, but our situation now was more precarious than ever. We couldn't afford any mistakes.

WE GOT to the hospital twenty minutes later and Xander and I ushered Erik in through a back entrance the hospital had provided for us. Xander veered off to go scout out the lobby and perimeter while Erik and I continued up to the birthing suite Casey had reserved. Chains was outside the door and gave us a nod as we approached.

"Morning, mates." He shook our hands. "Sounds like things are getting going in there, so you're just in time."

"I appreciate you looking out for her," Erik said. "Where are the kids?"

"All at the house with Joe and the perimeter security team, everyone on lockdown until the delivery is over."

He nodded. "Thank you."

"You want me here or back at the house?" Chains asked me.

"Here for now. I'll let you know."

We walked into the room and Erik hurried to his wife's side. Her eyes lit up when she saw him, even mid-contraction, and my gaze was immediately drawn to the brunette standing off to the side. She met it without wavering, approaching me with an outstretched hand, and a pair of catlike golden eyes that momentarily transfixed me.

"Lennox Briggs."

I shook her hand. "Thanks for your help while I was away, but you're relieved of duty today. You can check in with—"

"Relieved?" She arched one perfectly rounded eyebrow. "I'm here at Casey's request."

"I'm head of security. What I say goes, over everyone else, including Her Royal Highness, the Queen." When the hell had she become so familiar with the family that she felt comfortable calling Casey by her name?

"*Her Royal Highness* asked me to call her Casey."

Damn, she read me like a book.

"Look—" I began, but was interrupted by Casey's voice.

"Lennox, come meet my husband."

Lennox didn't say a word and merely walked over to where Erik was standing.

"Your Majesty." She held out her hand. "Lennox Briggs."

"It's good to meet you. Joe speaks highly of you."

"And he of you."

"Please call me Erik when we're in private."

"Thank you."

"Sandor, what are you doing over there?" Casey called out. "Come say hello."

"Hey." I walked over and leaned down to hug her. "How are you doing?"

"This little prince or princess is taking their time coming into the world, but it hasn't been too bad yet. Thanks for getting him here on time." She motioned to Erik.

"My pleasure. Well, I'll leave you two to it. I'm taking over security here so I'd like to reassign Lennox."

Casey frowned. "Sandor, she's part of my team now. I'd like her to stay."

"I know you would, but we have a process, and she hasn't gone through it. Unless and until she does, she can't be with us when you—and Erik—are vulnerable."

"Sandor." The look she gave me normally would have made me back down, but not today. Not under these circumstances.

"Sandor, maybe—" Erik began.

"We can't argue about this now. She's already in labor. I'm sorry, Casey, but my job is to protect you and Erik, and I can't do that if I don't know who has my back. If we'd gotten back earlier, or Joe had told me Ms. Briggs had been assigned to you, I could have vetted her. But I haven't, so she can't stay."

I met Erik's gaze firmly. This was what I'd spent the last twenty years doing, and he had to let me do it when we had the most at stake. Even when it made Casey unhappy.

Erik looked annoyed but he nodded. "He's right, babe. I'm sorry, but if he doesn't trust her, we can't have that kind of distraction while you're in labor."

Casey set her jaw and glared at both of us. "I trust her and I'm the one in labor. God dammit, I—oh!" She let out a shriek as another contraction started, and her knuckles turned white as she gripped the sheets.

No one moved as she breathed through the contraction, her face turning a little red and her breath coming faster and faster until she leaned back with a sigh of relief.

"Casey." Lennox spoke quietly once Casey was done. "It's okay. I'll head back to the house and regroup with Joe. Mr. Gustaffson is head of security, and if he's uncomfortable with my presence, I'll go. I'm here to help, not make things difficult."

"You're not the one making things difficult," Casey muttered.

"Casey." Erik leaned over and whispered something in her ear. She narrowed her eyes slightly but then nodded. "I'm sorry, Lennox. We'll see you soon, okay?"

"Of course." Lennox squeezed Casey's shoulder and nodded at Erik. "Your Majesty." She ignored me as she turned and walked out of the room.

When was the last time anyone had gotten under my skin like this? She was spectacularly pissed, which was equal parts annoying and entertaining.

"I'm sorry, Casey," I said, noting how irritated she was.

"This is *your* fault," she said to Erik. "If you hadn't been so determined to pass the education bill before coming home, he would've had time to do whatever he needs to do to vet people. Now I'm the one in labor, not either of you, and he sent away someone I'm comfortable with."

"I'm sorry, love." He blew out a breath before glancing at me. "Give us a minute, please?"

"Absolutely."

I walked out into the hallway and leaned against the wall. That hadn't gone the way I'd wanted it to. The last thing I ever wanted to do was upset Casey or put her and Erik at odds. It was an interesting dynamic because, in a sense, I'd had Casey all to myself for eleven years. Not inappropriately, of course, and she'd even been married to two other men in that time, but I hadn't had to check with either of them when it came to her safety. She and I had dealt with each other directly, and she trusted my judgment. Now that Erik was back in the picture—and I was extremely glad to have him back in both of our lives—it was different.

"Everything okay?" Chains asked me. "Lennox blew out of here like a typhoon. What'd you do to piss her off?"

"I haven't vetted her," was all I said. I didn't understand why I had to keep explaining myself. I was the fucking head of security and my job was to protect everyone. Fuck me for trying to keep them safe.

"Lennox is Joe's number two," Chains said, frowning at me. "She's been with him about five years."

"How come I've never met or heard of her until recently then?" I challenged.

"Joe has handpicked her assignments." Chains paused. "And she stays under the radar." He gave me a look. "Is it because she's a woman?"

I bristled. "Of course not."

Shit, who was I kidding? It was partly because she was a woman and that made me a little ashamed. I wasn't that kind of man. Was I?

"Then what?" Chains wasn't going to let this go.

"I don't know her, and with two attempts on Erik's life in six months, a new face makes me suspicious. I'd be suspicious if she was a man too."

"Fair enough. Talk to Joe. He'll straighten it out."

"Yeah, okay." I turned and walked back into the room. We had a triple line of protection at the hospital. Security posted outside the entrances and in the two stairwells, Chains outside the door, and if, god forbid, someone got past all of them, they'd have to take out both me and Erik, because he was always armed as well. Hopefully, it would never come to that.

4

———————

L*ennox*

I WAS HOT. Full-blown, outrageously pissed off. Sandor Gustaffson was an asshole, and the fact that he was going to be my direct supervisor if I chose to stay on this assignment didn't sit well with me at all. I stormed into the house, calling to Joe. He looked up from his laptop, eyebrows raised.

"Sandor threw you out?"

"This isn't how I work," I said firmly. "Either get whatever stick he has up his ass out, or I'm out."

"Lennox, I told you it might take him a little time to come around."

"He embarrassed me in front of the king and queen and made me look like an incompetent fool. I won't do it, Joe. I don't give a fuck who he is or who he works for. Send me somewhere else."

"Casey and the kids want you here," he said gently. "And so do I. Look, go for a swim and cool off, and I'll talk to Sandor as soon as I get a chance."

"I'm going home," I said. "I just wanted to pack my shit."

"Lennox." He got to his feet and approached me, putting a gentle hand on my shoulder. "Come on, I need one of you to trust me. Sandor's under a lot of pressure, so he's overreacting, but I'll give him your file and we'll have a talk and everything will be okay. This is a great gig for you, something that requires both brain and brawn, but also doesn't put you in the middle of a firefight every day. Trust me. Please?"

I sighed. Joe was like an older, wiser big brother and I trusted him completely, but Sandor had pissed me right the fuck off.

"Fine. I'm going for a swim." The water was one of my happy places, where all the bad things in my life disappeared. I could swim for hours.

BY THE TIME I changed into my suit, put on sunscreen and got outside, the kids were there. Casey and Erik were a blended family, since she had a son with Erik, an adopted daughter who was an adult and in college now, twins with her ex-husband Jayson, and of course the new baby. Erik had been married during the years he and Casey had been apart, and he and his ex had adopted a daughter named Leni, who was here for the summer. Casey's most recent ex, Jayson, had married Erik's ex, Liz, and they lived in Monte Carlo. There were a lot of moving pieces in this family because the kids were close and would all be going back and forth between Las Vegas, Monte Carlo, and Limaj.

It made me shudder just thinking about it, but from what I'd seen so far, the kids were sweet and well-adjusted, moving from situation to situation with ease. And they seemed to really like me, which was odd because I'd never been a fan of kids.

"Hi, Lennox!" Casey and Erik's son, Luke, waved before jumping into the pool and splashing his sisters. The twins, Joss and Jessie, immediately retaliated, splashing him within an inch of his life, all while Leni sat on a lounge chair laughing. Casey's adopted daughter, Sasha, peered at me over her sunglasses.

"Please come sit with me. The amount of giggling happening out here today might kill me."

I smiled and put my towel down on the chair beside her. "No giggling from me," I promised.

"I thought you were staying with my mom for the birth?" Sasha asked curiously.

"With Sandor, Chains, and the perimeter crew, it was overkill. We figured I'd be better served here with you guys since you outnumber Joe five to one."

Sasha chuckled. "Uncle Loco was being overprotective, right?"

I smiled. "Something like that."

I found it hysterical that the kids called Sandor Uncle Loco. It had something to do with an old Star Trek episode and a character named Locutus, but I'd never watched the show so it didn't mean anything to me.

"Come play keep-away with us, Sasha!" Leni called out.

Sasha glanced at me. "I will if you will."

I opened my mouth to protest but then realized I might be out of here tomorrow, and I didn't get to have innocent fun like this very often. "Okay," I said, getting to my feet. "Let's do it."

I PLAYED in the pool with the kids for most of the afternoon, and by the time they were ready to go inside to shower and eat, I was tired, but I opted to enjoy a little time to myself in this gorgeous, massive swimming pool. It was big enough for me to swim laps, which was what I'd come out here to do in the first place, even though I'd enjoyed spending time with the kids.

I dove in, swimming the length of the pool underwater before turning and coming up for air. I could do fifty laps without breaking much of a sweat, so to speak, and I put some effort into it since this would be my only workout today.

When I got to sixty, I slowed down, flipping onto my back and using my legs to propel myself a little more slowly as my heart rate gradually decreased. I always felt better after a swim, and this qualified. I had a membership at a local gym that everyone who worked for Joe used, but they didn't have a pool, so I was relegated to the one at my apartment complex. That meant getting up early, before the rest of the tenants took over. I was an early riser anyway, but I liked to eat and stretch before I did any serious working out so jumping in the pool at six in the morning was a hassle on a day off.

I finally got out of the pool and wrapped myself in a towel. I sat on one of the lounge chairs, squeezing water out of my hair, and noticed a shadow heading in my direction. I glanced up and managed to hide my scowl when I recognized Sandor. I'd just de-stressed and he was probably going to get me all worked up again.

"Good swim?" he asked. "You did a lot of laps."

"It's a good workout on a day when I can't hit the gym," was all I said.

"Not much for the water myself," he replied.

"Shame." I got up and let the towel fall, unwilling to make some phony show of modesty. I was in a one-piece suit that covered everything. If that was a problem for him, I didn't give a shit. "How are Casey and the baby? Everything go well?"

"It's a little boy," he said. "Nine pounds, one ounce, twenty-one inches long. They're both resting now."

"Big baby," I said, gathering my things. "I'm glad they're okay."

"So." He cleared his throat. "I thought perhaps we could talk."

"Sure. You first." I turned as I pulled on my shorts.

"Perhaps you'd like to shower and change and then we can get to know each other."

"I'd prefer to talk now." I dropped into the nearest chair. "What's on your mind?"

It amused me to see that he was uncomfortable. Whether it was because I was in a bathing suit or because I was wet or something else, I had no idea, but he didn't look happy as he sat across from me.

I met his gaze unwaveringly, noting his fine patrician features, full lips and...hazel eyes? Something about the color was off but I couldn't very well lean closer to look at them.

"Joe gave me your file and I'd like you to fill in some blanks for me," he said after we seemed to take an inordinate amount of time sizing each other up.

"Finished college in three years, was in ROTC, spent six years in the Marines, Special Forces, and have been with Joe for five. That makes me thirty-two. I did one tour and multiple missions in the Middle East. I left the military because I was tired of being broke and there was a hell of a lot more money in the private sector. I was also tired of following orders I didn't always believe in. I'm not big on missions with collateral damage, and I decided I'd be happier separating from the military."

"Okay."

"I'm a black belt in jujitsu and do a lot of mixed martial arts, but my specialty is Muay Thai. I'm proficient in pretty much every weapon known to man, from guns to knives to nunchucks." I paused. "Is this a job interview? Because I already have one. If you'd like to meet me at the gym, I'd be happy to kick your ass all over the mat to show you I'm competent, but otherwise, this is kind of a waste of time. I'm sure Joe already told you most of this stuff."

"He did, and yeah, it kind of is a job interview because even though you have a job, Casey wants you to have *this* one, and that only happens if I say so."

"Well, then, by all means, fire away." I'd met a thousand guys like him both in the military and the private sector, so I wasn't impressed, intimidated or amused.

"What happened in Qatar?"

5

____

S *andor*

I HAD to give it to her, she was good. She didn't react at all to my question, merely continued to fix those yellow-gold eyes on me with zero expression on her face. If I'd hoped to catch her off guard, either it hadn't worked or she was an excellent actress.

"My commanding officer's daughter was taken by a human trafficking ring. He went after her and I went after him because there was no way he was going to take them down on his own." She paused, a tiny flicker of vulnerability in her eyes for the first time as she looked away and stared off at nothing. "We tracked them to a billionaire sheikh in Qatar and chased them from Doha to Abu Dhabi. Unfortunately, by the time we got to her, we were a couple of hours too late. She was bleeding out from a botched abortion someone had performed on her after the sheikh got her pregnant, and there wasn't enough time to get her to a hospital. She died in my CO's arms."

"And?"

"And I killed the sonofabitch." She didn't hesitate and the look in her eyes was steely. "He walked in, realized she was dead, and laughed. I snapped and shot that asshole right between the eyes."

"Good for you," I said softly. "I'm sorry for your friend, and his daughter."

"Thank you." She set her jaw and looked at me. "Why did you want to know about that?"

"It's in your service record that you went AWOL but were cleared of all wrongdoing. I wanted to know what made a dedicated Marine go AWOL and Joe wouldn't tell me. So, I asked."

"My CO pulled some strings, told them he ordered me to go, so he was the one who got in trouble, not me. I tried to deny it but he said I'd made the ultimate sacrifice for him, so he would do this for me, because Carly—his daughter—was dead no matter what. We didn't honor her by ruining my life too."

"That was the honorable thing for him to do."

"I guess. He's dead now. Committed suicide in Leavenworth."

"I'm sorry." Shit, this wasn't the story I'd been expecting.

"Anything else?"

"Tell me about your personal life."

"Like?"

"The basics. Do you have a boyfriend? Are you straight? Do you—"

"Joe has all this info in my file," she huffed, shaking her head. "You're trying to bait me to see how much shit I'll put up with. So, let's save a little time. I'll put up with all the shit you have to dish out if it's related to the safety of a client. However, sitting out by the pool, asking questions you already know the answers to, just because you can? Nah. I'm done." She got to her feet.

"Seems to me you have a problem with authority," I said, leaning back in the chair and looking up at her.

"Joe and Casey would beg to differ."

I blew out a frustrated breath. What was it with this woman? I'd never had such a visceral reaction to someone who hadn't actually done anything wrong. "If it was up to me, you'd already be gone, because I don't like your attitude, but for some reason, Casey, Joe, and even Chains seem to think you'd be an excellent addition to the team. You could try to meet me halfway, Lennox."

"I could try to meet *you*?" She laughed. "You started busting my balls the second you got to the hospital, so how about you try to meet *me* halfway and stop acting like working with a woman somehow emasculates you."

I got to my feet and looked down into her golden eyes. "Nothing emasculates me, sweetheart."

"I'm not your sweetheart, but it sure doesn't seem like it."

"I believe you offered to meet me at the gym, so I'd like to take you up on that offer."

"Name the time and place. I can get us mat time at the gym Westfield Security uses, but I'm down if you'd rather do it elsewhere."

I nodded. "That's fine. I've worked out there a few times with Chains and Joe."

"Tomorrow?"

"I can't commit just yet," I replied cautiously. "Casey and the baby are coming home but I don't know what time. Until they're settled here and we have the security schedule set up, I can't make any plans."

"And am I going to be on that schedule or am I packing my shit and going home tonight?"

"Let's see what happens at the gym."

"Works for me." She disappeared into the house and I wanted to punch something. What the fuck had just happened? I'd come out here wanting to talk, and we'd wound up in another pissing contest. I had no idea why we continued to butt heads, but if she wanted to work with us, she was going to have to get used to the fact that I was the boss. Plain and simple.

I WAS UP EARLY after a restless night. I was worried about Casey, Erik, and the baby, worried about the shit going on in Limaj, and still thinking about the brunette with the golden eyes who was making me a little crazy. I didn't know which of us was being more stubborn, but after digging into every part of her life I could find a digital trail for, I had to admit Joe was right. She was clean, had more than enough experience, and was pretty badass for a girl —woman.

Dammit, I had to stop doing that. I'd never thought of myself as sexist, but I was. Even if I'd never admit it to anyone else, I couldn't hide the truth from myself. The fact that she was a woman, and that I hadn't vetted her, bugged the shit out of me, and the only thing different about this from all the other people Joe had sent me was that she was a woman.

She was also beautiful. I preferred brunettes to blondes, in general, and I liked a woman with meat on her bones. Tiny Hollywood-style size zeroes just didn't do it for me. There was nothing wrong with women like that, I'd been with my share, but the women who really turned me on were bigger. I liked some muscle, strong legs, sculpted arms... And Lennox had all of that in spades. Her body was in-fucking-credible and I was going to have to work hard to keep from staring because there wasn't a single reason not to hire her on permanently. I mean, I was willing to let her show me what she had at the gym, because it would be fun to spar with her, but Joe and Chains had already vouched for her, and her record spoke for itself.

I'd been a little surprised about what had happened in Qatar, but I probably would have done the same damn thing. Human traffickers were the scum of the earth, and for a man with that kind of wealth to let a young woman die because he didn't want to take her somewhere to get a safe abortion, well, he'd deserved everything he got. Especially since she'd only become pregnant because he'd raped her. I was sure it had been hard for Lennox, because killing someone one-on-one was a totally different thing than shooting at unknown enemies in a firefight in enemy territory, but the fact that she'd done it showed what she was made of.

The work we did, providing security for the royal family, meant putting our lives on the line every single day. Someone squeamish, or unwilling to die to save Erik or his family, wouldn't cut it. Lennox would be a good fit, no matter how resistant I seemed to be to working with her, and Casey and the kids liked her, which was important.

My phone buzzed and I reached for it. Joe's name flashed on the screen.

Joe: We're ready to bring them home. Decoy SUV is leaving now; Casey and Erik will be in the next one leaving in ten. Everything ready at the house?

I was already up and getting dressed as I typed.

Sandor: I'm ready. I'll wake Lennox as well.

I left my room and padded down the hall to where she'd been sleeping. I knocked quietly, wondering if she was a light sleeper. Five seconds later, she opened the door.

"Casey, Erik, and the baby are on the way. Can you keep an eye on the house while I do a perimeter check?"

"Of course." She was already dressed in cargo pants and a black tank top, but her feet were bare and it looked like she'd been brushing her hair. "Give me two minutes to put my hair up and get some shoes on."

"No problem." I headed out to the garage, checking the alarm system and breakers. We had an extensive system, with two backup generators in two separate locations. Should the power go out and if someone were to breach the perimeter and take out one of the generators, the other would automatically kick in. We'd built a steel reinforced safe room on the ground floor that would withstand a C-4 explosion and multiple grenade blasts. There was a cabinet in the den with bulletproof vests for the whole family and I had an arsenal of firearms in a locked safe in the garage.

The house wasn't nearly as secure as I would have liked, but it was a lot better than it had been six months ago. Hopefully, Casey would agree to move to the palace at least half the year. We were in a difficult situation with the kids, though. There were no schools in Limaj that taught in English, so the kids would have to attend boarding schools outside of the country, and if they were going to be gone anyway, Casey insisted they stay where they were comfortable, which was here. It made sense, but it was a security nightmare.

That was one of many reasons Erik had been so intent on getting the education bill passed. The situation with schools in Limaj was currently a disaster, even for the natives, and he wanted to change that sooner rather than later. He already had plans in motion to build an exclusive private school with an international baccalaureate program, which would cater to the wealthy in that region of the continent, as well as provide a way for all of the children in our extended family to go to school in Limaj. It wouldn't be possible until the public schools were sorted out, though, so that had been his focus. Between Casey's due date and the two attempts on his life, he hadn't been able to get it done, so we were back to square one.

Lennox joined me in the kitchen a minute later as I made a cup of coffee. Her hair was pulled back in a tight ponytail and she looked ready for anything. I probably didn't need to test her beyond our upcoming challenge at the gym, but she was far too sure of herself, and I had to be absolutely positive she'd follow my orders in an emergency.

"I'll need you outside, watching the front gate," I told her as she poured a cup of coffee into a travel mug.

She turned to look at me, her face back to the inscrutable mask she usually wore when we were in the same room together. "You want me to watch the front gate?" She looked like she might say something else, but instead, picked up her coffee mug and walked out the kitchen door, letting it shut behind her.

Oh yeah, she was pissed.

For some reason, that made me smile.

6

———————

L *ennox*

THE SUV CARRYING CASEY, Erik, and the baby arrived about thirty minutes later, Chains pulling it through the front gate about ten minutes after the decoy SUV driven by Xander had arrived. With the family safely inside, I got out my walkie-talkie and gave the all-clear to Sandor. He'd been testing me by putting me out here instead of somewhere I could actually help if something bad went down, but if he wanted to play games, I was good at them. I'd dealt with overbearing, condescending men my entire career so it barely fazed me.

The problem with Sandor was...he was hot. Not just handsome or sexy, but panty-melting, ovary-exploding, heartbreakingly hot. He was tall, six-six to my five-nine, and probably two-fifty, if not more. And almost all of it was muscle. He was covered in tattoos, which was a fantasy of mine, and every time I'd seen him, his dark blond hair had been pulled back in a ponytail. His full beard wasn't my favorite thing, but the rest of him was pretty close to perfection, and every time he looked at me, I wanted to lick his lower lip.

Jesus. I needed to get over this nonsense sooner rather than later. Sex wasn't a big part of my life. I had it on occasion, but it was usually a disappointment, so I was happier using a couple of expensive toys that took care of my needs. Hell, my fingers did a better job than most of the men I'd slept with. Military guys seemed to be big on ego and small on...other things. Not to mention selfish as fuck. I hated to think that way about my brothers-in-arms, but that was my experience so I'd just started shying away from casual hookups. It had been years since my last relationship, and while the sex had been better than some, it had still been disappointing.

Sandor, my gut told me, would not be a selfish lover. Even if he was a love-'em-and-leave-'em kind of guy, he would leave them screaming for more. I knew from Joe he was single and that his whole life had been devoted to protecting King Erik, Queen Casey and Luke, but I wondered how a guy that hot stayed single. He was in his late thirties, thirty-eight or thirty-nine if I remembered correctly, and in fantastic shape. I would've paid good money to see what he looked like without a shirt.

Shit.

What the hell was wrong with me? He was probably another selfish dick, just like the rest of them. I'd given up on men completely, because dating was painful and sex was such a letdown. If I ever gave it another chance, it would have to be with someone really fantastic. Maybe Erik had an older, distant rich cousin who wanted a trophy wife. I'd be down for that.

I almost chuckled at the thought of me being anyone's trophy anything. What the hell was wrong with me? I wasn't a gold-digger, and the last thing I needed was a man to take care of me. I'd been doing a good job of that since I was seventeen, so I sure as fuck wasn't going to stop now.

I got inside and Casey came over to hug me. "I'm so glad you're here," she whispered.

"Well, where is he?" I demanded. "I need to get my yearly baby fix and then I'm good."

"Just once a year?" Casey teased, turning to take the baby from Erik. "Here he is—Prince Levi Maxim al-Hassani."

"Oh my god, he's beautiful." I carefully took the swaddled bundle and rocked him against my chest. I truly had never had baby fever and I was pretty sure I didn't have a biological clock, but I did enjoy the occasional cuddle with a newborn. And this was one of those Gerber babies, not at all shriveled or goofy-looking, like some.

"He's pretty perfect," Casey agreed.

"And holy hell, you look amazing," I told her, looking her up and down. "You barely have any belly left. How do you do that?"

"Good genes?" She laughed. "I stayed in shape through all of my pregnancies, doing as much as my health and the size of my stomach would allow, all three times."

"I don't think babies are in my future, not in my line of work, but I think I'd probably go insane if I couldn't work out for nine whole months."

"Exactly."

We stood there a few minutes, gushing and grinning over the baby before I gave him back to his mother and finally looked up at Sandor. "So, where do you want me today?"

He glanced at Casey and then back at me. "Casey probably wants you inside the house with her. So, for now, the first few days until we get a feel for how overzealous the media is going to be, you're to be in the room with Casey at all times, except when she goes to bed for the night. We'll adjust accordingly, as we get into a new routine now that the baby's here." He turned to Erik. "Is there a new nanny coming?"

Erik shook his head. "Not yet. Marisol said she'd take overnight shifts for the time being. She doesn't have a lot to do now that the kids are older, and you guys will just have to pick up the slack driving them to activities, which will be limited for at least the first week. We want to minimize exposure for now." Marisol was the family's long-time nanny and housekeeper.

"There will be a lot of people coming and going," Casey said. "My mother is on her way over and I'm sure the rest of the family will be in and out constantly this first week, so let's just keep things mellow. We're going to do a small press conference on Friday, to announce the new member to the royal family, but other than that, no fanfare."

"Marisol has enough food in the refrigerator and freezer to feed a whole army," Erik said, "so it's just going to be a matter of defrosting and warming things up. My lovely queen nixed the idea of bringing in a chef, which means we're all on our own."

Casey laughed, nudging him. "Because you hate Marisol's lasagna."

"I never said that," he said, also laughing.

"All right." Sandor looked at me. "You're with Casey. I'm with the kids. Joe and Chains have gone home to sleep since they were up all night at the hospital. Xander, I want you in the control room monitoring the surveillance videos. We need to try to be relaxed because of the kids, but we have to stay diligent."

Everyone scattered and I followed Casey into the family room, where she dropped onto the couch and put her feet up.

"I'm going to do some work," Erik said, placing a kiss on her forehead. "Let me know if you need me?"

"Of course." She smiled up at him.

I took the baby from her and put him in the bouncy chair thing they'd set up and then I sat across from her.

"Do you need anything?" I asked her.

"Just for you to tell me how it went with you and Sandor."

I resisted the urge to roll my eyes, trying to stay professional, though I had a feeling that's not what she wanted from me. "He's a pain in the ass," I said finally. "Condescending and arrogant, but I get it. His job is to keep you and your family safe and that's a lot of pressure."

Casey laughed. "Wow. Politically correct much? This is me. And our relationship can't be that stuffy. So tell me the rest."

"I did." I laughed too. "He's an arrogant ass who thinks I'm not up to the job because I'm a woman. I challenged him to train with me so I can show him what I'm made of, but it's hard for both of us to get away with you in the hospital and now getting settled with the new baby. It'll happen, though."

Casey smiled. "I get the feeling you're going to kick his ass."

"I have a few tricks up my sleeve, but the point isn't to kick his ass, it's to show him I'm the real deal and the fact that I'm a woman doesn't factor into the equation."

"Have you always had to work this hard to prove yourself?" she asked softly.

I nodded. "Oh, yeah. Becoming a Marine and then Special Forces? It was a constant battle, and instead of getting better, it's gotten worse as I've gotten older because I'm thirty-two now, so I must be old and decrepit, and by the way, isn't your biological clock ticking? It's a nuisance, but it's made me tougher, I guess, so that's something."

Casey shook her head. "Believe it or not, it was very similar in the music biz. Being a female guitarist is rare. I mean, there are some exceptions like Joan Jett and Lita Ford, but they're both also lead singers, so that makes a difference. Lzzy Hale is badass, but she's a singer too, so being a guitar player that doesn't sing is pretty unheard of, and I had a lot of pushback in the beginning. Being the daughter of a rock and roll legend helped smooth the way for me, though, so I had it easier than most. When I was forming Pretty Harts, a lot of guys wouldn't play with me because I was the big-name star, and they didn't like it. I own a fucking recording studio and every so often we get a client that would come in and want to talk to 'the boss.' It drives me nuts."

"I used to get really worked up about it, but I've come to realize that all I can do is do what I do. I'm a bodyguard. I'm a trained professional and really good at what I do, so if I have to get in the gym and kick a hot security officer's ass once in a while, I do it because I can."

Casey paused. "You think Sandor is hot?"

Yikes. She was no dummy, and that was a stupid mistake on my part. I'd have to be more careful when I talked to her, because even though we got along well, she was still the boss. "Well, yeah, I mean, look at him. I'd have to be dead not to notice. Pretty boy or not, though, I'm going to kick his ass all over the gym when that happens."

"I don't know how to make it happen," Casey giggled, "but I really need to be there for that."

"Maybe we can arrange it."

We grinned at each other, but then she sobered. "Just do me a favor, though."

"I won't hurt him bad," I teased.

She shook her head. "I know you won't. But never forget what a great guy he is. I mean, the kind of guy who put his life on the line for Luke and me even though he didn't have to. Back then, he barely knew me, but he did it anyway. They don't come any more honorable or loyal than Sandor, and while he's being a little difficult right now, it's because of the stress he's under. He's not a bad guy. Keep that in mind."

"I will. Thank you." She'd given me something to think about, but I'd think later. Maybe in the shower or something. The arrogant ass I knew and the man she was describing weren't the same, and it was hard to reconcile the two.

7

————

S *andor*

With the kids settled, I'd been planning a quiet afternoon of catching up on paperwork, but around three o'clock Erik asked me to meet him in the library. When I arrived, Joe and Chains were there as well and I shut the double French doors behind me as I joined them.

"What's up?" I asked, slightly suspicious because usually I was the one setting up meetings.

"It's time to get serious about a permanent move to Limaj," Erik said, "and now that the baby's here, I have to be diligent about letting the people know that I'm their leader and going to be there for them. Of course, we'll always travel and do some commuting because of the kids and Casey's business interests here in Vegas, but on the outside, we have to create a home."

"All right." I sat in a chair and poured myself a cup of coffee. Something told me I wasn't going to like whatever was coming.

"You are and always will be my right-hand man," Erik said. "But you can't do everything. In the grand scheme of things, I'd like you to be my Chief of Staff, even though I know that's not the role you want."

I shook my head. "No, it's not. I'm not cut out for—"

"Hear me out." Erik interrupted me gently. "I need you to be my right hand, all the time. Day, night, personal and professional, and that's the position that allows for it."

"I understand that, but I'm not cut out to be a glorified assistant."

We stared at each other and Erik sighed. "Chief of Staff is a respected, high-level position that puts you in the middle of everything in my life. If you don't want it, I'm going to offer it to Jesper."

"He's perfect for that," I said gruffly. Jesper had been an ambassador to the U.K. before our crazy cousin, King Anwar, had taken over. Jesper's post had been taken from him and he'd gone underground, working with the rebellion. Now that Erik was in power, he'd made Jesper the temporary Minister of Commerce because we needed trustworthy people in Parliament, but that wasn't his forte and he would make a great Chief of Staff. Especially since he had small children at home and that position would allow him to be at the palace full-time. I felt bad that I hadn't checked on him after the bombing, but we'd been busy and I would have heard if anything had happened to him.

"Here's the thing," Joe spoke up. "I'm selling Westfield Security, and Chains is interested in buying it. Erik needs you to be flexible, which means heading up security isn't a good place for you, but it's perfect for me. I'm thinking of moving to Limaj and taking the job."

"You'd move to Limaj permanently?" I asked in surprise.

Joe leaned back in his chair. "I'm fifty-eight this year. I have no partner, no kids, very little family. I have money and a very specific skill set, which is best utilized working with Erik. I'm a middle-aged gay man with no roots, and it's time for me to set some down. Maybe Limaj is the place to do it."

"Seems like everything is already decided," I said, giving Erik a look.

He smiled at me. "Don't be a baby—you're the person I rely on most. You take care of my family and there isn't a position anywhere more important than that, but at the end of the day, you can't be following Luke and the twins around all day unless there's a specific threat to them. I need you to be flexible, and if you won't take the Chief of Staff position, you still need to be more flexible than the head of security position would allow. You can have any damn title you want, but I need you with me, Casey, or Luke, and that'll change every day so I don't care what we call it."

I nodded. "That's fine with me." I didn't care about titles either, I just didn't want to be tied to an office or have anything that was even remotely administrative.

"If this is all good, I'm going to buy Westfield Security," Chains said in his clipped British accent. "We'll provide security whenever any members of the family are here in Vegas, and of course, in an emergency, I'll be on the first plane. Unfortunately, much as I'd love to get in on the ground floor of security for a country and a government that's rebuilding, I have a life and a family here. My wife would move anywhere if I asked her to, but two of our children have other fathers, so that wouldn't be fair to them. We all agreed this would be our home base and I can't change that plan now."

"Understandable," Erik said. "And also a perfect solution for all of us. Knowing we have you guarding the house, the recording studio, and Sasha, since she won't be moving to Limaj, takes a load off my mind. Now I can focus on what we'll need in Limaj."

"I'll be changing the name to Westfield & Carruthers," Chains said with a grin. "In case anyone was interested."

"Why not Carruthers & Westfield?" Joe asked.

"Because you built up your name and brand, so it would be foolish of me to give that up."

We talked logistics and legalities for a little while and then Joe and Chains both went to do other things, leaving Erik and me alone.

"What's going on with you?" Erik asked after a minute. "And don't say nothing. I know you and you're not yourself. There's a lot going on, but usually you handle everything without batting an eyelash. This feels different."

"It's nothing I can put my finger on," I said slowly. "I spent a decade as someone else, living a completely different life, and now I'm suddenly thrown back into the fold as a member of the royal family while still performing bodyguard duties, taking care of your family, and acclimating to a dozen new changes, sometimes multiple every day. Different homes, cities, countries, continents. I'm sorting it out."

"You know you don't owe me your entire life, right?" he asked after a moment.

"What the fuck are you talking about?" I asked, narrowing my eyes.

"I mean, you gave up eleven years to take care of Casey and Luke, and maybe it's time for you to find yourself a woman and settle down in the suburbs somewhere."

I burst out laughing. "Do you even know me? That's never going to happen."

"You don't want a family? Or at least a woman by your side? Come on, that's not natural, not for men like us, and you know it."

"If it was to happen, sure, but where the hell am I going to find a woman? And with what time? Whether I'm here or in Limaj, my job is seven days a week, sixteen to eighteen hours a day. And even if I did meet someone, when would I see her, much less any kids we have?"

"Which is exactly why I'm offering you the option of getting out, doing your own thing. You could move here and work for Chains, taking individual gigs, so you don't work twenty-four seven. You could live in the house here and keep an eye on Sasha while actually living a little bit. I wouldn't blame you."

"You're a fucking nut job," I said, shaking my head at him. "You really think I'm cut out to settle down in the Las Vegas suburbs working part-time as a bodyguard?"

"I don't know, but I think it's time you thought about the future. In a few years, things are going to settle down and life is going to be more normal. Yes, as a king I'll always have to be diligent about security and such, but once I get the country back on track, Parliament will run things and I'll be more of a figurehead. What are you going to do then?"

"Exactly what I'm doing now," I responded blandly. "Except hopefully with less death threats and explosions."

Erik sighed. "When was the last time you took a vacation?"

I stared at him. I hadn't taken an actual vacation since we'd been in college.

"When was the last time you got laid?"

I scowled. I wasn't even going to answer that because it had been a long time. For me, anyway.

"What about the last time you did something fun?"

"I do fun stuff," I muttered.

"What? Watching Luke's swim meets? They're great, but that's not actual fun."

"Look, I get what you're saying, but I don't know the answer. I do what I do because I have to. Since you gave me my fucking title back, I'm Prince Sandor of Limaj and currently a member of Parliament. I have responsibilities in addition to keeping all of us safe, and I don't have time to think about all that other shit. Like you said, in a few years, things will calm down and maybe I'll find myself a twenty-year-old who'll want to pop out a bunch of babies for me, but for now, it's not in the cards."

"A twenty-year-old?" Erik laughed. "You didn't like 'em that young when you were twenty, and you're going to date them now?"

I shrugged. "I don't know. It's been so long since I've been in a relationship, I have no idea what I would look for in someone serious."

"Well, maybe you should think about it because I see you struggling, and even though you'd never admit it out loud, something is missing in your life."

"Thanks, Dr. Phil," I said wryly. "Can I go now?"

"No, you may not." Erik grinned at me. "I hear there's going to be a challenge happening at the gym in the near future."

"Seriously? This is what you're focused on?"

"Of course not. I focus on work, but then I take breaks to enjoy life, something you should try once in a while. And when I do, I hear things that make me happy."

"It makes you happy that I'm going to test out the skills of your wife's new bodyguard?"

"It does. Because I think she's going to surprise you."

"Maybe, but let's break this down scientifically. Physically, she can't come close to competing with guys like me, Chains, or Xander. Women simply don't have the muscle mass we do, and in my case, I've practically got a foot on her, not to mention a hundred pounds. In a case of life or death, even though I'm physically larger than all of you—Joe, Chains, Xander...would all give me a run for my money. I'm twenty years younger than Joe and six inches taller, but his training and experience would compensate for that. A woman like Lennox, who I'm sure is extremely skilled, simply couldn't compete physically."

"You think she made the Special Forces team because she couldn't compete physically?" He raised his eyebrows.

"I just think in a situation where everything else is equal, and I'm talking about trained assassins, which is something we genuinely have to worry about, she'll be at a disadvantage. It's not personal, it's science."

"I disagree," Erik said quietly. "I don't think Joe would have hired her if he thought she would ever be at a disadvantage."

"Erik, I need you to trust me when it comes to security measures."

"I do. And at the hospital, when we didn't have time to debate things, I took your side. However, we are no longer in an emergency situation, and I think you're wrong about Lennox. Now, if you tell me you found something sketchy in her past, or links to our enemies, or whatever else, that's a different story and I won't hesitate to kick her to the curb. But because she's a woman? That's not like you, and the truth is, with us having female children, I want *more* women on the staff, not less. It's not only more comfortable for them, it sets an excellent example for our people, that we're forward-thinking and ready to join the twenty-first century."

"As long as they pass whatever tests I set up for them," I said testily, "I'm fine with that."

"I think you're a bit of a curmudgeon deep down," Erik chuckled. "And you hate every word I just said."

"I don't hate it, but I worry that it's too much too soon. You know I'm not really sexist, but when it comes to my job, to your safety, I'm a little anal. I'll cop to that."

"It's why we make a good team. If I can get you to relax a little and you can get me to be a little more uptight, we'll be unstoppable."

That was something I agreed with.

8

———

L*ennox*

I'D INITIALLY BEEN a little nervous about this whole challenge I'd issued to Sandor, but now that I was here at the gym, everything else melted away. I was confident in my skills, and though this was technically a training exercise where no one would get hurt, I wasn't going to hold back. Sandor wanted me to fail, to prove that I wasn't as tough as he was, and that was bullshit. I'd been trained by the United States Marines Special fucking Forces and there was no universe where I'd embarrass myself. Could he take me? Sure. But there was every chance I'd take him as well. This wasn't about winning and losing; it was about respect. And I'd earn his today or I was done with this whole assignment.

Joe was annoyed I'd challenged him like this, so he was at the house with Casey and the children, but Xander, Chains, and even Erik were here to cheer us on and get in a good workout to boot. A handful of guys from the local professional hockey team, the Las Vegas Sidewinders, were here as well, since I was a big hockey fan and occasionally worked out with a few of them. Chains was close to them as well because one of the current players was his brother-in-law, and I thought I'd heard another was his wife's ex-husband. I shied away from gossip, so I wasn't sure what the connection was, but a bunch of them were here now and I itched to get started.

Sandor, of course, was late. Another calculated move to keep me off my game, but it wasn't going to work. I did better under pressure because the longer I waited, the calmer I got, and then I would explode with energy when the time was right. I jogged in place, warming up and making sure I'd stretched properly. We didn't always get to stretch before a fight during a mission, but this was training and no one wanted to get hurt.

"Hey." One of the Sidewinders I knew pretty well because he was single and we worked out together during the off-season, was a player named Dax O'Day. He approached me with a grin. "What's the big deal today? Some guy challenge you or something?"

I dropped my voice and gave him a little grin. "My new boss thinks I'm too much of a girl. I'm about to prove him wrong."

Dax grimaced. "Damn, you scare the crap out of me, so yeah, he should watch his ass. Who is it? Do I know him?"

"Sandor," I said.

His mouth opened a little and then he snapped it shut. "Hon, you're badass and all, but he's like, twice your size."

I gazed at him in irritation. "Whose side are you on?"

"Yours. Always." He held up a fist and bumped it with mine.

"Ready to get started?" Sandor came up behind me and I turned.

"Let's do it."

We headed for the mats where a lot of guys practiced mixed martial arts. We had a fucking entourage today, and for a second I let my nerves get the best of me, but then I looked up into Sandor's smug face and remembered why I was here. This wasn't about winning or losing. All I cared about was respect. I'd kicked and clawed my way through the ranks to get it in the Marines and I sure as hell wasn't going to allow some prince from an eastern European country that was barely on the map tell me I didn't have his.

We pulled on our gloves and then, holy fucking hell, he took off his shirt. Just as I'd suspected, his torso was amazing. But if he thought it would distract me, he was dead wrong. Pretty boys were a dime a dozen and meant less than nothing to me when I was working. And technically, I was working.

I was much smaller than him, about eight inches in height and a hundred pounds, but he had no clue what I was capable of. We circled each other like predators, eyes locked, bodies poised for battle. I was in the zone, but his shirtless torso made my mouth water. I unconsciously licked my lips, whether it was in anticipation of the fight or my subconscious imagination going wild, I didn't know. He was both formidable and enticing, which was confusing as hell. On the bright side, his eyes had darkened, watching me intently. If I didn't know better, I would have thought he was just as enthralled as I was with this little battle of wits, and it was a huge fucking turn-on. Unfortunately, I didn't have time to indulge myself in a fantasy today.

As I sized him up, planning my takedown, we continued to circle each other, fight ready, as if we had all the time in the world. His body was hard and toned, and every time he moved, I watched his muscles flex slightly. Damn, he was beautiful, and I had to dig deep to keep myself focused on the task at hand. He finally threw the first fake and I almost breathed a sigh of relief. It was a little jab he probably thought would catch me off guard so he could clobber me with a cross. Typical. I parried his half jab, slapping it out of the way and slipping down low to avoid his cross. Yeah, he was a tough SOB, and I made a split-second decision not to risk letting this drag on.

Fuck him. Hot or not, I had to take him.

I swept his leg, taking him down to the mat, where I knew I could beat him. His grunt told me I'd taken him by surprise, but I wasn't finished. My best bet to end this would be the rear naked choke. I circled his neck with my right arm, his trachea positioned at the crook of my elbow. I grabbed my left bicep with my right hand and put the palm of my left hand against my own shoulder, making it a lot tougher for him to break away. I brought my legs around, planted them inside his and applied pressure. I could render most people unconscious in a few seconds with this move, because of the pressure to the carotid artery, but that wasn't the goal here.

He obviously knew I could do it, too, because I held on to the strong bastard for dear life and he tapped out just as I was about to let go. I jumped back to my feet, meeting his gaze steadily, the hoots and hollers from our friends and others at the gym not penetrating my intense concentration. He was probably going to be pissed, but at least he now knew I wasn't just some *girl*. That I could kick ass and take names. That I'd earned my place on Joe's roster and was someone he could count on to protect the family. At least I hoped so.

To my surprise, he chuckled. "Very nice," he said. "That'll only work once with me, but I appreciate the way your mind operates. Care to go again?"

I shrugged. "I'm always up for a good workout and training, but I'm not going to risk injury because you have something to prove."

He shook his head and held up his hands, palms out. "Not the way I operate. You've proven to be a formidable opponent and we're on the same side. If you want to train with me, I could probably teach you a few things, and apparently there are a few skills I can still learn as well."

"Then let's do it." I lifted my hands, fight ready once again.

. . .

WE SPARRED and drilled for another hour, switching out with Chains, and even Dax joined the fun. It was hard work and a great workout, but enjoyable too. Sandor was fast for a man of his size, with instincts that matched my own and a quick mind. He wasn't a dirty fighter either, though I imagined he could be in a life-or-death situation. Getting into it with Dax was fun too, since he was a professional athlete. He'd asked me out a couple of times, but the timing hadn't been right and now I was glad we were just friends. He was a good guy but life as a professional hockey player kept him on the road a lot, which would never work with my crazy schedule. He'd taken it well and now we hung out on occasion, though I didn't see him much during hockey season.

He was the first to leave, high-fiving me and taking off with one of the guys on the team that I didn't know very well. I grabbed my water bottle and chugged some down, taking a few seconds to cool off a little. Chains and Erik had just left and within a few minutes, it was just Sandor and me.

Great.

Hopefully, he didn't have something stupid to say or I might deck him just because I could. I'd gotten in a handful of good shots today during the workout, but again, hurting each other wasn't the goal and though he could take a hit, what would giving him a black eye or a fat lip prove? That wasn't who I was anyway. When I hit someone, it was either to inflict damage because someone was in danger or just for practice because we were training. You could train hard and increase your skills without hurting each other and Sandor worked that way too.

"How often do you work out?" he asked me, reaching for his own water bottle.

"Usually six days a week, but intensity varies depending on availability, what my work schedule is, and who's around to spar with."

He nodded. "Same."

"On days when I absolutely can't get away, I'll do sit-ups, push-ups, and if possible, I swim laps."

"Never been a fan of swimming as part of my workout, but I also grew up in a country where it's cold eight months of the year."

"Makes sense." I wrapped a towel around my neck and dried off a little since I'd sweat like a lunatic. "Anyway, if there's nothing else, I'm going to take off."

He smiled. "Just FYI, I could've broken free if I really wanted to."

Was this guy for real? I turned to look at him, narrowing my eyes slightly. "Then you should have. I didn't ask you to take it easy on me."

"You had something to prove and I've been an asshole, so I figured I owed you."

"Oh, fuck you." I grabbed my bag and headed to the exit. I didn't have time for his egotistical bullshit and now I was spectacularly pissed. If I didn't get out of here right now, I was going to punch him right in the throat.

9

———————

S *andor*

Uн-oн. I'd gone too far. She was really pissed now and there was no reason for it. Why the hell had I said something specifically to piss her off? She was tough as hell and she'd impressed me, but instead of saying something to that effect, I'd insulted her. Shit. I had to fix this.

"Lennox, wait," I called out, walking in the direction she'd gone.

She stopped but didn't turn around. "What?"

"I apologize. I was trying to bust your balls but it came out wrong." I held up my hands in a placating gesture. "Honestly. I didn't mean it. You're extremely skilled and I only meant to tease you, but I realize we don't know each other well enough for that."

She turned, her eyes meeting mine suspiciously, though she inclined her head. "All right."

"Work out again tomorrow if we can get away?"

"Sure." She walked out without looking back. I'd been trying to bust her balls but she was the one who was a ballbuster. The weird thing was, I kind of liked it.

THE NEXT WEEK was quiet but busy as the family adjusted to the new baby and Erik did his best to spend quality time with everyone while still dealing with everything going on back home. He was being pulled in a bunch of different directions, but having missed Luke's birth because he'd been in hiding then, he hadn't wanted to miss anything this time and the medical care in Limaj couldn't come close to the care Casey would get here in the States had there been any complications with the delivery. However, now that the baby was born, we were both anxious to get back to Hiskale. We had to get the kids settled, though, and that was the biggest problem. Until Erik could get that private school up and running, there was literally nowhere for the kids to attend, short of hiring tutors and bringing them with us, and that wasn't fair to them.

Luke was twelve now and involved in swimming, hockey, and band. The twins took fencing together and while Joss was taking piano and saxophone lessons, Jessie was serious about art and sculpting. Sasha was going to be a junior in college this fall, and poor Leni had been dragged back and forth between Monte Carlo and Las Vegas multiple times in the last year. At some point, something was going to have to give and Erik didn't yet know what it was.

"Uncle Loco?" Luke came padding into the room we now used as a sort of command center, where the surveillance equipment was located, as well as a ton of ammo in case we needed it during an attack on the grounds.

"Hey, buddy." I turned, smiling at him. The kid always made me smile. I'd known him his whole life and he was truly the child I'd probably never have. I loved him as much as I could love anyone and he was the one thing that brought me happiness when things were difficult.

"I'm bored."

"How come?" I cocked my head. "You have a pool, at least a thousand video games, books, computers, music and, most importantly, food. How can you be bored?"

"Because I don't have any friends."

"What happened to all your friends?"

"Their parents aren't willing to let you do background checks, which means I can't go to their houses, and they feel weird coming here because we have armed guards."

I sighed. This was an unexpected complication and there wasn't much I could do about it.

"I'm sorry. You want me to take you somewhere, like the arcade, where you could meet a friend or two? Just me and you?"

He shrugged. "I guess, but no one is around right now and...I don't know." He sank into one of the chairs. "This summer has sucked."

"There's a lot going on."

"And, you know, my real dad is back in my life but I never see him, never spend time with him. I mean, he might as well still be dead."

I winced. It would kill Erik if he knew Luke felt this way.

"You know he's not doing it on purpose, right?"

"I know. But the new baby is getting all the attention and the rest of us are just kind of existing."

"What do you suggest?"

"Can't we go on vacation like a normal family?"

"The baby's only a week old and he can't be around that many germs yet."

"For like six weeks, which means school will have started and then we won't be able to do anything."

"You should be talking to your mom and dad about this."

"I just told you—they're busy."

"I can take you out with a friend or two or three, but other than that, I'm not sure how to help. You want to play air hockey or something?"

His eyes lit up. "Do you have time?"

"I can take half an hour. Let's go." I got to my feet and we went down to the basement. I was going to have to find a way to mention this to Erik and Casey. They didn't have a lot of time, but they'd made a conscious decision to live this life, which meant they had to make sacrifices. And Luke wasn't supposed to be one of the sacrifices.

THE NEXT MORNING, I was up early and stopped by Lennox's room to see if she wanted to go to the gym with me. It was only five thirty, so we'd be back before the rest of the house was stirring, though I knew Erik was already up and on the phone to Europe. We could probably get in a good hour of hard-core training if she was ready to go.

She opened her bedroom door in surprise, though she was wearing workout clothes, so she was probably planning to go for a run. "What's going on?" she asked.

"I wondered if you were up for a workout. We have the time."

"Oh." She glanced at her watch. "Sure. Give me five minutes to brush my teeth and get socks on."

"I'll meet you at the car."

Fifteen minutes later we were warming up at the gym. I watched her out of the corner of my eye, trying to be a little more respectful of her as a colleague and trying to stop critically assessing every move she made. She was damn good, her body strong and sure as she did a few tai chi moves that were part of her warmup routine.

We started sparring, a few jabs here and there to get into it. She then followed with a kick to my shin that made me wince. She was stronger than I gave her credit for.

"You kick like a girl." I said it with a grin on my face, to let her know I was kidding.

She raised her eyebrows and then smirked. "And if you train a little harder, you probably could too."

I snorted out a laugh; she was a pain in my ass, but I was warming up to her. "I'll keep that in mind," was all I said as I braced for another blow. She hit hard, I'd give her that much, and she was fast. She moved like a panther, sleek and sneaky and with purpose, eyeing me as if I was her prey. And with catlike precision no less. I loved watching her move and I allowed her to get in an extra kick as my thoughts moved to a place they shouldn't, imagining her naked. Damn, she was probably fucking fantastic without clothes on.

Now why had I gone there? She kicked me twice more before I snapped out of my lusty thoughts and got back into the session. I wasn't the kind of man who sexualized women in my life just because I could. Twelve fucking years living with and protecting Casey and I'd never gone there, even though my heart had eventually begun to betray me. Falling in love with my best friend's girl had been a huge failure on my part, but I'd never let it show, never let her know, and god knows, never acted on it. We'd come close once, one night when loneliness, betrayal, and vulnerability had morphed into an emotional intimacy that could have gone in a very bad direction. Luckily, we'd managed to keep it platonic, and now she was back with Erik and I was sparring with a sexy bodyguard who'd almost knocked me unconscious last week.

"Tell me the truth," she said, coming at me with a cross that would've hurt had it connected.

"Shoot."

"Could you have broken free last week?"

I shook my head. "No way to know. Had it been life or death? Had Luke been five feet away from me with a gun to his head? Maybe. Probably. I'd like to think I would've found the strength to break free before I passed out, but hindsight is twenty-twenty."

She nodded. "That's fair. I can't imagine how it would feel to be protecting someone I truly loved, the way you obviously feel about Luke, in a situation like that."

"I worry about it every day," I admitted. "And that's a big part of the reason why I've been so hard on you. One slip-up, and he, or any of them, could be gone. We've fought through so much, worked so hard to get our country back, and to find our way back to each other, I can't let anything happen to them." I dropped my hands, meeting her eyes. "It's also why I'll always bust your balls. Why I'll always push you—and the others—to be better, stronger, faster."

"I understand." She stopped moving and looked at me intently. "And I give you my word I'm up for the task."

WE GOT BACK to the house to hear yelling coming from the family room. Erik and Casey were arguing in a way I'd never heard them fight before and it was a little disconcerting.

"This isn't what you promised!" she was saying.

"I can't help what's going on in Limaj," he countered.

"You've been so upset over how much of Luke's life you missed, and now that he's here with you, you barely spend any time with him. You didn't see him as a newborn and now that we have another one, you pick him up, like, once a day. Why are you even here if you're not going to actually be here?"

"That's not fair."

"I asked you for two goddamn weeks! Two weeks to bond with our baby and be a couple, a family, new parents...and you can't even give me one. We lie in bed at night and you don't talk about our family, you talk about the education bill. I get it. I want to get to work too, but we missed out on eleven years together as a couple. The people aren't going to fall over and die if you only devote two hours a day to work instead of twelve for a week or two. If this is how it's going to be, I'll stay here and you might as well go back to Hiskale."

"Casey." Erik sounded hurt, which wasn't like him, and I struggled with whether or not to intervene.

"What do we do?" Lennox whispered.

"Nothing. I've literally never heard them fight, so it's new for me too."

"Honey, I'm sorry. I'm just under so much pressure..." Erik's voice dropped.

"And I'm not?" Casey's voice rose again. "New country, new marriage, new baby, four fucking kids, and I'm a queen now, something I was never trained to be. You think I'm not under pressure?"

"I know, but—"

"But what? Push something that weighs nine pounds out of your ass, after carrying it around in your belly for nine months, while taking care of your family, your business and learning about a whole new culture, and then come tell me how hard it is for you."

"Okay, stop. I know you're upset, but I don't want the kids to hear us fight."

"Why not? It's *normal*. What you and I had twelve years ago was a stolen interlude. *This* is real. This is what forever is and, so far, I'm not liking it all that much." There were footsteps and then a slammed door.

Lennox and I looked at each other warily.

"I'll go talk to Erik, and you get in the shower. Casey needs a little time to cool off and it'll be okay."

"Got it." She disappeared and I went into the family room where Erik was standing with his hands on his hips, staring off at nothing.

"Rough morning?" I asked him.

"You have no idea," he muttered.

"Give her a break," I said gently. "You're both right, but she did just go through pregnancy and labor, and all the hormones are going wild as her body readjusts."

He turned to stare at me. "You always take her side. You ever notice that?"

"I didn't at the hospital when she wanted Lennox to stay in the room."

"Okay, you always take her side unless it's safety-related."

"She's my friend," I said gently.

"You're in love with her."

And there it was. I'd wondered how long it would be before he threw that in my face. He knew me better than almost anyone, so hiding it from him hadn't worked. But it wasn't true anymore, either.

"Was," I corrected him. "Not anymore. And it was never tangible, never something I articulated, not even in my head. You left me alone with this gorgeous, talented, strong, amazing woman. I'm only human, and I won't apologize for that. But I never touched her and never let her know. It's also ancient history. All of that dissipated when you came back."

He sighed, looking away. "I'm sorry. For everything. For putting you in an untenable situation. For tasking you to do something I should have done."

"You did what you had to do, as did I."

"But you still take her side." His green eyes twinkled with a combination of mirth and resignation.

"I take her side when she's right. She's probably got a touch of post-partum depression going on, but you wouldn't know that because you weren't here the last two times. She's exhausted because even though Marisol gets up with Levi at night, she wakes up every time he makes a sound. She's been like that with all the kids. And she's probably lonely because you're here but you're not. You're on the phone five, six hours a day, maybe more. You're on your computer almost all day. Log off, man. Engage with your family. You won't get these weeks back. Before you know it, you'll be back in Hiskale and lucky to see them an hour a day. Luke complained about it to me too, so fix this before it's too late."

"Shit." He blew out a breath. "Thank you. As always. For being my sounding board."

"We good?" I asked him carefully. And I wasn't talking about his fight with Casey anymore.

"You thought I didn't know how you felt about her?"

"It came up once before but we didn't address it much, and I'd like this to be the last time. It's different now that you're back. Before, we were alone, and it was hard to watch her suffer. Now you're back and I know she's happy —this morning's episode notwithstanding—so it doesn't hurt me to see her because she has what she needs."

"I get that. And yes, of course we're good. Always." He drew me into a brief hug, a rare show of emotion for us, and then he looked toward the stairs. "So, since you're the Casey whisperer, how do I fix this?"

"You go up there and say 'I'm sorry. I love you. I'll do better.' And then hold her."

"Got it." He gave me a wry smile before taking the steps two at a time.

I hadn't lied about my feelings for Casey lessening since they'd gotten married, but it didn't completely negate a decade of unrequited love either. At some point, I was going to have to move past all that, even though I had zero idea where I'd find someone to get involved with or even go out on a few dates with. How did you do that in my line of work? I didn't think I had the time or energy to find out.

10

—————

L*ennox*

THE NEXT COUPLE of days were quieter than usual. Casey didn't come downstairs much and Erik stayed with her. There hadn't been any more fighting but I'd heard her crying earlier this morning and I did my best to stay invisible. It was my job to know everything going on around her, but I didn't want to be intrusive. We were fairly safe sequestered here in the house, so I didn't need to be nosey. Mostly, I kept an eye on the house, the grounds, and the family, worked out, and slept. Late at night I usually watched TV or read for an hour before falling asleep, but there wasn't much in the way of free time and I wondered if this was how other people lived.

Today was Sunday and I was supposed to have half the day off, but I had nowhere to go and no one to do anything with, which was kind of weird. I could call Dax, see if he wanted to watch a football game somewhere, but that might give him the wrong idea and I really wasn't interested in dating him. I had a handful of friends, but everyone was married or lived somewhere else, and I so rarely did anything for fun that I'd almost forgotten how.

I wandered into the kitchen to get something to eat, my hair down instead of the usual ponytail and my feet bare. I was dressed for a day off and thinking about binge-watching something after a swim. I was waffling between a spy show called *Jack Ryan* and a miniseries featuring Tom

Hiddleston called *The Night Manager*. I hummed to myself as I put a pod in the Keurig machine and brewed myself a cup of coffee, thinking I should call my friend Sabrina. We'd served together overseas but she'd left the military right after I did and was now working as a physician's assistant in New York.

"Morning." Sandor's deep voice made me jump and I turned, shaking my head.

"Morning."

"What are you up to on your day off?"

"It's only half a day since I have to be on duty after dinner," I said, "but not much. I have a handful of friends here in Vegas, but there's not much to do unless we've made plans ahead of time. I'm going to swim and then maybe watch some movies."

He arched one golden brow. "You get half a day off a week and you're going to watch movies?"

I took a sip of coffee. "What do you suggest? Shopping? Spa day? Lunch with the girls?"

"Maybe. That's what most women do."

"I'm not most women." Our eyes locked and for a moment I had the strangest pull, tugging me to him. It was so real I practically felt it, and I quickly looked away, in search of food. I normally ate a protein bar in the morning, but I'd have eaten a piece of cheesecake if it meant getting away from that smoldering gaze. Why couldn't I ever tell what the man was thinking?

"So what's fun for you?" he asked, apparently not willing to let this go.

"Lots of stuff I rarely have time for. I only have part of today and I want to swim, so reading and watching a movie or two will relax me and that's plenty."

"But if you had time off," he pressed.

I gave him an exasperated look. "I like to hike, and snorkel if I'm near a beach. I also like fast cars and motorcycles, and will rent one if I have the time. And I love hockey."

"Why am I not surprised?" He gave me a lazy smile that made my insides do a weird jiggly little thing. "You date that guy from the Sidewinders?"

"Dax?" I shook my head. "We're just friends. I don't have time to date and, honestly, between his schedule and mine, when would we see each other?"

"I know the feeling. My sister asks me every time I talk to her if I've met anyone."

"Well, you're good-looking, rich, and are actually a prince, even if you don't use the title. I'd think women would be crawling out of the woodwork to get to you."

There was an awkward pause as our eyes met once again, and he finally shrugged. "Not the kind of women I'd want to get involved with."

"No?" Now I was the one pressing. "What kind of women do you get involved with?"

He put his coffee mug down and added water to the Keurig machine. "The kind who aren't after my money or my title. The kind who might understand how many hours I work and how important my job is to me. The kind who'd be willing to make huge sacrifices so we could be together." He pressed the button to brew a cup. "So essentially, the nonexistent kind."

"You don't know that," I said softly. If there was such a thing as vulnerability in Sandor, this was probably as close as I'd get to seeing it.

"I haven't been out on a date, like dinner and dancing or a movie or even a hand-holding thing, in thirteen years."

"I... What?" I gaped at him. "Really?"

"Don't get me wrong, there's been sex, but an actual date? I'm beginning to think it's impossible for a guy like me."

"Well, if it makes you feel any better, you're probably older than me, but I haven't been out on a date in five years."

"I'm thirty-nine," he said. "So seven years older, and seven and five is twelve, which makes us almost even. What's your excuse?"

"Well, since I moved to the private sector, all I do is work. And frankly, sex is so disappointing most of the time, I don't even want to bother with the dinner and movie that goes with it."

He'd been taking his first sip of coffee and sputtered over the top as his eyes snapped to mine for the third time.

"What?" I asked with a laugh. "Guys can be selfish in that department."

"Then you're sleeping with the wrong ones," he said quietly.

"Are your eyes blue?" I blurted out.

He paused and then a small smile crossed his handsome face. "They are."

"Then why..." I squinted and leaned closer, something I'd been wanting to do since the first time we met. "You're wearing hazel contacts?"

He nodded. "My eyes are incredibly blue and very striking, something my enemies would notice, so when I was training to be a bodyguard, they suggested hazel contacts to help me be less conspicuous, and I've been wearing them ever since. I don't need them to see, so in a pinch I can take them out and toss them, but I've never had to."

"And you wear them at home too?"

"I never know where I'm going or what I need to do, so I buy dailies and make it a habit to put them in first thing every morning."

"Interesting." I nodded. "I couldn't figure out why your eye color was so different."

"Now you know." He leaned against the counter and I had the strangest urge to lean against him, feel that rock-hard body against mine.

Oh boy. Nope. Bad Lennox. Bad, bad Lennox.

"Well." I cleared my throat. "I'm going to go sit outside and read the newspaper on my laptop while I enjoy my coffee."

"Have a good half-day off," he called after me.

WHEN I GOT OUTSIDE, I was surprised to see Casey already sitting there. She had a coffee mug in her hands and she was staring off into the distance. Her face was a little red, telling me she'd been crying again, and I wasn't sure what to do.

"It's okay," she called out. "You can join me."

"I don't want to intrude," I said slowly.

"It's fine. Were you going to swim?"

"After I have coffee and read the paper."

"Make yourself at home." She motioned to the empty chairs next to her.

"Are you okay? You've been crying."

"Erik and I have been fighting again, just without the raised voices." She sighed. "It's been a rough week."

"I'm sorry."

"Yeah, me too." Casey leaned her head back. "I waited so long for him to come back to me, and now that he's here, he's still gone."

I didn't know the whole story, but the background I'd been given was that Erik had faked his death to protect her and their unborn child. Only a handful of people—like Sandor—had known he was alive and Casey wasn't one of them. They'd reunited last summer and were now married and had another baby. I didn't know much of anything else so it was hard to have a conversation without asking stupid questions. "I know you don't want to hear it, but he must be under enormous pressure to rebuild Limaj, right?"

"I understand that. I asked him for two weeks. That's all. He was in Limaj from January until he got here just before Levi was born. Six whole months with us barely together at all, letting him focus on what he had to do while I was taking care of my own thing and the kids. Two damn weeks, Lennox. Is that so much to ask?"

"No." I shook my head. "It's not. But maybe in his mind... I don't know. I don't understand men at all. That's probably why I'm spectacularly single."

"I've never truly loved anyone else," Casey said. "Even when I thought he was dead, my heart never moved on. I'm not sure why this is so upsetting since I've barely seen him the last few months, but it's become really bad the last few days, so I'm guessing it has to do with having just had a baby."

"Postpartum depression?"

"Probably. I barely had any with Luke, but I probably wasn't aware of it since there was a lot going on since Erik faked his death not long after Luke was born. I had a little with the twins, but it passed within a few weeks. What I'm feeling this time is intense, but I can't let it get out that something is wrong with me. Limaj is a small, old-fashioned country and it would be a big deal. I don't want to give Erik anything else to worry about so—"

"You should let Erik worry about what he has to worry about," a gentle voice spoke from behind us.

We both jumped and I felt like an idiot for not realizing he'd snuck up on us.

"Eavesdropping is impolite," Casey told her husband.

"So is hiding an illness from the man who loves you," he countered, leaning down to kiss her forehead and squatting beside her, one hand lingering on the side of her face. "Is this something you should see a doctor for?"

"Probably."

"Then let's make an appointment. Babe, I don't give a shit what anyone thinks. Mental illness, especially situational like this, isn't anything to be ashamed of. We have to be forward-thinking so that the people of Limaj— and anywhere else—understand that it's okay to talk about these things. I can't let them lead me. I have to lead *them*."

"I don't want to add anything else to your plate," she whispered.

"You *are* my plate," he whispered back. "And my utensils and my everything..."

I didn't hear the rest of what they said because I slipped back into the house, leaving them to their intimate moment. In spite of their current struggles, there was no doubt they loved each other deeply, and I wondered if anyone would ever love me that way.

11

S *andor*

CASEY'S official postpartum depression diagnosis seemed to snap Erik out of his work-induced coma and he put almost everything aside that week to immerse himself with her and the kids for a few days. It was becoming urgent for us to get back to Limaj, but they needed time to work out whatever had been brewing between them, and I was glad he'd finally realized his family had to come first sometimes. Not that I was one to talk, but at least I knew what I hoped I would do if I ever had a family.

I chuckled to myself, fully aware of how easy it was to be an armchair quarterback when you had no skin in the game. I had the TV on in my room, watching a documentary about World War II, and I couldn't decide if I was ready to sleep or not. It had been quieter than usual the last two days, with Erik, Casey, Luke, Leni, and the twins watching movies and playing games like a regular family. It was nice to see, but I was a little bored. Probably more than a little envious as well. I'd never craved a family, not the way Erik did, but the older I got, the more I realized how much I was missing.

I stared up at the ceiling, trying to remember the last time I'd gotten laid. That always helped remind me I wasn't the white picket fence kind of guy, but I hadn't met anyone interesting in a long time.

Okay, that was a lie. There was a very interesting and sexy woman in the house right now, and the thought of sleeping with her made my dick hard instantly. But she wasn't an option for a whole bunch of reasons. First and foremost, I was her boss and in our line of work, distractions could be deadly. Second, she didn't seem even a little bit interested. Well, okay, maybe a little. That whole thing about my eye color had caught me off guard. I'd had no idea she'd noticed and it was a little disconcerting how astute she was because not a single woman I wasn't related to had ever noticed. The fact that Lennox had picked up on it told me she took a somewhat deeper look than the others had. Maybe it was purely professional, but I doubted it.

Lennox. I'd never heard of anyone with that for a first name before and it rolled off my tongue like silk. Damn, I was sporting a boner so hard it was getting painful. I was going to need some relief and I slid my hand into my shorts, giving it a slow, firm stroke. I closed my eyes, picturing her pretty face, with those incredibly full lips. I'd thought about little else since she'd said sex was disappointing to her... What foolish men had been lucky enough to get her into bed and then...disappointed her?

I'd take my time if I ever got the chance to touch her, explore every inch of her body while simultaneously taking the opportunity to discover what she liked, what made her hum with desire. I loved women's bodies, and I already knew hers was delectable. Picturing her beneath me got me so close to the edge, I nearly laughed at myself. It had definitely been too long because it usually took me forever to get off by my own hand.

I shifted on the bed, getting more comfortable, and tightened my grip just as a noise caught my attention. My hand froze as I waited. Whatever it was had been subtle, so it could've been anything. One of the kids coming down for a snack, someone dropping something on the floor upstairs, one of the security guys letting a door slam behind him. I'd almost convinced myself everything was okay when I heard it again and this time I realized it was coming from outside. No one should be outside this time of night other than our security guards, and they wouldn't be making noise without giving me some kind of signal.

I shot straight up and swung my legs over the side of the bed, grabbing my gun and yanking on a T-shirt before opening my bedroom door and stepping into the hall. I hated carrying a gun in my hand in the house, but I trusted my gut and right now something was wrong. I'd taken out the earpiece that kept me in touch with everyone since I'd been in bed, but there was no help for that now.

I padded down the hall and peeked into the living room, which was empty. I slipped into the dark kitchen and switched on a light. Also empty. Then I heard another noise.

Shit. I'd left my phone behind too, but we had a lot of contingencies, so I pushed two buttons on the underside of the island, something we'd done on purpose since we had a house full of kids. There were three buttons, and pressing one by accident wouldn't do anything. However, pressing two specific buttons at the same time sent an alert to everyone's phones, including Joe's and Chains', even when they weren't on site. Erik would see it and protect the family upstairs since he was always armed, and the team outside would know something was up as well.

I'd let my guard down tonight because Lennox had overnight duty and I trusted her, but now I was regretting that decision. I followed the sounds coming from outside, going into the garage and then out through a side door just as someone went running past me, followed by Lennox flying through the air and taking down whomever it was. She had him pinned and restrained in the two seconds it took me to point my gun, and she looked up in annoyance, a drop of blood dripping down her lip.

"There's at least one more of them," Lennox said. "Went that way."

I grabbed the man on the ground, hauling him to his feet just as Xander came running out.

"What's going on?" he demanded.

I pushed the man she'd captured toward her, and then Xander and I both went in the direction she pointed. We separated when we got around back. I motioned for him to go around the pool while I dropped into a crouch and hugged the back wall of the house, my bare feet quiet on the floor of the patio. I heard the rustling of bushes and knew it wasn't Xander making that much noise, so the other intruder was on the move.

I heard a howl and then Xander's all-clear whistle. He had him handcuffed and dragged him to his feet, a grim look on his face.

"Armed," he said. "No ID."

"Who are you?" I barked at the man, who remained stoically silent.

I repeated the question in Limaji and though he didn't respond, the man's eyes shifted slightly, so that confirmed my suspicion he'd been sent by someone in my country.

"You have no protection here," I told him. "The royal family doesn't deal with the police, so I can make you disappear and no one will ever know."

The man swallowed but still wasn't talking.

Oh, this wasn't good.

"Get him into the garage," I told Xander. "I'll see if there's anyone else."

"Looks like Chains is here," Xander said, yanking the man by the arm and nudging him forward.

I did a scan of the perimeter before meeting everyone in the garage. We weren't set up here for interrogations and the like, not with kids and civilians in the house, so I was going to have to count on Chains and Joe. They had space at the office they used for things like this, but it had never happened as far as I knew.

I walked into the garage and found both men bound and gagged, sitting on chairs, surrounded by Lennox, Xander, Chains and Erik, who looked furious.

"We can't do this here," I told him firmly. "Let me get some clothes on and we'll move this party elsewhere."

"Damn straight." He glared at the men.

"We need to secure the grounds before we do anything, though," I said. My gaze swung to Lennox. "You okay?"

"I'm fine." She had a bruise forming under her eye and her lower lip was cut, but she looked badass as hell standing there with her hands on her hips.

"Walk with me," I told her.

She immediately followed me into the house.

"What happened?" I asked her as we went into my room and I started pulling on clothes and socks.

"I went to check on the gate guards and neither of them were there. These two knuckleheads jumped me and immediately pulled out my earpiece, so they knew what they were doing and that I'd be on my own once they did that, but as soon as they realized I wasn't going to be easy to take down, they split up, so I chased one and then you came out."

Pros," I said, shaking my head as I stepped into my boots. "You sure you're okay? Your eye is starting to swell shut."

"I'm good. I'll get some ice on it in a minute."

"Sandor?" Casey's voice made me spin around and I found her in the doorway looking scared and confused.

"Hey, what are you doing down here? Everyone okay?"

"Erik called upstairs and said we were good, so I figured I should come see what's going on."

"We're not sure yet," I told her, "but we can't interrogate them here."

She shuddered. "No, not with all the kids in the house."

"Why don't you go upstairs?" I suggested.

"The kids are hunkered down with Sasha and Sylvia. I need to know what's what in my own house." Sylvia was Levi's new nanny. "I'm still a black belt in karate, you know."

I smiled. "Yes, you are, but you just had a baby and are out of practice. Go back upstairs, okay? I'll send Erik up as soon as we know what we're going to do with these guys."

"Not until I know what's happening." She glanced at Lennox. "Your eye is swelling shut. Get some ice on it right away."

"I will. Thanks." Lennox nodded.

WE WALKED into the garage after stopping in the kitchen for an ice pack and found Joe and Chains talking in hushed tones.

"I've sent their pictures to Ace," Chains told me. "He has access to a wider international database than we do."

"Good." I looked down at the men, trying to ascertain whether or not I'd ever seen them before. One of them, the one Lennox had tackled, looked familiar and I glanced at Erik. The look on his face told me he was having similar thoughts.

"We have to decide what we want to do," I said carefully. "If we interrogate them on our own, we have to do something with them afterward, and I don't think letting them go is an option. However, if we call the police, we can do a brief interrogation now, and then they're their problem."

Erik looked at Casey. "It's up to you. The kids are home and if we call the cops, they'll know something is up."

"They already know something is up," she said quietly. "Let's call the cops. We don't want to be responsible for dead bodies, and if I find out they were here to hurt my children, that's what there's going to be."

"I'm on it." Chains grabbed his phone.

As he moved out of the room, Erik dropped to his haunches and removed the gag from one of the men's mouths. "Who put you up to this?" he asked in Limaji. "Just give me a name and we can say it was a misunderstanding."

"Liar." The man responded in Limaji as well. "You don't care about me."

"I don't, but I'm willing to compromise to find out what I need to know."

"Your illegitimate rule will soon be over," the man hissed, "and a true monarch will replace you."

"Omar?" Erik tested out the name, and the man's eyes momentarily flickered with surprise. Then he slumped down, going quiet again. "Well, thanks for that."

Erik turned to me. "At least now we know Omar's not dead."

12

———————

L *ennox*

IT TOOK hours for the police to come to the house, arrest the intruders, take all of our statements, review video surveillance and make us jump through a dozen hoops. They wanted me to go down to the station for an official state-ment, so I didn't get home until almost dawn. My eye had officially swollen shut and my ribs were killing me from when the two guys had jumped me. Erik had sent an attorney with me, just in case, but I hadn't done anything wrong. Those guys had been trespassing and we'd found our two security guards drugged and stuffed in the bushes on the grounds. The whole ordeal had taken forever and I was tired.

I stopped in the kitchen to get some water and more ice, but paused to rest for a minute. I put my hands on the counter and let my head drop to my chest. Tonight had been scary. Not because those two men had gotten past our security, but because they'd gotten right up to the house and if I hadn't been so diligent, they could have gotten inside.

I sensed his presence before he spoke, and his voice soothed me for some reason. "How bad is it?"

"Not terrible, just sore." I glanced over my shoulder at him.

"Let me see." He put a big, warm hand on my arm and it gave me goose bumps, which of course, I couldn't hide from him.

"It's okay," I said in a rough voice, unsure why he impacted me this way.

"Let me see the damage," he said, not moving.

I sighed but turned and lifted my shirt. "I haven't seen it yet," I said. "So you tell me."

"Ah, yeah, that has to hurt." He didn't touch me, but having his eyes on my naked torso, despite the sports bra I wore, was like a caress nonetheless. The look in his eyes exuded a tenderness I'd never seen in him, and the yearning to have his hands on me intensified. Especially once I saw his eyes. They were as blue as the Mediterranean, shockingly so, and for a moment I was completely mesmerized.

He met my gaze and I couldn't look away. His eyes were absolutely breathtaking—no wonder he'd been encouraged to hide them—and I took a few seconds to get lost in them. It wasn't often I allowed myself to feel vulnerable, but my ribs hurt like a bitch and having Sandor this close was somehow comforting. "I, uh, a hot shower will help," I finally managed to say.

"Soak in the tub," he said. "I've got some special Epsom salts with essential oils in them. And a muscle relaxer."

I shook my head. "No. I can't take anything that'll knock me out."

"You can and you will. It's probably not a serious injury, but you need to rest and let your body heal. We're covered here. Joe, Xander and Chains are all here, along with Erik and me. We're calling Logan back from Limaj as well, and one of our CIA friends, Ace Ross, is en route. We're covered for now, so you should take advantage of this opportunity."

I hesitated but then nodded. "Okay. Thank you."

"Thank you for being diligent tonight."

"They still got the drop on me by pulling out my earbud."

"You took one of them down and you probably would've taken the other one as well. It's obvious we need a bigger security team, and we can't use rent-a-cops anymore to patrol the front gate."

I nodded. "I agree."

"Come on, let's get you that muscle relaxer and run your bath. I'll take care of everything while you're sleeping."

"I don't like to sleep that soundly," I said again, even though I followed him to his room.

"And under different circumstances, I would agree. But it was a long night and we might have a lot going on in the coming days, so don't argue." He turned abruptly, and his arm brushed against mine. It was a brief moment of contact but the skin he'd touched was practically on fire.

"I'm not used to anyone taking care of me," I said in a throaty whisper.

He hesitated a fraction of a second before saying, "All of us can use someone to rely on now and again."

"Who do you rely on?" I asked quietly.

"Mostly Erik."

"Who did you rely on when he was in hiding?" He was standing close enough to me that I saw the uncertainty flicker in his eyes, his large body almost frozen as our gazes remained locked, an invisible force keeping us from moving.

"No one," he admitted. "I couldn't. It was too dangerous."

"Wasn't it lonely?" I wasn't sure why I wanted to know, but I did.

"You get used to it, I think." He paused. "At least that's what I told myself."

"I don't know if you get used to it so much as become resigned to it."

We were standing beside his dresser, the room bathed in semidarkness. I'd never been as acutely aware of the loneliness in my life until this moment, when this monster of a man beside me admitted to his own.

"People like us," he said slowly, "often don't have a choice. Loneliness is the cross we bear. But it makes the moments when we're not alone that much more poignant. You know?"

Wow. Who was this thoughtful guy and what happened to the asshole version of Sandor?

Somehow, I managed to nod, wishing I had something equally insightful to add to the conversation. But he'd turned his back and was rummaging on his dresser for something. He handed me a pill out of a bottle in one of the drawers and then followed me to the guest bathroom I used. He dug around in the linen closet and pulled out a plastic bag filled with Epsom salts.

"My special blend," he said, dumping about half a cup's worth into the water.

When I looked up he was smiling, something I didn't see him do very often, so I smiled back. "Thank you."

"You're welcome." He touched my arm, for another split second of contact, and then he was gone, shutting the door behind him.

I woke up at noon feeling like a new woman. Sandor's bath and muscle relaxer recipe had been just what I needed and though my ribs were still sore, I didn't feel nearly as bad as I had eight hours ago. I took a quick shower and dressed in my usual uniform of cargo pants, tank top and boots, attaching my ankle holster since we didn't like to flash guns in front of the kids unless absolutely necessary.

The kitchen was busy when I walked in, with the kids at the island having lunch, Marisol cooking, and Casey sitting in a chair by the table holding Levi.

"Hey." Casey looked up. "How are you feeling?"

"Much better, thanks." I turned on the coffee maker, something I seemed to do a lot.

"What happened to your eye?" Leni demanded. "Did you get beat up by the bad guys last night?"

"Actually, she did the beating up," Casey said gently. "He just got in one lucky punch."

Leni high-fived me. "You rock. Thanks, Lennox."

"You're welcome." I smiled at her. She was precocious as hell, but she cracked me up.

"Will you teach me karate?" she asked.

"I'm a black belt in jujitsu," I explained, "which is a little different. But any time you'd like to learn some self-defense, I'm happy to teach you."

"We could all use some self-defense classes," Sasha said. "Personally, I'd like to be able to defend myself."

"We can arrange that," Casey said, looking at me. "Would you be willing, Lennox?"

"Absolutely. I'll talk with Sandor about my duty schedule."

"What about it?" Sandor came in smiling at everyone.

I told him about the girls wanting to learn self-defense and he nodded. "Absolutely. Whenever everyone is ready to start."

"Would you teach me, Uncle Loco?" Luke asked, looking at him. "I don't want to train with the girls."

"Why not?" Sandor turned toward him and leaned against the counter. "Lennox is an extremely skilled bodyguard and her credentials are actually more impressive than mine. I'm bigger than she is, but she took me down at the gym a couple of weeks ago, and if we had actually been fighting, instead of training, she would have knocked me out."

Luke's eyes rounded and he stared at me with surprise. "Oh, wow. That's kind of cool... I guess I could train with her too. I mean, I just want to learn to protect myself now that I'm part of the royal family and all that."

"Of course." Sandor ruffled his hair. "We can arrange something."

It warmed me in ways I didn't want to think about to hear praise from Sandor, and I dug around in the refrigerator looking for some fruit. After last night's incident, I didn't feel like a protein bar. Once in a while, I needed real food, and an omelet with fruit on the side sounded good.

"What can I make you?" Marisol asked me.

"I feel like an omelet," I told her. "But I can do it."

"Don't be ridiculous. One of your eyes is practically swollen shut. You sit and let me cook. Bacon and tomatoes sound good?" She already knew me well.

"Yes, thank you."

"How are you feeling?" Sandor asked me.

"Much better. You were right about the hot bath and the muscle relaxer."

"I'm glad." He left the room and I couldn't help but allow my gaze to follow him, taking in the broad shoulders that tapered down to a small waist and an incredible ass. Damn, he was hot and I was in heat. What was that about?

I tore my eyes away and looked up to see Casey watching me, a small smile playing on her lips. Thank god I had a black eye that hopefully covered the fact that I turned bright red. Then Marisol put a plate in front of me and I dug in.

"He's nice to look at, isn't he?" Casey murmured in my ear as she brushed past me.

I nearly choked.

"O. M. G." Sasha was staring at something on her phone. "Mom!"

"What is it?" Casey rushed to her side.

"I was voted in as this year's belle of the ball." Her eyes were wide. "Holy shit."

"That's awesome!" Jessie said, looking up, her eyes twinkling.

"Wow." Casey smiled at her oldest child. "That's really exciting. Are you going to do it?"

Sasha bit her lip. "Should I?"

"I'm sorry," I interrupted. "What are we talking about?"

"My ex-husband owns the Charleston Hotel and Casino," Casey explained. "Every year they do a big charity ball, raising money for cancer and other children's charities, and they choose a belle of the ball, who's kind of like the main attraction. It's someone single and either a celebrity or royalty or something like that. It usually costs about ten grand per dance to dance with the belle, so it's a huge honor. And I totally think you should do it. Especially since you haven't gotten back on the dating horse again since Anton."

"It's kind of scary," Sasha admitted, "but fun too. I think I will. I'm going to call Dad." She grinned at us and dialed a number as she left the room. Sasha had been adopted when Casey was married to Nick Kingsley, who owned the Charleston. I'd had to read the background on the family several times to wrap my head around it all, but I was glad I had because everyone in the family was close, including exes.

"This is going to be a huge deal for her," Marisol said, smiling. "I hope she meets someone wonderful, because she still thinks about Anton far too much."

"Who's Anton?" I asked. There hadn't been anything about him in my notes.

"Her ex," Casey said. "He's the son of one of the Sidewinders, Anatoli Petrov. They were hot and heavy last year and then things went south. It's kind of complicated, but my gut tells me those two will see each other again."

"Love is wasted on the young," I said ruefully.

"Sometimes." Casey gave me a knowing smile. "But other times you just know. I was twenty-two when Erik and I got together, but I'd had a crush on him for years. Love is a mysterious thing."

I focused on my food, deciding not to comment. I couldn't imagine being with anyone I'd dated in my late teens or early twenties. Hell, I couldn't imagine being with anyone I'd ever dated. The nice guys had been boring and/or terrible in bed; the rest were just jerks.

The wistful, romantic part of me that rarely surfaced gave me a nudge, and I smiled at the thought of being with Sandor. He wouldn't be a jerk. I knew that as sure as I was breathing. He might not be the relationship type, but if he was in one, he would be one of the good ones. Too bad neither of us was in the market for something like that.

13

S *andor*

THE KIDS STARTED BACK to school in mid-August, and it was time for the rest of us to move back to Limaj. Erik had been dealing with the aftermath of the bombing of Parliament House from here, but he had to be back on Limaji soil, interacting with the people and settling the nerves of the politicians. The building had been razed and there were plans in place to build something entirely new, but in the meantime, the government didn't have an official meeting place and Erik had to take care of that relatively soon.

He was torn because of his family, and while that made sense, there were people counting on him. I was torn too, because going back to Limaj meant more death threats, heightened security, and being away from the kids. With no schooling options in Limaj, Luke was going to live with Nick and Skye, with Chains overseeing security, and the twins and Leni were going to Monte Carlo to live with Jayson and Liz. Liz had been CIA up until this year, so we weren't worried about their safety, and at least they'd be a lot closer than Las Vegas. Sasha was staying here, getting ready for her junior year of college, and Sylvia, Marisol and her husband were going to Limaj with us, to care for Levi and help everyone settle in at the palace. There was a lot going on that had nothing to do with ruling the country, and it was going to be busy.

I was immersed in email when Lennox came in.

"Hey." She sat down across from me.

"Hi." I looked up curiously.

"The family wants to go for ice cream... What's the protocol for that?"

"We send out the SUV with one of us driving and no one else in it, and then we use one of the Westfield vehicles to actually go. I assume we're leaving the baby home?"

She nodded.

"And everyone is going?"

"Erik, Casey, Luke, Leni and the twins. Sasha's not interested."

"All right." I got to my feet. "I'll call Joe or Chains to bring one of the Westfield trucks, send Logan out with the SUV about five minutes before the rest of us leave, and then we'll do it. No one knows we're going out or where we're going. I don't foresee any issues, but I'll drive and I'd like you to follow with one of the other cars, just in case."

She nodded. "I'll make sure everyone is ready. Let me know when the second vehicle arrives."

We headed out thirty minutes later and it was interesting to watch the family dynamic in this instance. They weren't royalty, or a blended family, or any other label—they were just two parents with their children. The twins and Leni giggled almost ceaselessly, while Luke told terrible jokes and Erik and Casey indulged them all. Once we got to the ice cream place they loved, Erik ordered and they stood in line like anyone else. Erik and Casey both had on baseball caps and dark sunglasses that hid their identities fairly well, and the kids were just...kids.

"What do you want?" Erik turned to me.

"Chocolate fudge ripple," Luke answered for me.

I laughed and nodded. "The boy knows me." I turned and scanned the lot for Chains, who was driving the family SUV, and Lennox, who'd taken Casey's Corvette. Impulsively, I texted her.

Sandor: What flavor?

Lennox: I'm good.

Sandor: What. Flavor.

Lennox: You're going to have to work me out extra hard later if I do ice cream now.

I nearly swallowed my tongue thinking about what that could mean, though I was sure she hadn't meant it that way.

Sandor: Deal. What flavor?

Lennox: Butter pecan.

I added her order to everyone else's and when the server brought it, I took it over to her. She rolled down the window and reached for it.

"This was unnecessary," she said. "But thank you."

"You're welcome." Our eyes locked for a minute and I momentarily forgot everything but her. She was so damn pretty it was hard not to look at her. What the hell was wrong with me? Every time I got close to her weird things happened in my boxers as well as my brain.

I walked back to the others and ate my cone with them, smiling and joking with the kids as if I was one of them. In a way, I was. They'd grown up considering me their uncle, and Erik and I were first cousins, so we were actually family. But this wasn't my life. I didn't have a family of my own and while I didn't dwell on it, I'd been thinking about it lately. Maybe it was because I was in the last year of my thirties and somehow forty seemed old. It was also possible it was because Casey and Erik were together now, and I no longer had the sole purpose of keeping her alive. While I protected the entire family, I didn't have a single focus like before.

I'd also never met someone I couldn't stop thinking about in more than a decade, but Lennox occupied a lot more of my thoughts than I was used to and it was frustrating. Why did I always get infatuated with women I couldn't have?

"Okay, let's go," Erik said to me under his breath. "I think some teenagers just recognized Casey so I don't want to push it."

"Absolutely." I put the last of the cone in my mouth, wiped my hands and got to my feet. We headed back to the SUV and everyone piled in.

"Do you have ice cream in Limaj?" Joss asked as we got on the road.

"We mostly have gelato," I told her. "But it's basically the same thing."

"Cool."

"What about pizza?" Leni asked. "'Cause we can't move someplace that doesn't have pizza."

Erik laughed. "We have pizza. We also have a personal chef at the palace who can make anything we want."

"My mother used to make homemade pizza," I mused aloud. "It was the best. My sister, your Aunt Elen, has the recipe. When you come for the holidays, perhaps we can try to make it together."

"That would be fun!" Leni said.

"We're going to do Christmas in Limaj?" Jessie asked quietly.

"We're thinking about it. Why?" Casey asked her.

"I don't want to do Christmas there. I want to be here with our grandmas and grandpas and all our friends. I don't want to leave Las Vegas." And Jessie burst into tears.

. . .

WITH ERIK and Casey dealing with Jessie's meltdown, I went to my room to start packing. I'd keep a handful of things here, but I would be in Limaj seventy-five percent of the time going forward, and I needed a home, some place to feel settled. Erik and I had discussed living arrangements and I wanted my own suite in the king's wing of the palace. I had to be close enough to get to him and his family in an emergency, but we all needed privacy. Luckily, the palace was big enough to provide that. He and Casey had started some renovations back in January when they'd gotten married, but contractors were hard to find in Limaj right now, so it was slow.

Their master bedroom suite and bathroom had been done, but the kids' rooms were still in progress and my suite was next. We would be moving into the palace en masse right now, which meant finding comfortable quarters for myself, Joe, Lennox, Xander, Logan, and the new guy we'd just hired, Axel. Not to mention Marisol and her husband, Bill. It was going to be a full house.

"I don't suppose you feel like working out."

I spun around, so lost in thought I hadn't heard Lennox come in.

"Oh, hi. Tomorrow's going to be a long day, you sure you want to hit the gym?"

She nodded. "Yeah, I'm restless and I hate long flights, even if I'm on a private jet."

"Give me ten and I'll meet you at the car."

"Great." She ducked out and I went back to the task at hand.

I hated packing and I'd been living out of a suitcase more often than not the last year. I finished up quickly, deciding I could get anything I left behind when we returned in October for the charity ball. There was no doubt we would come for that, with Sasha as this year's belle of the ball, so I left my tuxedo behind as well. I didn't think I'd need one in the next two months in Limaj.

I left my large suitcase by the door in my room and quickly changed into workout clothes. I really didn't want to work out tonight, but if Lennox needed it, I was happy to comply. We'd fallen into an easy, comfortable working relationship that bordered on friendship. We didn't get too personal, but there was something there between us any time we were alone and I wasn't sure what that meant. It's not like I could ask her if she liked me. I was her boss and that would be unprofessional as fuck.

At least, that's what I kept telling myself.

14

———

L *ennox*

THE ONLY PERSON at the gym when we arrived was Chains, who was leaving. He handed Sandor the keys and told him to lock up.

"Since we dominate the gym ninety percent of the time," he told us, "Joe worked out a deal for us to have a set of keys. This way, our guys can work out night or day, depending on their schedules."

"Perfect." Sandor put the keys in his bag. "We'll make sure it's locked up tight before we go."

"Safe travels tomorrow." Chains waved and took off.

I was already bouncing on my toes, ready to go. I couldn't explain my restlessness, but I was anxious to throw some punches. I'd been taking it easy because of my bruised ribs but I was ready to up my game again. Especially with Sandor. He always pushed me when we sparred, but in a good way.

"Ready?" He was bouncing too, jabbing at nothing as we danced around each other.

"Let's do it."

"How are the ribs?" he asked me.

"Still a little sore, but I think I'm good."

"I'll avoid that side. Last thing you need is to aggravate it before a long trip."

"Okay." I faked with my right hand and swung hard with my left, catching him in the stomach. His rock-hard, flat-as-a-board with all kinds of sinewy muscles stomach. He was wearing a shirt but I knew what it looked like without one and I'd had a few fantasies about what I'd do if I ever got to see him completely naked. In reality, I had to keep it professional, but my dreams were my own. And he'd invaded all of them.

I was so lost in thought, I didn't see him make his move, and without warning, I was on my back, his massive body covering mine. Instead of fighting back, though, I just lay there, staring up at him. He was so close, so fucking close, and he had me pinned down. I could get away, but that wasn't the point. I didn't want to. I just wanted to feel his body on mine for a few more seconds. As many seconds, even fractions of a second, as I could get away with.

"You okay?" he asked slowly, though he didn't move, didn't let me up, didn't do anything.

"Yeah." My brain apparently was on the fritz because I couldn't seem to do anything either. We just stared at each other, our eyes locked, neither of us moving.

"You have to say or do something," he whispered, his Adam's apple bobbing slightly.

"I can't," I whispered back, even though there was no reason for us to be whispering.

He slowly released my wrists but still didn't get up. And when I didn't move either, he dipped his head, his lips gently grazing mine. It was featherlight, as though he was giving me every opportunity to move away, but I was firmly rooted in place. There was no way in hell I'd do anything that would prevent him from kissing me.

When he did, it was the sexiest thing I'd ever experienced. Sandor didn't just kiss me, he made love to my mouth. He started slow, pressing closed-mouth kisses to my lips, before sliding his tongue along the seam, and then seeking out mine. And still, he didn't rush. His tongue worked mine like an artist, exploring my mouth with tender precision, stroking and gliding until I wrapped my arms around his neck and pulled him down. His body dwarfed mine, but all I felt was sexy. He was big and covered in tattoos, with a bushy beard and muscles on his muscles, but it was glorious. I wanted him to devour me, fuck me into another world, because I already knew that's the kind of lover he would be.

"Damn, baby, what are we doing?" He broke away slowly, his eyes glued to mine, one big hand on the side of my face.

"I don't know," I responded, trying to still the crazy beating of my heart, "but I like it."

He kissed me again, this time flipping us over so I was lying on top of him, and strong fingers kneaded my ass, my back, my neck. I might have moaned, but when he edged up my T-shirt, revealing my sports bra, the sound he made was one of sheer desire.

"You're fucking beautiful," he said softly, trailing his hands along my flat stomach.

I'd had to sit up for him to get my shirt off and he was taking full advantage of my half-dressed state.

"You are too," I whispered, unconsciously licking my lips.

He tugged off his tank and I sighed happily. He was a big guy, but his body was perfection, all hard angles and muscles and holy fuck, his happy trail consisted of golden hair. I dropped my head and kissed my way down, from his chest to the rim of his shorts, which I merely nuzzled, enjoying the view for now since I didn't think I could rip his pants off right here at the gym.

He dug his fingers into my hair and pulled at my ponytail holder.

"I love your hair," he said, running his fingers through the locks as they tumbled around my shoulders.

"You're so blond," I said needlessly. "It's sexy as *fuck*."

"Glad to oblige." He gently pushed me onto my back and reached for my shorts.

"What are you doing?" I gasped, looking around and wondering if anyone could see us from outside.

"Hopefully, something that isn't going to disappoint you," he chuckled, tugging my shorts the rest of the way off.

"Sandor, what if someone—"

"No one can see in from outside; the windows have two-way glass."

"Are there video cameras?"

"No idea...but what are they going to do with the video if there are? We're both single, consenting adults. You think we can make money on Pornhub?"

I chuckled but it quickly turned into a groan as he moved the fabric of my thong and slid one naughty finger between my legs.

"You're so wet," he said, though I wasn't sure why he needed to since I was more than aware of how aroused I was.

"What did you think would happen with all that kissing?" I mumbled.

"Just wait." He pulled my thong free of my legs and then crouched between them.

"Oh my god…" My breath escaped in a rush when his lips touched me there. It had been years since anyone had gone down on me, and when his tongue slid inside of me, I arched right into his face. He was wicked, too, licking and tongue-fucking me while holding my hips firmly in place so my movements were limited but the enjoyment was heightened.

"Sandor…" I was so close to coming, it was embarrassing, but this was exquisite torture. When his tongue found my clit and he softly bit down, it was all over. My body jerked and a scream escaped me that I'd never heard before. My orgasm was so hard, I saw white lights, and he didn't let up, wringing out every last ounce of pleasure until I whimpered from the over-load on my sensitive clit.

"Disappointed?" he asked with a grin as he sat up.

"Shut up," I muttered.

15

———

S *andor*

FUCKING HELL, had I just gone down on Lennox right here on the mat at the gym? Yup, I definitely had, and she'd come so hard my beard was coated with her juices. And it was fucking awesome. She was beautiful and sexy and I was so goddamn hard, I needed to get inside of her now. She was still shivering slightly, in the aftermath of her orgasm, and I crawled over her so I could kiss her. I wanted her to taste herself on my tongue, feel how much I wanted her.

Her soft little whimper was a plea for more, telling me she wasn't nearly finished for the night.

"How many times can you come in one night?" I asked her, tracing her gorgeous lips with one of my fingers.

"Not sure. Once is my record," she chuckled.

"Just once?" I made a face. "I guess we'll have to fix that."

I looked around and then got to my feet, holding out my hands to her.

"Where are we going?" she asked in confusion, letting me help her up.

"There's a couch in the office and that'll be a lot more comfortable than this rough vinyl mat." I took her hand, grabbed my wallet, and led her into the back. The office door was open and I sank into the nearest chair, playfully pulling her over my knees.

Her body went rigid as she said, "I don't like to be spanked."

My hands stilled, giving her the ability to get up if she really wanted to. "I'll never do anything you don't want me to do."

She glanced back over her shoulder at me but didn't say anything.

I met her gaze. "But I'd like you to give me a chance to find out exactly what you *do* like."

"Okay."

"I made you feel good a few minutes ago, yes?"

"Oh, yes." This time she smiled.

"Then tell me your fantasies."

She looked confused. "What?"

"Your fantasies. What do you fantasize about sexually?"

"Well..." She finally relaxed across my lap. "A man who understands the sensuality and romance of kissing. Who knows that sex is more than just sticking it in and getting off."

I rumbled out a laugh. "Have you slept with many men who *don't* get that?"

She hesitated. "Pretty much all of them."

Bloody hell. Was she for real? My dick got even harder just thinking about all the ways I wanted to make her feel good. And she liked to kiss. I could suck on those beautiful red lips of hers all day.

"Tell me more," I said softly.

"I want a man who knows his way around a woman's body, who cares enough to take the time to learn every little thing I like. And finally, I want a big, strong man who can make me feel good, without making me feel like I'm a lesser person just because I'm a woman. A man who can make love to me—or even fuck me—without taking away my power. I don't know if you can understand what I mean by that."

Take away her power? Jesus, what kinds of jerks had she been sleeping with? "Baby, I don't know what your love life has been like, or your sex life for that matter, but this—what we're doing—is all about mutual pleasure. And taking away your power? Why *the fuck* would I do that? The fact that you can kick my ass all over the gym is one of the things that attracted me to you. The last thing I want to do is diminish your power because that's what makes this—and you—sexy." I ran my hand along her smooth, firm ass.

Her hazel eyes turned to liquid fire as she continued to look at me over her shoulder, unconsciously licking her lips. "What about you?" she asked, her voice husky and deep. "What are your fantasies?"

She caught me off guard with that. I'd often asked women I was having sex with to tell me their fantasies because I liked making them come true. But no one had ever asked me mine.

"I just bared my soul to you and you can't tell me yours?" she asked after a moment.

I ran my hand up her back and dug my fingers gently but firmly into the hair at the back of her head. "One set of fantasies at a time," I said quietly. "If we do this again, I'll tell you mine. But tonight is all about yours."

"Okay." She let her head drop so that I was holding it by her hair, but my touch remained gentle.

As tough as she was on the outside, she needed something different with this kind of intimacy, and I was okay with that. I'd had more than my share of wild, kinky, over-the-top sexual encounters and I was ready for something a little more meaningful as well, even if it wasn't going to be long-term.

Deciding to change tactics, I let go of her hair and lifted her by the waist, setting her on my lap again, but this time on her bottom. She wrapped her arms around my neck and I took a moment to really look at her. I already thought she was beautiful, but having her almost naked, in my lap, was spectacular. Her face was still flushed from the orgasm she'd had a little while ago and her hair was a wild halo around her face, making me want to kiss her just the way she'd fantasized about.

So I did. I leaned in and took her mouth with a sweetness I hadn't felt in a long time. Maybe ever. Her lips were delectable, soft, sexy, and so incredibly feminine. She worked hard to be badass and competed with men professionally every single day, so bringing out her feminine side, something I was positive not many people ever managed with her, did something to me I couldn't quite articulate.

She made a little sound, deep in her throat, and I deepened the kiss. My tongue stroked hers with carefree, tender glides, enjoying every second of this rare taste of intimacy. I would probably regret it tomorrow, but tonight I couldn't have cared less. Being with someone like Lennox was a rare treat, like cheesecake to a diabetic, and I'd become acutely aware of how little true pleasure I had in my life. I'd never imagined a woman could make me feel this way, like a man with needs instead of a man who took care of others. But Lennox had already become part of my life, and though I probably wouldn't have her forever, I could have her for now.

"Sandor." Her lips were swollen from how thoroughly I'd kissed her, and I met her gaze with a smile.

"Yes, sweetheart?"

"Why am I the only one naked?"

"But you're not," I replied. "You're still wearing that bra."

Without a word, she removed it, tossing it to the side and showing me the most perfect, round, handfuls of breasts I'd ever had the pleasure of touching.

"You were saying?" she teased.

"I was having so much fun enjoying your luscious body," I said. "But I can get naked too."

"Yes, please." Her eyes danced with a sexy combination of mischief and desire and I leaned down to taste her lips one more time.

"I'm glad you like to kiss," I told her as I set her on her feet, "because it's one of my favorite things."

"I actually don't usually like to kiss," she admitted, her eyes never leaving my body as I tugged my shorts down. "It's always been a fantasy to find a guy that made me want to, but you're the first to make me enjoy it."

I kicked my shorts free of my legs. "That's good to hear."

"Holy hell, are you kidding me?" She was staring at my crotch, her eyes wide, and when she looked up at me, she was shaking her head. "Seriously? Smart, rich, good-looking, honest-to-goodness royalty *and* a big dick? Do other men hate you?"

"Probably," I responded, "but not for any of the things you just mentioned."

She reached out and slowly wrapped her hand around my cock. "I can't close my hand around it," she said, chuckling. "Handsome, I don't know if this is going to fit."

"Oh, it'll fit. Promise." I reached for her and pulled her to me. "Do I need to bury my face between your legs again to get you ready?"

She licked her lips, something I noticed she did whenever I said something that turned her on, but she shook her head. "I think it's my turn to pleasure you."

"I already told you, tonight is all about you. If there's a next time, we can make it all about me."

"You're really something," she murmured, leaning up for another kiss that blew me away because she took the lead, her tongue sliding between my lips almost urgently. Our mouths moved together with ease, as if we'd been kissing a lot longer than half an hour.

She walked us back onto the loveseat against the wall, pushing me onto it and climbing onto my lap after me. She straddled me like a woman who knew what she wanted and I struggled to pull away long enough to grope around for the wallet that had been abandoned on the floor with my shorts.

"Do guys still carry condoms in their wallets?" she asked, amusement on her face.

"Where else would I carry it?" I countered, opening the package and sliding it down my throbbing erection.

She glanced down at it and then back at me. "I'm really having doubts about...how that's going to work."

"Trust me." This time when I kissed her, I let her know just how much I wanted her. What was foreplay before became a prelude to something more, something so superb I wasn't sure I would have been able to describe it. Her body moved with mine even though I wasn't even inside of her yet. She was completely immersed in our kiss, her hands in my hair, tugging at my ponytail and letting it fall free.

"God, that's hot," she whispered, gazing up at me lustily.

"Glad you like it." I shifted my hips so my cock was poised right where I wanted it. She was a little nervous, though, so I wouldn't rush. I had every confidence she would be begging me for more in short order, but I could wait until she was ready.

She sank down until I was a couple of inches inside of her. Her eyes closed and she tensed slightly. That wasn't what I wanted, so I slid one hand between us, searching out her clit and rolling it between my thumb and forefinger with enough pressure to make her breath catch.

"Oh my god." Her head fell back.

I ran my hands along her back, taking a moment to nibble her breasts. They weren't large, but they were literally perfect. For me anyway. I could hold them in my hands and the second I touched them, her nipples pebbled beautifully. Someday, I'd make her come just touching her breasts, but for right now, we both needed something else. I didn't know how long I'd last after the twenty minutes I'd spent kissing her and the fifteen minutes I'd spent between her legs. My dick was beyond ready for some action and I rocked my hips forward, edging deeper inside of her.

To my surprise, she sank down, taking all of me at once and letting out a gasp as I filled her.

"Jesus, Mary and Joseph," she panted. "I think you're going to split me in half."

We both chuckled and she leaned in, kissing me, trailing her lips across my cheek, to my ear, and then to that soft spot behind it that made me shudder.

"Easy, baby, I'm so close...and I need you to come one more time for me."

"Oh, I'm going to come," she said.

I pulled halfway out, shifted my hips, and thrust back in. I did it a few times, getting a feel for what she liked, and every time I bottomed out, she made the sexiest little noise, a cross between a cry of pain and a plea for more.

"You okay?" I asked, slowing down so I could look into her eyes.

"Soooo okay," she whispered, drawing out the words and starting to ride me like a rodeo queen. Her firm, gorgeous body rocked back and forth, her hips undulating in a rhythm that matched mine. When she sped up, I knew she was close and I felt a familiar tingling crawling down my spine. My balls drew up tight and I grunted from the exertion of holding back.

"Let go, handsome," she whispered, placing her hands on my chest. "Fuck me a little rougher and I'm going to come harder than before."

I jackhammered up and into her, down and out, over and over, until her pussy convulsed around me, squeezing and milking us both into paradise. I roared through my orgasm, filling the condom as we exploded together. She was quieter this time, but her short fingernails dug into my shoulders as she bucked on my lap, almost falling over backwards before I caught her around the waist.

She collapsed against me, her head in the crook of my shoulder, her beautiful torso pressed to mine. My arms closed around her of their own volition, and I held her, a little starstruck by how good it had been. Sex was usually good, for me anyway, but this had reached another level of pleasure, something that transcended a simple orgasm. I could do that on my own, but this, well, this didn't happen very often. Not in my lifetime anyway.

"I think we broke something," she murmured, stirring slightly.

"What do you mean?"

"I feel something...wet." She slowly pulled free and, sure enough, the condom had broken.

"Oh, hell." I met her gaze. "I'm sorry. But I promise you, I don't have any diseases."

"You'd better not." She playfully smacked my shoulder. "And don't worry, I have a birth control implant, so we're good."

I held out a hand to her and she took it carefully, meeting my gaze almost worriedly. I pulled her back onto my lap and touched her face. "Are you upset about the condom?"

"No." She smiled. "I was kidding. I mean, I'll take your word that you didn't just give me the clap, but I'm not mad. It happens. That's why I'm also on birth control."

The strangest twinge of disappointment ran through me, but it was quickly replaced by concern as she started to pull free.

"Where are you going?" I asked.

She paused. "Um, I don't know. I guess to clean up. I figured since we were done..." Her voice trailed off with uncertainty.

"I'm not that kind of guy," I said, getting to my feet and pulling her against me. "I don't treat a woman I've just made love with like an afterthought. I mean, I have, but those were strangers, women who were looking for exactly what I was looking for and nothing else. But you don't fall into that category. We work and live together, have a relationship beyond sex. I don't want you to feel awkward."

"We don't have a relationship beyond work," she said quietly. "Do we?"

"I think we do now."

Our eyes locked meaningfully, like they had for weeks, and she trailed a finger down my stomach, tracing the V of my oblique muscles. "Then I think this is going to be a whole lot of fun."

"You can say that again." I scooped her up and carried her to the back where the showers were.

16

L *ennox*

LIMAJ WAS BEAUTIFUL. As we rode in the limousine from the airport to the palace, I stared out at the countryside in a little bit of awe. The country was a fantastic mix of old and new, with modern buildings interspersed with ancient churches and cobblestone streets in some places. The sun was shining and it was hot today; eighty degrees in late August was a little warmer than average but I was glad because I wasn't ready for winter. Living in Las Vegas the last five years had me spoiled and I didn't know how I'd react to so many months of winter. From mid-September until the end of May, it was chilly and often wet. The weather was a little warmer in the southern part of the country, near the sea, but the rest was colder and winter lasted longer.

Although I'd known what I was signing up for, it was an odd feeling to be moving to a foreign country for an undetermined length of time. Would I be here forever? I'd never thought much about my future in terms of how long I could be a bodyguard, whether or not I'd ever get married or have a family, where I'd put down roots. My job as one of the bodyguards to the royal family was long-term, and since there was nothing keeping me in Las Vegas and the pay was fantastic, I hadn't given it a second thought when they'd presented me with the opportunity.

Things might get complicated now, though. I didn't know what Sandor's thoughts were about what had happened between us or if we were going to do it again, but I hoped so. Good sex was rare in my experience, and the more time I spent in his company, the more I enjoyed it. He was smart and dedicated, loyal and hard-working, not to mention hotter than the Vegas sun with a dry sense of humor that often made me laugh. They'd definitely broken the mold with Sandor, because I'd never met anyone like him and I probably never would again.

I doubted I was anything special to him, but good sex went both ways and he'd said we had a relationship that went beyond the professional. I didn't know exactly what that meant, but I wanted to find out. Nothing would distract me from my job, of course, but I deserved a little fun too. Especially the kind that ended in mind-blowing orgasms from a sexy, tattooed prince.

"Wow," I said aloud as we passed what appeared to be a very old cottage with a sign in the front yard. "Is that place for sale?"

Sandor nodded. "The building has been there since the 1600s, so anyone who buys it has to keep the original integrity and as much of the interior as is practical in order to be habitable. So far, no one has wanted to take on that much work. The inside is a disaster, the plumbing and electrical need to be updated, new roof, stuff like that."

"I'd buy it," I said automatically. "How far are we from the palace?"

"About ten miles." He smiled. "I can see you puttering around an old inn like that."

"It was an inn in the 1600s? That's so cool!" I loved everything historical, from architecture to romance novels, so a house like that would be a dream come true to own.

"Maybe once we're settled, I can make a few calls and see about getting a tour. Would you like that?"

"That would be great. Thank you." I smiled at him and he smiled back.

Oh, boy, I was in deep shit. Just the thought of what we'd done at the gym the other day made me a little...damp down there. How on earth was I going to work with him day in and day out with all this sexy passion between us?

"Casey and I are going to be spending a lot of time out and about with the people," Erik said. "Build on good will and some public relations, and since you and Sandor will be with us, just keep notes on anything like that, that you'd like to see. If Sandor or I can arrange it, we will. This is going to be your home for the foreseeable future, so I'd like you to get to know the area and some of the country. Not only will it be interesting, it'll help you do your job better, becoming familiar with back alleys and side streets, small towns, etc. You never know when the motorcade might need detours and such."

I nodded. "Sounds like a win-win plan to me."

"Is the music shop still there?" Casey asked Erik. "The one near Timur's Café?"

Erik frowned. "You know, I haven't looked. We'll have to check into it."

"I'll call around tomorrow," Sandor said.

"Oh, and there's a tutor coming that's going to work with all of you," Erik said. "I'll need everyone to speak at least rudimentary Limaji."

"I can curse in Limaji," Casey murmured. "Thanks to a certain tattooed bodyguard who shall remain nameless."

"You taught my wife to cuss in Limaji?" Erik arched his brow at Sandor.

"Nope. I taught your ex-fiancée to curse. Since you've been back together, I haven't taught her a single bad word."

"*Mahan ma cuolo.*" Casey giggled as she spoke.

Sandor snorted as Erik rolled his eyes.

"What did she say?" I demanded, joining in their laughter.

"She told me to kiss her ass," Erik said with a wry smile.

"I can teach you to say 'fuck you,' too," Casey said, still giggling.

"*Lubia ta,*" I responded with no expression.

"Where did you learn that?" Sandor demanded as Casey and I burst out laughing.

"Google," I told him.

Sandor shook his head but was smiling at me.

"I've been learning some the last six months or so," Joe said, joining our conversation. "I think it'll be a lot easier now that we're here."

"Honestly, I have a handle on the language as well," Casey said. "I wanted Luke to have a little something of his father, so Sandor would teach him words when he was a toddler, and I'd learn them too. Mostly, I struggle with nouns. Like bed, or table, or car... I know the basics like 'where is,' or 'when' and such. I'm looking forward to becoming more proficient."

"I'll have the tutor coming several times a week," Erik said. "He or she can work with you and Lennox one day, and then with Joe and the others on opposite days.

We talked and joked the rest of the way to the palace and when we drove up, I was a little mesmerized by the beauty. A huge, sprawling castle made of cement blocks and what looked like gold carvings and marble pillars. It was massive, which surprised me even though I wasn't sure why.

"This is the back entrance," Erik explained. "We'll go in and out of here because the front of the castle is always being watched by tourists. This is my entrance and over the next few days, I'll show you every nook and cranny of the building. Emergency exits, safe rooms, private areas, and the tunnel. All of us, including me, need to know this place inside and out, in case of an emergency. Sandor and I know it pretty well, but we're in the process of constructing an alternate tunnel that runs parallel to the one that's been here for years. So if someone like Omar, someone who knows about the original tunnel, manages to get inside the palace, they won't find us."

"I'll arrange for the security team to do some drills," Joe said. "We need to be prepared for anything."

"Everyone needs to take a day or two to get settled," Erik said. "I want each of you to get me a list of things you'll need because the palace is pretty sparse right now when it comes to the comforts of home. Once you've settled, let me know what's missing. I've been working on my quarters and I had to buy all kinds of basics, from towels to lamps to desk furniture. I guess Anwar got rid of everything from the other suites during his reign, so we're slowly restocking."

"It's going to be busy," Casey said gently. "But the priority is to make sure everyone is comfortable before it gets cold."

"It'll be cold before we know it," Sandor said. "We'll have our first snow in the next six or seven weeks, I think."

"How cold is cold?" I asked.

"January, February and March are bad," Sandor replied, meeting my eyes. "We'll stay below freezing for a solid three months in eighty percent of the country. The coast will be a little warmer, probably in the forties during those months, but that's not where we are. And the northern part of the country will have snow starting in October and going straight through until early May."

"We're not going to be there, right?" I laughed.

"Hell no."

THE PALACE WAS huge and Sandor and I went down several hallways before getting to an elevator that took us to a top floor where I'd been told my room was. There weren't a lot of options and Erik had chosen one he thought would be most comfortable, though I'd been told I could pick another if I was unhappy with his choice. Sandor unlocked a door around the corner from the elevator and we stepped inside. Erik hadn't been kidding about how bare everything was. There was a bed, a nightstand, a dresser that had seen better days, and a threadbare chair by the windows. The bed had no linens or pillows, there were no window treatments, and what had once been a beautiful fireplace was now framed by a crumbling carved mantel.

"Fuck." Sandor looked around with distaste. "This is unacceptable."

"I'll need some sheets and stuff," I said quickly, "but it'll be okay."

"No, it's not okay." He turned and grabbed my suitcase, which had been delivered for me. "Come with me."

"Sandor, it'll be fine," I protested.

"I wouldn't sleep in this room and neither should you." He gave me a wry smile. "Even if I wasn't a prince."

I grinned at him, loving the easy banter we'd morphed into since we'd slept together. "Are you taking me to your room?" I asked, raising my eyebrows.

He glanced down at me. "You have a problem with that?"

"No, but..." My voice trailed off.

"But what?"

"People are going to know we're hooking up and I don't know that we're at a place to be so...public."

He seemed to hesitate. "You may be right, but at the end of the day, you're not sleeping in that shithole. I can speak to my sister about you sleeping on the couch in her room, but until your room is renovated, you're not sleeping there."

"I don't want to inconvenience anyone," I protested.

"What we do is no one's business," he said after a moment. "We made some adjustments before we arrived, and this is now my wing of the palace, so technically, no one is going to know who's sleeping where. If it comes up, we can say I'm sleeping on the couch and I gave you my bed. Or we can let people assume whatever they want. We're adults and deserve a modicum of privacy."

I nodded. "Okay."

His suite of rooms was much nicer than mine. He had a massive four-poster bed made of mahogany, with expensive furniture and elegant decorations. The massive windows along one wall overlooked what appeared to be gardens, with a beautiful fountain and bushes containing colorful flowers.

"Apparently, my sister did some decorating while I was gone," he said, as if reading my mind. "She wanted to surprise a few of us so she busted her ass to get a few rooms done. I'd be happy with a mattress on the floor, but I have to admit she did a good job to make this feel homey."

"It's beautiful," I agreed.

"We'll talk to Erik tomorrow about the timeline for more renovations and we'll figure out what to do from there. In the meantime, make yourself at home. We have a security meeting planned over dinner so we can set up the duty roster and such, but that's not for another four hours." He met my gaze with a sexy smile. "Any idea what we could do to pass the time?"

I laughed and turned to wrap my arms around his neck. "No ideas at all. You?"

He looked over at the bed. "Well, there's a bed over there that's never been broken in."

My eyes widened in faux horror. "O. M. G. We should remedy that *immediately*."

He pulled off his shirt.

17

———

S*andor*

FRESHLY FUCKED WAS a good look on the woman in my bed. Hell, just having a woman in my bed was a great look, but Lennox was intoxicating, and the chemistry between us was intense. I couldn't keep my hands off of her, and the feeling seemed mutual. I loved a woman who wasn't shy about sex and gave as good as she got. Sexually, we were made for each other. Her hard, toned body was gorgeous, and her silky skin kept me going back for more.

"I'll need a shower before dinner," she whispered, curling into my side.

"We can do that." We were quiet for a few minutes before we finally moved apart.

"Do you have any idea what your duties are going to be? Aren't you technically still a member of Parliament?"

I grimaced. "Yes, but Erik's bringing everyone in for a meeting of the General Assembly soon. We're doing it here because Parliament House is essentially gone, but it's time to get things going."

"I don't know a lot about how things work here," she said. "But is the country...running itself?"

I sat up and stretched before holding out my hand to her. She took it and I led her into the bathroom, turning on the shower before answering. "The only thing Anwar did that was good, was keep the oil trade going. And even though he stole a lot of that money, he was arrogant enough to keep it all in his personal account. Since the royal family is one large entity when it comes to finances, that money reverted to Erik when he became king. He's since brought in a forensic accountant to go through the last ten years' worth of books and records to find out exactly where the al-Hassani family money ends and the country's money begins. Half of our oil belongs to the people, so the money brought in from selling it is supposed to be used for the people—roads, military, schools, etc. Anwar used the bare minimum to keep things afloat, so Erik has been drawing from that account to get things back in motion. Tourism this summer made a huge impact, allowing many shop owners to reopen, hotels to hire more staff. Things are changing for the better, but it takes time."

I stepped into the shower and pulled her against me.

"That's fascinating," she said. "It's really exciting to be part of something like this."

"I agree."

"Maybe you should stay in Parliament," she said after a moment.

I hadn't been expecting that and cocked my head. "Why?"

"Well, the country has been through a lot and Erik needs all the help he can get to turn things around. I'd think someone like you—a member of the royal family as well as his most trusted confidant—would be the perfect person to work with."

I frowned. "In theory, you're correct, but I've never wanted that life."

"It seems to me it's your calling, whether you wanted it or not. You carry the royal bloodline so you automatically earn respect, and more than all of that, you and Erik are a team."

I smiled, lowering my head to kiss her lightly, my lips lingering on hers for a few seconds. "That's incredibly insightful," I said. "And I'm sure it's going to come up when Erik and I meet."

She smiled up at me, and for the first time in a long time, something inside of me that had been wound up as tight as a drum suddenly loosened. It was faint, this feeling of emotional intimacy, but it was there and I wasn't sure if I was terrified or excited.

OUR DINNER MEETING went late into the night, going over blueprints of the renovations going on at the palace, strategizing escape routes in an emergency, and trying to set up a duty schedule that would allow all of us to get some sleep.

"We need more help," Joe said at last. "There simply aren't enough of us to cover the whole palace, as well as Casey and Erik, seven days a week, twenty-four hours a day."

"I can protect Casey at night," Erik said firmly. "But the stairs and elevator to our floors have to be monitored regularly, all night long."

"And the grounds, the main gate, the entrances…" Joe shook his head. "We'll need to bring in at least five more people. Short-term, everyone is willing to work seven days, but that's not sustainable."

Erik nodded. "Agreed. It's going to take time to find the right people, though, so for now, everyone's going to have to sacrifice. However, there will be hefty bonuses for everyone."

"I like bonuses," Xander said with a grin.

"There's a cottage outside the city I might buy," Lennox said, grinning. "So bonuses will be gladly accepted."

We talked for a while longer before we called it a night. Erik pulled me aside, though, asking me to stay behind. He poured two snifters of brandy and we settled in chairs next to the fireplace. Neither of us spoke for a minute and then Erik turned to me, a serious look on his face.

"Uh-oh," I said knowingly. "Now what?"

"Is there anything you want to tell me?" he asked, his eyes twinkling.

Jesus fuck. I mentally grimaced, though I kept my face neutral. "Like what?"

Erik grinned. "I went looking for you earlier. You were so busy you didn't hear me knock."

Double fuck.

I didn't say anything, merely let him continue.

"How long has this been going on with you and Lennox?"

"A week or so."

"Were you going to tell me?"

"Since when am I supposed to report to you about my sex life?"

"Since the woman you're having sex with is tasked with protecting my wife and newborn son. Not to mention the fact that she fits in well with all of us, and we trust her, so if things go bad with you romantically, it could cost us a key player in the staff, which we can't afford."

I sighed. I'd had these very same thoughts, but I didn't know what to do about that. Lennox and I were still feeling things out and we didn't have a label or status yet. I was attracted to her both physically and mentally, but I wasn't sure about the emotional stuff yet because it was too soon. "I don't know what to tell you," I said aloud. "It kind of started by accident and we're taking things one day at a time."

"So it's not just sex."

"I don't know yet. I mean, we work and live together, so it's definitely not just a casual hookup, but it's not anything serious either."

"Could it be?" Erik's voice was low, steady, because he knew how uncomfortable I was with this kind of conversation.

"I... Yes." I took a sip of brandy and looked away. I wasn't sure where that moment of clarity came from but it felt right when I said it.

"Casey and I like her a lot, so that would make us happy for both of you. Just promise me if you change your mind, you won't do it in a way that makes her want to leave."

"I'd never intentionally hurt her," I said. "You should know me better than that."

"I do, but affairs of the heart can get messy. Please be cognizant of that."

"Of course."

"Okay, now that that's out of the way, I have something else to discuss with you."

"This is about my role in your administration, yeah?"

"I need you, Sandor. Your talents are wasted as a bodyguard."

"This again."

"I'm overwhelmed, to be honest. I don't know how long I'll continue to do double duty as King and President, but until we sort that out, I need to surround myself with the most trustworthy people possible. Our circle has to stay small."

"Okay."

"You sacrificed more than a decade of your life for me, so I owe you. Anything you want, you just have to ask. But this is about duty and our people. They need someone like you in a prominent position."

"What position are you thinking of?"

"It's not a final decision yet, but somewhere in Parliament."

"You know that's uncomfortable for me."

"I know. But if you give me two years, you can take on any other role you want after that. Deal?"

"Deal." I paused. "But I still work with Joe on security matters."

"Absolutely."

"And you do not, under any circumstances, tell anyone about Lennox and me."

"Dude, half the palace heard the noise coming out of the bedroom. That ship has sailed."

I didn't know for sure, because it had never happened before, but I might have turned red. Jesus *fuck*.

· · ·

I WAS UP EARLY Sunday morning and I rolled over to look at Lennox, who was asleep beside me. Renovations on her room had started but it was far from finished, and frankly, the thought of her sleeping elsewhere made me a little crazy. Maybe I was a selfish prick, but the sex was beyond my wildest dreams and the more time we spent together, the more I liked her.

Today I had a surprise for her, and I leaned over to nuzzle the curve of her neck. "Wake up, sleepyhead."

"Mmm." She moved against me. "What time is it?"

"Almost eight, but we have meetings at noon, and I wanted to show you something this morning before we start our shifts."

Her eyes fluttered open. "Do I need to get dressed?"

I chuckled. "Yes. We're going somewhere. Jeans and a T-shirt are fine, though."

"All right." She sat up. "I can be ready to go in fifteen minutes."

"I'll call down to have Dena bring us coffee."

"Perfect."

AN HOUR later we were on the back of a motorcycle I'd borrowed from a palace guard I'd known since childhood. I headed out of Hiskale, toward the highway, and it occurred to me how much I enjoyed having Lennox behind me on the bike. I picked up speed as we left the city limits, and her arms tightened around my waist, so I opened it up, loving the feel of the engine between my legs and the beautiful woman draped across my back.

I slowed down as we hit the village of Ryskala, cognizant of small children and pedestrians.

"Hey, I recognize this street," Lennox yelled in my ear.

I grinned and turned into the driveway of the cottage she'd seen when we'd first arrived in Limaj.

I heard her squeal of excitement even through my helmet and I stopped the bike, waiting for her to climb off before I joined her.

"Do we get to go inside?" she asked.

"Absolutely." I secured both of our helmets on the handlebars and took her hand as we approached the door. I dug the key Erik had obtained for me out of my pocket and unlocked it. It was made of solid oak and squeaked as I pushed it open, but Lennox was so excited she brushed right past me.

"Oh wow," she said. "This is amazing. Look at the fireplace!" She went in that direction, marveling over the carved wooden mantel.

"Look at the bannister," I said, motioning to the stairs. It was made of cherry wood with lions carved into the ends.

"This is amazing," she said, inspecting every inch of the main room.

"I did a little digging," I told her, "and it appears this was an inn for about two hundred years before the last family abandoned it and it became a historical site."

"Who owns it now?" she asked, moving toward the kitchen.

"We do."

"We who?"

"The royal family. We didn't realize that the other day, but I pulled some records and that's what I found out."

Her face fell. "So that means I can't buy it."

"Well, it's for sale, so technically you can, but there are a lot of restrictions and the biggest thing is that the government would like it to become a working inn again. I don't know that you'd have the time to take on both extensive renovation and run an inn."

She nodded. "That's fair. I guess it's something to think about."

"I just have one question."

"Sure."

"Why would you want to buy an old, beat-up house like this in a foreign country?"

"Because it's really cool and I've never had a home as an adult. I mean, a place to lay my head, sure. But not a home. I left home before I turned eighteen and headed to college, where I lived in a dorm. Then I went into the Marines and slept in barracks and such. I got out and moved to Vegas to work for Joe and rented a tiny efficiency apartment that I pretty much only use for sleeping. I've never had a place of my own and it's time. Even if I'm only here a few years, it would be a great project to renovate the house and have something that's mine."

"Do you think you'll stay in Limaj a long time?" I asked, something unfamiliar stirring inside of me. Was this...emotion? Fuck. I didn't like it.

"Casey asked me if I would be willing to commit to five years because trusting your life to someone new is stressful. And I don't have anything to go back to in the U.S. other than a job and a handful of friends that are scattered all over the country."

"That's how I feel too," I admitted. "I spent twelve years in the U.S. and it was all about protecting Casey and Luke. I lived where Casey lived, went where she went. Now that I'm home, it's a little overwhelming to think about staying in one place."

"Do you consider yourself more American than Limaji now?" she asked. "Your accent is almost undetectable and you speak like an American in the things you say."

"I don't feel like an American, but I also don't feel like a Limaji prince anymore."

"I can't imagine what it was like for you." She moved close to me, putting one hand on my shoulder. "So many years living in hiding, keeping huge secrets, and carrying the weight of responsibility for Casey and Luke. You must have lost so much of yourself doing that for so long."

18

L*ennox*

HE WRAPPED one arm around my waist and held me against him. "Honestly, I'm still trying to figure out who I am. Erik wants me to stay in Parliament and I don't know how I feel about it."

"Maybe it would be good for you to try something different, you know?" I gazed up at him, trying to read the play of emotions on his face. "Kind of like me right now, opting for big changes because my life before had stagnated."

"We have that in common, for sure." He leaned down to lightly press his lips to mine, and as always, the moment we touched, fireworks went off around us. I slid my tongue into his mouth and instinct automatically took over. I practically melted into him, my body curving against his like we were one. He palmed my ass with his hands, pulling me closer and closer as the world seemed to disappear around us.

I slid my hands under his T-shirt, anxious to feel the warmth of his skin against mine, even if it was just my hands. We hadn't been involved long, but I was already addicted to his touch, to his very presence in my life. I'd been trying to keep my feelings in check, but it was almost impossible. He was that intoxicating.

The fact that he'd arranged this tour for me today made me stupidly happy, and I'd never been the type of woman who got all sappy when a guy I liked did something nice for me. But Sandor wasn't just any guy and even if I managed to get hold of my emotions, my body was going to betray me at every turn. I simply couldn't resist him.

He'd backed me against the nearest wall now and we were all over each other. Like we hadn't made love multiple times every day since we'd been in Limaj. Like he was as addicted to me as I was to him. Like this was more than a casual hookup. God, I was an idiot.

I didn't resist when he dropped to his knees and lifted my T-shirt, nuzzling my stomach and pressing light kisses around my belly button. His beard tickled my skin and I squirmed a little, but then he started unbuttoning my jeans and my heart rate kicked up a notch with anticipation of what was to come.

He slid my jeans down to my knees, all while nuzzling my stomach, his hands skimming my thighs.

"What are we doing?" I whispered, trying to retain some semblance of control.

He rumbled out a laugh. "What do you think?"

"Yeah, but what if someone comes in?"

"No one is coming except you." He pressed his face to my crotch as he pulled my panties down, and I sighed. I was wet just thinking about what he was about to do, a tiny whimper escaping me when he pulled away. He slid off my sneakers and pulled my jeans and panties the rest of the way off, leaving me naked from the waist down.

"Wh-what are you doing?" I gasped out the words because his mouth was dangerously close to the place that would drive me wild, but he was taking his time getting there.

"Trust me," he murmured.

I didn't even try to hide my moan when he snaked his tongue out between my legs. Before I could wrap my head around where this was going, he'd taken my right leg and brought it up and over his shoulder. Then he used his fingers to separate my folds and tease my clit.

"Oh, fuck, fuck, fuck," I gasped, frantic for something to hold on to, because doing this standing on one leg was the craziest thing ever.

"I won't let you fall," he said, his breath warm against my leg. "Just relax and enjoy."

He moved back between my legs and my eyes fell closed. He was an absolute master at oral sex, usually wringing at least two orgasms from me before he was done, and today was no different. His fingers and tongue were pure magic, making the leg I had on the ground start to shake uncontrollably My first orgasm came quickly, so he gentled his touch, working me up expertly, until I lost control for the second time, my fingers digging into his hair and scalp.

My knees were shaking so hard I could barely stand up and Sandor just scooped me up in his arms when he was done, sinking into a chair with me on his lap. I settled against his shoulder, simultaneously unnerved at how much he affected me and contented with our deepening relationship. I wished I knew what he was thinking, but I wasn't comfortable enough to ask. Not yet anyway.

"How do you do this every damn time?" I asked him.

"It's not hard to figure out what a woman enjoys," he replied, one of his big hands on my bottom. "Guys who don't bother are just lazy."

"You're definitely not lazy," I whispered, arching my neck so I could kiss his throat. His skin was a little salty but I ran my tongue over his Adam's apple, anxious to give him back even a fraction of the pleasure he always gave me.

"I try not to be."

"I want to make you feel as good as you make me feel," I told him.

"You don't have to," he said, a smile playing on his lips. "I didn't go down on you expecting something in return."

I skimmed my hands along his chest. "Are you ever going to tell me your fantasy?"

He smiled. "Maybe someday."

"But not today?"

"Probably not."

I chuckled, curious about his secrecy but more interested in pleasing him than talking about fantasies. "Then I guess I'll have to improvise."

"Well, far be it for me to stop you." He leaned back in the chair, a playful smile still on his lips.

I dropped to the floor and waited impatiently as he undid his jeans and slid them down over his hips. Yup, still huge, still my favorite thing to suck on these days, even though I could barely take half in my mouth. He didn't seem to mind, though, and I started with the head. I licked it with firm strokes, something I noted he liked, and then closed my lips around him, taking as much of him as I could. He never pushed or tried to go deeper, as if he instinctively knew it wouldn't be possible at his size. I gave it my best shot, until my eyes watered and I started to gag.

"Hey." He gently pulled away. "It feels good no matter how deep you take me, so do what's comfortable. I don't get off watching you struggle."

I backed off a little and used my hand, moving it in time to the rhythm of my mouth. He groaned, wrapping my hair in his fist though he didn't try to guide me. He just held on as I sucked and stroked him. I loved this feeling, loved the salty taste of the pre-come leaking from the head, and even the way he tugged at my hair while I was doing it. I'd reciprocated oral sex in the past because it was expected; with Sandor, it was my pleasure.

The sound he made as he came was pure masculine power, coming from deep in his chest, and I swallowed around him twice, until he finally relaxed.

"Damn, baby, that felt good." He tugged me back onto his lap and we sat there like that for a while, my arms wrapped around his neck and his wrapped around my torso.

"Thank you for today," I whispered.

"The pleasure was mine."

WE GOT BACK to the palace and he went to find Erik while I went up to his suite to freshen up since my hair looked like a chicken had just laid an egg in it. Once I was presentable, I went to find Casey since she'd asked me to stop by today when I had a chance. I found her in her office, which was really a private den just off to the side of the master bedroom. She looked up from her laptop as I came in and motioned for me to join her.

"Hey." She smiled. "Where did you and Sandor get off to this morning?"

"We went and saw that cottage I fell in love with on the day I arrived."

"And?"

"It's lovely. Needs a lot of updating as far as plumbing and electrical and such, but it's amazing. So much natural charm and historical character. I'm not in any hurry to buy it, since I don't have time to run an inn, but it's on my radar."

"So." Casey's eyes twinkled. "You and Sandor, huh?"

I groaned. "Are we that obvious?"

"Well, according to the staff, you're not exactly quiet about your late-night trysts."

I didn't normally blush, but this was my boss and, you know, a queen. "I'm sorry. We'll try to be quieter."

"Oh, please." Casey waved a hand. "That's ridiculous. Fuck to your hearts' content. It's been a long time coming for him, and I get the feeling you don't date a lot either."

"No, not much at all. Guys don't like women who can kick their asses."

"I think Erik fell in love with me *before* he figured out I had a black belt," Casey chuckled.

"I don't even know if I believe in love anymore," I admitted, perching on the edge of her desk.

Casey met my eyes curiously. "Really? You and Sandor are just knocking boots? Nothing else?"

"I don't think..." My voice trailed off. She was my boss. I had to play this off, no matter how interested she seemed. "It's just easier not to get too involved. He's...way out of my league."

Casey blinked. "Out of your league? Why? Because he has royal blood and a title?"

"Well, that's part of it. He's also rich and extremely good-looking. Rich, hot princes don't get serious with average-looking female bodyguards who have man hands."

"You don't have man hands." Casey laughed. "You have beautiful hands. Just because you keep your nails short doesn't make them man hands. My nails were almost always short because I played guitar for a living, but that didn't make them ugly. Just simple."

"Well, guys like Sandor probably don't marry simple girls like me, and I don't want to be nothing but a notch on his bedpost. I'm sure it'll burn itself out at some point in the next couple of months and he'll move on."

"You don't know him very well, do you?" Casey cocked her head. "Sandor is as loyal and kind as he is rich and hot. He wouldn't be sleeping with you if he didn't at least plan to give you a chance."

"He's really sweet under his gruff exterior," I admitted.

"Please tell me he's good in bed," Casey whispered.

"He's...*amazing* in bed." I bit my lip to keep from grinning too much.

Casey didn't hold back, though, and pumped her fist. "Yes! I knew it. Thank goodness. I'd be *so* disappointed if he was bad."

"No way. We're good in that department." I cleared my throat. "So, was there something else you wanted to talk to me about?"

"Yes. I want to hire an assistant of sorts and I know who I want, but she has to be thoroughly vetted, of course. Sandor is working on that part of it, but I'd like you to interview her this week as well, get a feel for her. You can make it seem like you had to outline the security protocols to make sure she understands them, but in reality, I want your gut feelings about her."

"Of course."

"Also, I'm flying in a dressmaker I know from New York. She's going to design dresses for us for the charity ball in October. Since my daughter is the belle of the ball, I figure we should all look special. And you'll need to dress up too, even as my bodyguard, because there will be a lot of celebrities there and we don't want to make them uncomfortable by having armed guards following us everywhere. We'll have her make you a dress you can wear a thigh holster with."

"Whatever you need," I said.

"You and Sandor should go together," she said with a teasing smile. "He looks fantastic in a tux."

"He looks even better naked," I responded.

"Well, I don't know about that, but I'll take your word for it."

"Okay." I got to my feet. "Is there anything else?"

"One more thing." Casey paused. "Are you planning to move out of Sandor's room any time soon?"

"I...don't know. Why?"

"Well, I don't want to make your room a priority if you're staying with Sandor, when there are half a dozen other rooms that need updating. Xander's room is a mess, and if we agree to hire Edita, she'll need somewhere comfortable too."

"Oh, go ahead and do theirs. I don't know what's going to happen with me and Sandor, but as long as the bed is clean, I can sleep anywhere if I have to."

Casey opened her mouth as if she was going to say something else, but apparently changed her mind.

"We good?" I asked after a moment.

She nodded and said, "Yup. See you later."

19

—————

S *andor*

MEMBERS OF PARLIAMENT began arriving just before nine on Monday morning, but I was still upstairs, adjusting my tie in the mirror. I wasn't looking forward to this and hadn't slept well last night. My gut was screaming at me today, warning me of danger, but I wasn't sure what to do about it since nothing bad was actually going on. My king, my *friend*, had asked me to sit at his side today, so what the hell else was I supposed to do? Joe was in charge of security, and he was damn good at what he did, but the control freak in me was having a hard time letting go.

"You okay?" Lennox leaned against the door to the bathroom, her eyes seeking mine in the mirror.

I nodded. "I'm heading down now."

"You look extremely sexy in a suit," she said with a smile, moving against me.

My arms circled her waist instinctively as I leaned down to kiss her. "Thank you." I playfully dropped my hands to squeeze her ass.

"I have to go," she said. "I'll be with Casey and the baby today."

She moved toward the door and I called to her. "Lennox."

She turned. "Yes?"

"Pay attention to your gut today. Even if it winds up being a false alarm, take Casey and the baby to one of the tunnels if you find even the slightest thing is off. No one is going to be upset that you erred on the side of caution."

She nodded. "Don't worry. I've got this."

She shut the door quietly behind her and I turned my thoughts to the task at hand. The more I thought about my place in Parliament, the more confused I became. I had the same education that Erik had—an undergraduate degree in international finance and a master's in business. I'd served more time in the military than anyone in the royal family was expected to since I'd done two years while Erik was finishing high school and then another year while he'd done his own required service. I had two different black belts and had trained with the CIA while I'd been in hiding, so I knew security, intelligence, and protection protocol like the back of my hand.

Because I'd taken my job of protecting Casey and Luke so seriously, I'd immersed myself in it to the point that I'd let everything else fall to the wayside. Other than sex here and there, when I couldn't stand celibacy anymore, the only thing I thought about was keeping my charges alive. Now it seemed I was moving on to a different part of my life and I wasn't sure I knew how anymore. My growing affection for Lennox had shown me just how inept I was as a...boyfriend? She hadn't said anything, and I suspected she wasn't all that experienced at romantic relationships either, but I didn't want to be another one of those guys who disappointed her. There was no problem in the bedroom, of that I was sure, but I struggled with everything else.

We'd been together a few weeks and had more sex than I'd ever had with the same person in my life. We also lived together, and while I hadn't planned to jump right to that level, we'd had no choice initially and now I couldn't imagine her moving out. She was easy to live with, get along with, sleep with... What else did I need? My feelings for her were growing exponentially, which could mean one of two things: that I'd found my soulmate and we were meant to be together, or that our proximity to each other, both personally and professionally, had thrown us into a situation that would most likely end badly. I was okay with the first, if not a little wary, but the second wasn't an option. Our lives were too closely intertwined.

Glancing at my watch, it was a minute before nine, so I grabbed my briefcase and headed down to the meeting room. Erik had transformed the formal dining hall into a meeting room of sorts, with tables set up that seated ten each, and a podium at the front of the room. Erik was already there, drinking a cup of coffee and greeting members of Parliament as they arrived. I spotted my brother and veered in his direction since we didn't see much of each other these days.

"Hey." Daniil looked up with a grin. "You're looking good, big brother."

"You don't look too bad yourself," I replied, giving him a hug.

"I hear there's a woman in your life."

I groaned. How the fuck had word gotten around so quickly? "Let's not do this here," I said quietly. "We're still new and people are starting to talk. I don't want anything to scare her away."

Daniil nodded. "Understood. So, is it true Erik's asked you to take a seat in Parliament?"

"It is, but we haven't finalized anything yet. Are you going to be the ambassador to the U.K.?"

"If that's what he wants from me, absolutely."

"Gentlemen." Jesper Vanta joined us and I shook his hand, wondering what was happening with him and Daniil, since they were now divorced but shared two children. Daniil and I had never spoken about his sexuality; I'd never known he was gay and still doubted it, but that wasn't the kind of thing we talked about. We were a fairly uptight family, in spite of our fierce loyalty to each other.

"Good to see you." I shook Jesper's hand.

"Is it true there's a woman in your life?" Jesper asked, his eyes twinkling with laughter.

I rolled my eyes and Daniil started laughing.

"On that note," I told them, "I'm going to get some coffee." I walked in the other direction, wondering if something was wrong with me, if I was truly an uptight prick, or if I was somehow ashamed to admit I had a girlfriend. I hadn't had one since college, and that felt like a very long time ago, so this was all new to me. Watching the love Casey and Erik shared had skewed my view of romance, convincing me I would never find someone to love the way they loved each other.

Except I'd asked a woman I'd only slept with a couple of times to move in with me. There had been reasons, excuses probably, but at the end of the day I didn't want her to leave. I liked waking up next to her, having her at my side, and her interest in my country warmed me in ways I didn't want to think about. She was as close to perfect, for me anyway, as anyone could possibly be. Which scared the crap out of me, and truth be told, nothing scared me outside of the thought of something happening to Erik, Casey or the kids.

"Morning." Erik smiled as I joined him, coffee in hand.

"Good morning." I nodded at the man beside Erik, General Sven Galante. He was a four-star general in our army, though he was probably only about five years older than I was. He'd risen through the ranks quickly under Anwar's rule, and once Erik had cleaned house after taking over, Sven had gone straight to the top. However, I wasn't sure what he was doing here since the military wasn't part of Parliament. Erik gave me a look, a tiny, subtle nod of his head that most people wouldn't see, but we'd shared this type of thing for most of our lives. It was part of what kept us alive over the years, our ability to communicate without words or motions.

In this case, he was letting me know there was a specific reason we'd brought in a general to this meeting, and I wrestled with disparate feelings. This almost definitely meant Sven was in the running for Minister of Defense and that Erik had something else in mind for me, which confused me since I'd been leaning in that direction.

"Shall we get the meeting started?" Erik asked.

"Let's do it." I sank into the chair beside his. We were at the head table, for lack of a better word, which included Erik, Daniil, Elen, Jesper, General Galante, and someone I didn't know. I glanced at Erik and he gave me another one of his looks, telling me he'd explain soon.

In the meantime, I leaned over and kissed my sister's cheek. "Good morning," I told her. "And so help me, if you ask about my girlfriend, I'll make sure Erik makes you ambassador to the Arctic Circle."

She laughed. "Why the big secret?"

"Because I don't want anything to jinx it."

"As long as she makes you happy." She turned to Jesper and started a conversation with him, effectively ending ours, and I was grateful for that.

"Good morning." Erik stood at the podium and got everyone to quiet down. "The breakfast buffet is set up on both sides of the room, and it looks like most of you have plates, so I thought I'd start with a few opening statements. You should all have an agenda in front of you. If you turn to the last page of the packet that's been provided, you'll see a list of all Parliament positions and those that are currently filled."

Our Parliament was made up of sixty members. There were two representatives from each region of the country, similar to state senators in the U.S., and we had twenty-five regions. Then there was the President of the General Assembly, a position currently held by Erik, and eight cabinet positions we called Ministers. Historically, the final position had been—ironically—that of historian, someone who was in charge of all the records of everything that went on in Parliament. As far as I knew, we didn't need one anymore because technology eliminated the need for it, but I wasn't sure what Erik's plans were with regard to that position, which meant there were fifty-nine positions that needed filling.

"To get started, we need to address the attack from the last time we met. Parliament House, sadly, is beyond repair. I've already started recon-struction, but without a budget for the year, there isn't a lot of money to play with. Our fiscal year is from the first of June until the thirty-first of May, and the current budget doesn't meet our needs for rebuilding the country. In that same vein, we also don't have a Minister of Commerce, who would be the one to put a budget together for us to make adjust-ments to. Angus Haverly is the man I'd like to see in that role, and his biography is part of your packet. I'd like everyone to take a few minutes to read it, while we finish eating. Then I'll let him speak and we'll have a vote."

He sat down beside me and I nudged him. "Is that him?" I asked under my breath in English, moving my eyes in the direction of the stranger at our table.

Erik smiled. "I don't think you two ever met," he said, turning to the man sitting across the table from us. "Angus, this is my cousin and closest confi-dant, Sandor Gustaffson. Sandor, this is Angus Haverly. He's half-Limaji, born to a Limaji mother and British father. We had classes together my freshman year at university, but he graduated that year and we lost touch. He's moved back since I took power. He worked on Wall Street for a decade and then moved to the U.K. as a financial advisor to some of the royal family. I think he's perfect for the role of Minister of Commerce."

"Thank you." Angus inclined his head. "I'm honored to have the oppor-tunity to work with you."

"Nice to meet you," I told him.

"Likewise." We chatted for a bit and then Erik got into the nitty-gritty of the meeting. Everything had to be debated, brought to a vote, and voted on. We started with some of the easier appointments, like Ministers of Commerce and Arts and Education. We deliberated through lunch and were now inching toward dinnertime. I'd loosened my tie, gone to the bathroom twenty-seven times, and drank so much coffee I probably wouldn't sleep for a week. And yet, we'd only accomplished a handful of things.

"Your Majesty." One of the men from the northern part of the country got to his feet. "With all due respect, I feel this has to be said."

"By all means." Erik inclined his head.

"Your rush to accomplish so much in a single day shows your inexperi-ence. We need to take the time to establish ourselves, create unity. Making rash decisions will only lead to more chaos."

Erik met the man's eyes and didn't say anything for a full minute.

Uh-oh. I dipped my head to hide my smile because this was classic Erik. He was about to give someone a dressing down they would never forget, and in such a way that they would most likely thank him for it when he was done.

"As you know," Erik said in a deadly quiet tone, "I spent nearly eleven years in hiding. I gave up my fiancée, our child, my family, and my birthright—all for my country, my people. I didn't have a plan, but I knew I had to protect the bloodline, so that when the time was right, we could oust Anwar from power. Since my return, I've devoted almost all of my time—again neglecting my family, my children, everyone that I'd already lost so much time with, in order to bring our country back to some semblance of normalcy after a decade of terror. I was instated as king with a unanimous vote of Parliament. I was elected President of the General Assembly with ninety-two percent of the vote from the general public, which is unheard of in a democracy." He paused, looking around. "If there's someone more suited, and also willing, to step up and replace me so that I can enjoy a little time with the family I just got back, as well as take on the role of rebuilding our country, please, step forward and we can arrange another vote."

The room was silent. The man who'd initially challenged him sat back down, his face a little red.

"We don't have time to jump through hoops," Erik continued. "While we'll still follow the rules of law and the tenets of our constitution, we don't have six months to debate every bill. We barely have a functional government. Omar Daishel, my former brother-in-law, has already made multiple attempts on my life. International relations are almost nonexistent. The people need us to reinstate trade, reestablish tourism, create jobs and a working economy. If you think we can do this in tiny incremental steps, you haven't been paying attention. So either get on board or get out of my way." He turned back to his notes. "Now, next on the agenda..."

With the education bill still on the table, I had a feeling we'd be here all night because that was one of Erik's priorities. It would take weeks to revamp the budget, but at least we'd already approved an emergency addendum that would release money to continue rebuilding Parliament House and keep the country's infrastructure running. Beyond that, we had so much to do it was daunting.

20

———————

L*ennox*

Being a bodyguard could be spectacularly boring. That was a good thing in this case, because it meant everyone was safe and sound, but it was hard for me to sit still for long periods of time. With nothing going on, my mind turned to the sexy prince I was presently living and sleeping with. I'd never imagined myself in the position I was in, and it was both exciting and scary. I was trying not to let myself get too involved too quickly, but it was hard not to. He was everything I never knew I wanted. Unfortunately, I had no idea what his take was on things between us.

Sandor kept anything that might resemble an emotion buried. Other than when we made love, he was tightly wound and always on alert. He didn't sleep well and the only time he was ever relaxed was the five minutes or so after we'd had sex. Once in a while he let his guard down, like the few times I'd seen him with Luke, but the rest of the time he was both physically and mentally tough as nails. Sometimes it bothered me, the way he kept himself closed off to the world, but I was becoming increasingly aware that he was letting me in. He laughed a little more often now and though he struggled with emotional intimacy, I'd seen signs of him trying. There were tiny moments of tenderness when we were alone, traces of feelings I tried not to read too much into.

I thought of myself as a loner and kept the circle I considered friends extremely small, but Sandor took that to another level entirely. He had Erik, Casey and the kids, along with a handful of colleagues like Joe and Xander, but that was all. He'd even lost touch with his brother and sister over the years, though they appeared to be reconnecting now that we were all in Limaj. I wasn't sure what demons he struggled with, but I also wasn't sure if we'd reached a place in our relationship where I could ask.

Not wanting to let myself get any more distracted, I headed back to Casey and Erik's living area and found her looking at something on her phone.

"Hey, Lennox, can you message Sandor and find out how much longer they're going to go? Erik isn't answering my texts, which means he's probably talking, and I need to know if I should go ahead and eat without him."

"Oh, um, sure." I pulled out my phone and sent Sandor the message. He responded a minute later.

Sandor: We'll probably be here half the night. Tell her to eat without him.

I relayed the message and Casey nodded. "Okay, well, I guess it's just you and me, then. Want to eat with me?"

"Sure. What's on the menu?"

"Really boring stuff," Casey sighed. "Grilled chicken and veggies."

"Welcome to my world," I said with a laugh. "That's how I have to eat if I want to stay in shape."

"Yeah, well, I've never had to worry about it before, but I guess having a baby at thirty-five changes everything."

"You'll get back in shape before you know it," I told her. "And once you're feeling up to it, we can start working out together. I'll get you into better shape than ever."

"I'll take you up on that." Casey called down to the kitchen and then turned to me. "So, how are things going with Sandor?"

I chuckled. "Nothing new. We're too busy to do much of anything but sleep and make love. We usually have about fifteen minutes a day to talk about stuff that isn't related to work, and other than taking me to see that cottage on the outskirts of the city, we haven't had much time together."

Casey scowled. "Well, that's lame. Has he even taken you out on a date?"

My face felt a little hot as I shook my head. "No, but there honestly hasn't been time. We got together days before we moved to Limaj and in the month we've been here, we've been going nonstop."

"But you're living together, even if it was only because of circumstances out of our control. That has to mean something, right? Are you happy? Does he make you feel good outside the bedroom?"

I sighed, sinking into the chair beside her. "Honestly, I try not to let him make me feel too good outside the bedroom because even though you don't agree, I still feel like he's way out of my league. Have you seen the gossip columns lately?" I shuddered a little. "The number of women interested in him, seeking him out, looking forward to seeing him when we go to Vegas for the charity ball, well, it's a little daunting."

Casey smiled. "I know. And that's why I'm having a custom gown made for you. You're also going to have professional hair and makeup done that day, right along with me and the girls. He's not going to know what hit him when he sees you."

I tapped my foot impatiently. "That's not who I am."

"And being the queen of an eastern European country isn't who I am, either, yet here we are. Erik knows who and what I am and loves me anyway. By the same token, I respect who and what he is, so I do my best to fit into both worlds. If you love each other, none of that other stuff will matter."

"I think it's way too soon to think about the L word," I muttered.

Marisol came in with a large tray of food, setting it down on the coffee table before leaving us to our own devices. We ate in companionable silence, each lost in our own thoughts, until we heard Levi start to cry through the baby monitor. Casey started to get up but I stopped her since I was done eating.

"I'll get him," I said. "You finish eating."

I went into the baby's nursery and picked him up. Sylvia took overnight shifts now since he wasn't sleeping well, but he was cute as hell. I held him against my chest, rocking him slightly, and for the first time in my life, I wondered what it would be like to have one of my own. I'd never really given it a lot of thought because between the military and my terrible luck with men, I figured it wasn't going to happen. But now I had this gorgeous, sexy, sweet man who actually liked me.

Damn Sandor. This was all his fault, making me think things I shouldn't and want things I hadn't thought about in a long time. I was going to have to snap out of this romantic haze I'd been in and be a little more realistic about the future. Maybe the smart thing to do would be to break things off. Except I didn't want to.

I carried Levi back into the living room and Casey looked up with a smile. "How's my sweet boy?"

"He's so beautiful," I gushed, handing him to Casey. "You and Erik make some pretty babies."

"You and Sandor would make some pretty babies too," Casey said, wiggling her eyebrows.

"Let's hold off on the baby shower, okay? I don't think either of us is ready for that."

"I wasn't ready either," Casey said quietly. "But I wouldn't trade it for the world."

WHILE CASEY TENDED to the baby, I opened my laptop and pulled up the cameras. Although there was a control room with a separate monitor for each camera, we also had direct links on our computers so we could access them from anywhere, at any time. I'd been checking periodically throughout the day because we'd been taught to look for either something completely out of place or something different that appeared too often. Like the same person going to the front gates repeatedly. There had been someone earlier today that caught my eye. And there he was.

I enlarged the frame so I could get a better look at him, chewing the inside of my cheek thoughtfully. Why did he look familiar?

"Casey?"

"Hmm?"

"Does this guy look familiar to you?" I turned the laptop so she could see.

She squinted and frowned. Then her eyes widened. "Holy shit."

"Who is it?" I asked quickly.

"That's Omar."

"Shit." I grabbed my phone and texted Sandor.

21

———

S*andor*

I WAS FIGHTING boredom and frustration from the lack of progress when a
text from Lennox came through.

Lennox: Need to see you NOW.

I got to my feet with no explanation; Erik knew me well enough to know
I wouldn't do it if I didn't have a damn good reason. I strode out into the
hallway just as she was coming down the main staircase at a fairly fast pace.

"What's going on?" I asked her.

"Omar. He's been casing the front gate. I've spotted him at least three
times today, but it took me until now to recognize him."

"Fucker." I started up the stairs. "I need you to take my place in the meeting. We need security in there. For protocol reasons, I need you standing at
the front of the room, close enough to Erik to get to him before anyone else,
should there be an attack of some kind."

"You sure you wouldn't rather—" she began.

"No. If Omar is nearby, it's better for me to be involved because I know
him and understand the language."

"Won't Erik wonder what's going on?"

"Say, 'Excuse me, Your Majesty,' and whisper what's going on in his ear.
That's all. He knows the drill."

"What about Casey and the baby?"

"I'll move Joe to be with her and take Xander with me. You're with Erik."

"Understood." She moved into the room without hesitation.

I was grateful she did as I asked without question, considering our personal relationship. I'd worried that we'd have a hard time separating the two, but apparently not. I should have known better, of course. She was a consummate professional and wouldn't let something like the fact that we were involved impact the safety of our friends and family. It was strange, how quickly she'd integrated into our family unit. Erik, Daniil, Elen and I were related by blood, and I'd had more than a decade to build relationships with Casey and the kids. Xander had been with us for a couple of years and was just now reaching the point where I trusted him implicitly.

With Lennox, though we'd had a rough start, we'd gelled quickly. In more ways than one. Even as I took the stairs three at a time to get to the control room and talk to Joe, she was in the back of my mind. Knowing I could trust her was worth its weight in gold and I was able to focus on the task at hand without worrying about Erik. Not only was she perfectly capable of protecting him, he was pretty adept at protecting himself, so I wasn't overly worried. Not yet anyway.

Joe looked up as I came into the room and I told him what Lennox had seen.

"Good eye," he muttered. "I must be losing my touch." He tapped a few keys to enlarge the front gate screen and, sure enough, someone that looked very much like Omar was peering through the security bars. He was dressed like any of the other tourists or citizens who often came to look at the palace, but now that Lennox had spotted him, it was definitely Omar. And he had no business loitering at the front gate. He was up to something and I needed to know what it was.

I yanked off my jacket and tie, grabbing a hoodie off the counter. We had matching emerald green hoodies for the palace guards to wear during regular shifts. We wanted to be able to identify each other without being too obvious and this had been our short-term solution. I yanked it on and headed out, cursing the dress shoes on my feet.

"Tell Xander to meet me out front," I called to Joe. "But don't alert the guards or it might spook him."

I took a back exit and lifted the hood over my head, scanning the area. I recognized the guard at the back door and nodded at him, muttering something about a perimeter check. He was probably surprised, but I was more concerned with finding Omar. Capturing him would eliminate our biggest threat, but he wasn't stupid, and I wasn't naïve enough to think it would be easy.

I skirted the side of the building, using the binoculars I'd thought to grab to scan the gate. He was still there. In my peripheral vision, I got a glimpse of Xander heading toward the gate from the other direction, but Omar must have had some sixth sense and quickly put up his hood, moving away from the gate. I picked up speed, sprinting across the grounds and past the two guards at the gate, who moved aside in confusion.

"He saw us," Xander muttered, coming up behind me.

"Let him go," I told him, coming to a stop. "There are too many people and he'll be lost in the crowd in seconds anyway."

"Shit." Xander looked around.

I motioned with my head and we walked back in the direction from which we'd come. I hated that he'd gotten away, but I wasn't surprised. He hadn't gotten this far by being stupid, so we were just going to have to up our game.

"I have to go back to my meeting," I told him, "so keep an eye on the surveillance cameras. It's getting dark now and I don't want to take any chances with the safety of our guests."

"Got it." Xander jogged off in the other direction and I yanked the hoodie off my head. I didn't bother getting my jacket and tie; I needed to update Erik and the rest of Parliament regardless of how I was dressed.

Everyone looked up as I entered the room and I felt a moment of discomfiture, unprepared to have that much attention on me. But my eyes sought out Lennox, who was standing a couple of feet behind Erik, and her presence relaxed me. Erik immediately rose to greet me, concern etched into his face.

"Was it Omar?" he asked under his breath.

I nodded. "But we lost him. As soon as he spotted us, he took off, and there were just too many people for us to safely give chase."

Erik sighed. "Well, at least now we'll be able to tell everyone to look for him. Let me debrief the Assembly on what we know and then I'm going to get this education bill passed if I have to tie them all to their chairs."

ERIK GOT his bill passed just after midnight and we finally adjourned. We'd accomplished a great deal, to be honest, and it would have been a good day had I not been preoccupied with Omar's appearance at the front gates.

"When are we leaving to go back to Vegas for the ball?" I asked him.

Erik hesitated. "Casey's still struggling. Her doctor upped her meds and she's hanging in there, but I'm worried about her. I'd like to go back a little sooner than we intended. I know it's inconvenient, but she needs to be able to check in with her doctor, see her mom...and frankly, my children will only be small once. I already missed most of Luke's childhood, and now I'm only seeing Leni a few times a year... I don't want to spend these years working ninety hours a week. I can be a statesman when they're older. I want to be a husband and a father too."

"I don't know if you can do it all."

"I don't know either, but I have to put a bit of a priority on my wife and children. Do me a favor, my friend."

"What's that?"

"Don't make my mistakes. Take time for your own needs and don't worry so much about mine. Or the country's."

"Coming from the man who literally gave up everything for his country and his people."

"And learned a very hard lesson." He gave me a meaningful look.

We parted at the bottom of the stairs and I watched him ascend toward his private residence before turning to my own.

When I got there, the suite was quiet and empty. I got undressed and stepped into the shower. Though I wasn't dirty, per se, I'd been in the same clothes for sixteen hours and felt grungy. Especially since I hoped to be balls-deep inside of Lennox in the next hour or so. Hopefully, she'd be up soon. Casey and the baby were undoubtedly in bed, so there was no reason for her to hang around, though she'd probably been waiting for Erik to return before turning in for the night.

The glass shower door opened and I felt Lennox's warm body up against my back. I reached back to slide my hands over the curve of her ass, smiling as she pressed a kiss into the middle of my back.

"Hey, babe." Her voice was soft.

I turned, looking down into her face. "Hi. How was your day?"

"Mostly uneventful. Except for that Omar thing."

I grimaced. "Yeah, we're going to need to put his picture all over the palace so guards and employees will recognize him immediately if he shows his face anywhere near the gate again."

"I get the feeling he won't make that mistake again," she murmured.

"You're probably right."

She turned her back to me, reaching for her shampoo, something that smelled like roses and lavender or something equally herbal that normally wouldn't have meant much to me. Except now that she used it in front of me and then usually crawled into bed with me, the scent had become something I associated with her, and made me want to surround myself in it. I leaned over to kiss the curve of her neck, inhaling the smell of her shampoo and tasting the saltiness of her skin. She continued to enthrall me and I wasn't sure whether or not it was time to verbalize something, to let her know how much I liked her.

Jesus, that sounded stupid even in my head. How was I supposed to initiate a conversation about liking her without sounding like a dumbass? Or was I just supposed to assume she knew?

Fuck. I had no idea how to do this and I felt ridiculous.

"What are you thinking about so intently?" she asked, startling me back to the present.

"What makes you think I was thinking intently?" I asked.

"You get this little crease between your brows... It's cute."

I chuckled. "Yeah, okay." I kissed the tip of her nose and then stepped out of the shower and grabbed a towel. She followed a minute later, after squeezing the water out of her hair. We dried off in companionable silence and she brushed her hair while I brushed my teeth.

Maybe I didn't need to say anything. Because this was easy and comfortable and felt really good. I'd probably muck it up if I said something this soon anyway. I was definitely better off keeping my mouth shut.

22

———————

L *ennox*

THE NEXT COUPLE of weeks were busy, keeping Sandor and me apart more than usual, except at night. But even then, we were surprisingly too exhausted for sex and usually just fell asleep in each other's arms. Which was weird, considering how casual the relationship was in general. There were more and more moments of intimacy these days, especially when we made love, but mostly we were just too damn busy.

On a Sunday morning, the day before we were leaving to go back to Las Vegas for the charity ball and whatever else we were going to do, I woke up to the hottest guy I knew between my legs, doing something that made my hips arch up and my entire body quiver from the pleasure. By the time I was capable of rational thought again, he'd crawled up and wrapped his arms around me, erection pressed against my back, apparently in no hurry to find release.

"Mmm." I shifted, my eyes still closed as I breathed in the faint scent of his aftershave. "Good morning."

"Good morning, beautiful." He kissed the top of my head.

"What did I do to deserve such a wonderful wake-up?"

"Nothing. I've just been neglecting you of late, so I thought I'd make up for it."

"I can't complain," I admitted.

We lay there in companionable silence for a while, his body wrapped around mine, one of his big, beautiful hands running through my hair.

As we lay there, I had a thought and I tipped up my head to look at him. "We've been doing the sex thing for a while now and—"

"Is that what this is?" he asked, palming one of my breasts with his hand, his thumb lazily stroking my nipple until I almost forgot what I was going to say.

"Well, we haven't really said what it is." Damn him, I was already squirming with the need for him to touch me more.

"Mm-hmm. We may not have used any specific words, but there's more to this than sex unless I'm way off the mark."

I paused. He always did shit like this, playing games with my heart even though that probably wasn't his intention. "We're friends who have an incredibly active and pleasurable sex life," I said, leaning into his hand. I loved his fucking hands. They were huge, like the rest of him, but he was so gentle with them.

"Uh-huh." His other hand had travelled down to skim the light patch of hair at the apex of my thighs.

"Could I finish my thought please?" I asked, chuckling.

"Of course."

"Anyway, we've been together for a while now and you still haven't told me *your* fantasy."

"You think there's just one?" he drawled, his eyes darkening slightly.

"I, er, well, you haven't told me any."

"I'm kidding. There's just one. I've done everything else I've wanted to do in the bedroom."

"Are you going to tell me what it is?"

Something I'd never seen before flickered in his eyes and he turned away. It wasn't possible Sandor was embarrassed, was it? I wouldn't have thought so but I knew what I'd seen and it had been there, albeit only for a second.

"You can't laugh," he said at last, stilling the movements of his hands.

"Of course not." I paused. "Well, I mean, if you fantasize about wearing a pink tutu and high heels and having me spank you with a red feather, I might giggle a little, but I'll still do it."

He chuckled. "Done all that. So to speak."

"I'd pay good money to see that."

He pinched my nipple hard enough to make me gasp but I wasn't giving up. His trying to distract me made me want to know more than ever.

"Let me preface this by saying I've never, *ever* had unprotected sex."

"Not even once?"

He shook his head. "Not as a stupid, horny teenager, not during any of my drunken nights on tour with Casey and Pretty Harts, never. As a member of the royal family, it was drilled into us from a very young age that we were targets for gold diggers and women looking to trap us, so it was never an option. And as an adult, of course, my life was too complicated to risk it."

"Okay."

He met my gaze, his piercing blue eyes finding mine with what I could only describe as a sudden burst of confidence. The strongest, toughest man I knew was actually nervous about telling me his sexual fantasy? I couldn't even fathom what that meant, although I could guess part of it after what he'd just said.

"I want to be bare inside a woman, a woman I care about," he said, his deep voice a little edgy now. "Fucking her harder than I've ever fucked anyone, and ending with putting my baby inside of her."

Oh sweet Jesus, my ovaries might have exploded with longing, and I had to rest my head on his chest to prevent him from seeing how badly I wanted that woman to be me.

"I know it's not very sexy," he said softly. "But—"

"It's one of the most romantic things I've ever heard," I whispered, keeping my face buried in his chest. "Which makes it sexy to me."

"You think my Neanderthal fantasy about fucking a woman so hard I imprint my seed in her is romantic?" He actually sounded confused. Poor, sweet, clueless Sandor. How had he gone so many years without an ounce of romance in his life?

"You said it at the beginning—with the right woman. *That* makes it romantic. That makes it the kind of fantasy a woman who loves you might want to share."

Our eyes finally met and we just stared at each other. It was right there, just beneath the surface, all that damn emotion we were both trying to hide. And we both knew it. The problem was that I was the only one who was cognizant of it.

"Are you sorry you asked?" he asked after a moment.

"Not even a little. It makes me appreciate the man you are even more." I ran my fingers through his hair. The hair I loved so much. I didn't know what I would do when this inevitably ended and I had to sleep with other men, men who weren't my Sandor.

"What did you think about just now that made you look so sad?" he asked.

There he was, my borderline sensitive, intuitive man. Too bad he pretended all his better qualities were a result of his bodyguard training. "Just wondering how you go backwards once you've had the best sex of your life."

"Backwards? What does that mean?"

"When we eventually move on and stop doing this... I've been with enough men to know this kind of sex isn't the norm. So it makes me sad to think someday I'll have to go back to mediocre sex and self-induced orgasms."

Instead of responding, he kissed me, his lips taking mine almost fiercely. Almost as if the thought of me being with other men made him jealous. Something obviously irritated him because within seconds I was flat on my back, he'd sheathed himself with a condom and was pushing inside of me, taking me with a possessiveness I'd never felt from him before. But he was all over me, kissing, touching, pulling my hair, practically swallowing my tongue, until I was a panting, quivering mess of passion.

"Say my name." He growled as he thrust in, this time staying firmly seated and forcing me out of my lust-filled haze.

"San-dor..." I licked my lips as he pulled out and pushed back in.

"Again."

"Oh my god, what—"

"Again. My whole name."

"Sandor."

"The rest." He was panting as hard as I was, but he didn't let up. Out, in, stop. Out, in, stop.

"Harrison."

"And?" This time he pulled out to the tip before stopping.

"Gustaff-son." I gasped out his surname, arching my hips to pull him deep again, though he continued to torment me.

"Don't ever forget it," he whispered, burying his face in the crook of my neck as he started to move again.

We came together, the timing so frighteningly in sync it might have shocked me had I not been completely caught up in this beautiful man. I came so hard I practically blacked out for a moment, my entire body tingling from the intensity.

It wasn't until he shifted slightly that I realized I'd dug my fingernails into his ass.

"Did I draw blood?" I asked when I finally let go.

"Nah." He shrugged, still pinning me down with his much larger body. "And if you did, it'll be worth every drop."

"What was all that?" I asked, wrapping my arms around him. "You were on a mission."

"Yeah—to make you come."

"You were jealous," I said, deciding to test the waters.

He stiffened but I wasn't going to let him off so easily.

"We agreed on complete honesty," I reminded him. "And the minute I started talking about fucking other guys, you threw me down and fucked me like a man with something to prove."

He blew out a breath. "Contrary to popular belief, I do have feelings. I'm not a complete boor. I have to keep a lot of things buried, it's the nature of who I am and what I do, but not everything. And right now, you're mine. I don't know what the future holds, but for the foreseeable future, I don't want to hear about, talk about, or think about you with anyone else."

I hesitated. "Does that mean we're exclusive?"

"You're damn straight it does."

I felt like a silly schoolgirl, but that made me stupidly happy. Sandor had become very important to me in a relatively short time and there was no way in hell I was going to sleep with anyone else, whether he said the words making it exclusive or not. However, hearing him say it, seeing his reaction to my mentioning being with someone else, was telling in so many ways. I didn't want to get ahead of myself, but maybe this was a good omen.

"No comment?" he asked after a moment.

"I can't think of exactly the right comment," I replied, hiding my smile. "But it makes me happy because I can't even fathom sleeping with anyone else now that I'm with you."

"Ditto." He wrapped his arms around me again. "I was thinking I'd like to take you out on a date. Or two or three. I feel a bit like a cad, ravishing your body every night but not treating you like a gentleman should."

"We don't have the kind of lifestyle that's conducive to dating like other people, but I wouldn't be opposed to a date now and then."

"We head back to Vegas tomorrow, and the following day I'll be interviewing a bunch of new guys that will potentially join our security team. However, after that, barring unforeseen circumstances, we could make some time. I was thinking we could go to dinner and a movie. I realize that's very cliché, but I haven't done it since college, there's a new Star Wars thing I'd love to see, and based on one of the T-shirts I've seen you sleep in, you're also a Star Wars fan."

I paused. "Actually, that week is the first hockey game of the season and my friend on the team invited me to go. And before you bend me over a desk or something, Dax and I are just friends. I can get another ticket for you; he won't mind. But I'd really like to see the season opener if you're into it."

He kissed me. "I love the Sidewinders. Sounds like a great date. Dinner before the game?"

"Perfect."

23

S *andor*

THE NEXT TWO days were a whirlwind between traveling to Vegas and interviewing the new candidates to come work with us, but I had to admit it was good to be back at the house in Las Vegas. For some reason, I felt safer here than in Limaj. In the U.S., we not only had our private security force, but the police and, in a pinch, the CIA since both Erik and I had ties to them. In Limaj, it was hard to tell who was loyal, the military was a mess, and the police force was small and overextended. I could relax a little here, and that was exactly what I planned to do. And I planned to make sure Lennox was right there with me.

We were going to the hockey game tonight and it turned out the whole family was going. Erik, Casey, and the kids had been invited to sit in the owner's box, which made security a whole lot easier, and Chains had told me to enjoy date night—he had everything under control. The fact that I would be at the game was an added bonus in an emergency, but we didn't foresee any issues.

Since the family would be using the SUV, I borrowed Casey's Corvette and Lennox and I took off for dinner late in the afternoon. She wore jeans and a Sidewinders jersey, which I thought looked sexy as hell even though it was big on her. I had a Sidewinders hoodie that I would put on over my button-down shirt after dinner, but I figured I'd make an attempt to look at least a little different than my usual cargo pants, black T-shirt and boots. She wore much of the same for work, so it was kind of nice for both of us to wear something different.

We walked into a quaint steakhouse hand in hand, and for the first time in a very long time, I wasn't thinking about Erik, Limaj, or work. I was a hundred percent focused on the woman with me and our date tonight. We settled into a booth, sitting next to each other because I wanted to be able to touch her, and she leaned into my side as we opened one menu and perused it together.

"They have crab-stuffed mushrooms," she said. "Let's get those."

"Sounds good."

After we ordered wine, an appetizer and our entrees, she glanced up at me. "I assume you know the story about Sasha and Anton Petrov?"

I knew the basics but not everything, so I nodded. "Yeah. They were hot and heavy last year. Apparently, he asked her to marry him and she panicked. I don't know the details, but it was pretty emotional for Sasha. Is she going tonight?"

"It's Anton's first game as a pro, and even though they're not together, she doesn't want to miss it."

"She did him a solid," I told her. "The one detail I do know is that he wanted to leave school without graduating and go to the Sidewinders early, but the team didn't think he was ready, so he probably would have been sent down to the minors, and she didn't want that for him."

"She did the right thing so he wouldn't crash and burn with his career." She nodded. "Poor kid. I bet that was hard."

"Casey did a good job with her," I said fondly. "The kids are all pretty great, but Sasha lost her biological mom, got adopted by Casey and Nick, then they got divorced and she had to adjust to another reality. Eventually, Casey married Jayson and had the twins, throwing more at her, and she just keeps on keeping on. Sasha's pretty badass, a lot like her mom."

"You and Casey must have gotten very close over the years," Lennox said.

I paused. This was a touchy subject. I didn't want to lie to her, but I also didn't know how to explain the complexity of that relationship and the depth of my feelings, though they'd remained platonic. "For ten years, she and Luke were my life," I said carefully. "Not the way that sounds, because there was never anything romantic or sexual between us, but Erik asked me to take care of them and I did. I gave up everything to protect them. I'd do it again in a heartbeat, but now that Erik is back, I'm trying to find myself again." I leaned over and brushed my lips against hers. "And I'm happy to have found you along the way."

She smiled back. "Me too."

"So tell me something about you that I don't know, that goes beyond what I can find on a background check."

"Well, believe it or not, as much of a tomboy as I am, I love getting my hair done. Like going to a salon and having it cut and washed and dried... Washing my hair is a huge turn-on. Just FYI."

I leaned over and nibbled her neck. "Why haven't you told me this before?" I asked, gently sucking on her earlobe. "We've taken a lot of showers together."

"I don't know. I've never had a guy wash my hair before." She eyed me. "But with your big hands, I think it would be a treat."

"I guess we're going to have to find out."

Our food arrived and we chatted as we ate. We'd both ordered big-ass T-bone steaks and she ate every bite, unlike many women I'd seen who picked at their meals or just ordered salad when out on a date.

"Prince Sandor, is that you?"

The voice made me turn and it was a damn good thing I'd been raised in the royal family because the woman coming toward me made me cringe.

Fuck.

She was a princess from some European country, I couldn't remember which one, and Erik had made me dance with her at an event we'd had at the palace last winter. She'd done everything but blow me on the dance floor to get me to go home with her and I had no idea what the hell she was doing in a steakhouse in Las Vegas.

"Hello." I inclined my head. "It's good to see you."

"Well, I bought my ticket to the charity ball as soon as I saw that King Erik was attending, since I knew you'd be there." She sank into a seat across from us.

Christ. I needed to nip this in the bud but I smiled politely. "The money goes to a good cause." I slid my arm around Lennox's shoulder. "By the way, I'd like to introduce you to my girlfriend, Lennox Briggs. Honey, this is Princess Veronique."

Lennox nodded politely, though I noted she'd stiffened when I introduced her as my girlfriend. Crap. I was going to have to address that now too. This was a huge pain in my ass and I still didn't know what the hell Veronique was doing at a place like this. I'd chosen it specifically because even though the steaks were fantastic, it wasn't a high-end place where I would automatically be recognized.

"Girlfriend?" Veronique looked Lennox up and down carefully, a smile quirking her lips. "Well, I suppose it's to be expected that you'd play the field a little before your cousin finds you a proper wife."

I scowled. "That's both impolite and inaccurate. I have no intention of finding a wife any time soon."

The waiter appeared, asking if he should bring another wine glass and I abruptly told him no.

"Well, I'll see you Saturday," Veronique said with a coy smile, sliding out of the booth.

"What the fuck," I muttered, shaking my head. I turned to Lennox. "Honey, I'm sorry. That was completely unexpected and I have no idea how she found me. I apologize."

"For which thing?" she asked, catching me off guard.

"Excuse me?"

"For. Which. Thing." She enunciated clearly.

Oh, hell, she was royally pissed and other than Veronique's rudeness, which I had no control over, I had no idea why.

24

L*ennox*

I'D KNOWN there were women clamoring for him. Rich, titled, gorgeous debutantes and princesses from all over the world. You only had to check on the Instagram page of the Royal Family of Limaj or his personal one, but the women came out en force whenever possible. He stayed fairly sequestered, though, so this was my first time being faced with it in person. However, having him conveniently use me as his decoy to thwart her efforts while simultaneously announcing he had no intention of marrying me, well, that was bullshit.

Not that I expected him to marry me, and certainly not at this early stage of the game, but to say it out loud like that made me look like his plaything of the month or something, and that was unacceptable. I didn't need any promises for the future, but he sure as hell wasn't going to disrespect me like that.

"I'm sorry for the things she said," he began.

"It's not what *she* said," I said, mortified to feel tears sting my eyelids. What the hell was wrong with me? I never reacted like this to men and hated feeling so vulnerable.

"What did I say?" he asked gently, lifting my chin.

I tried to jerk away but I was on the inside of the booth and he was a lot stronger than I was, even though he wasn't being rough.

"Think about it," I hissed, biting my lip to keep from smacking his hand away from my face.

"I called you my girlfriend without us discussing it, yeah?"

I rolled my eyes, which helped abate the tears. "No. I mean, yes, but no, that's not why I'm pissed."

He met my gaze, his eyes slightly narrowed as he searched my face. I could practically see the wheels turning behind those gorgeous blue eyes he no longer covered with colored contact lenses.

Neither of us spoke and I let him sort it out. It took a few minutes, too, our gazes locked intently as he probably went over and over his exchange with Veronique. I knew the moment it clicked because his eyes sharpened and then softened. Then he kissed me. The bastard. I pulled away, my pride refusing to allow me to give in that easily, but the moment we touched, my body betrayed me.

"The comment about not getting married," he said finally.

"*What* about the comment?" I pressed. He had to know, and understand, how insulting what he'd said was.

And there was the blank look again.

"You really have no idea, do you?" I sighed, disappointment flooding me.

"Not exactly, no." He reached for my hand and squeezed it gently. "I told you from the beginning that I'm not good at this stuff, so help me out, okay? I can't learn and be better if you don't talk to me."

I blew out a breath. "In the same sentence, for the most part, you called me your girlfriend and then reiterated the fact that you had no plans to get married. Which demeaned my importance to you in a very public way since that woman had already insulted me and made her intentions toward you very clear."

He looked horrified and I had to admit it was almost comical, watching the play of emotions on his face as he digested what I'd told him.

"Fucking hell," he groaned, dropping his head. "Forgive me, Lennox. You're right. That was awful, terrible, selfish—"

"Okay, enough with the self-flagellation. But seriously, Sandor, while we're nowhere near ready to talk about something like marriage, what you just did made me feel...*used*. She'd just insulted me, saying I wasn't wife material, and you reiterated it by saying you weren't going to marry me."

He grimaced. "No. It came out all wrong. I'm so sorry. She caught me by surprise. She was at the inaugural ball Erik threw last winter after he ascended the throne, and he told me I should dance with her. Her father is king of an important trade partner and at the time, I was single. So I danced with her, but she was pushy as hell. She practically stuck her tongue down my throat on the dance floor and I blew her off after that. I don't know how she found me here tonight, but I was trying to be as rude as she was and get rid of her. It never occurred to me..." His voice died off and he reached out to cup my cheek with his hand. "What I meant was that Erik has no say in who or when I marry, not that I wouldn't marry *you*."

I breathed in through my nose, sad and still incredibly embarrassed, but I knew him well enough to know he hadn't meant it the way it had come out. Even if it was true, that he would never get married or that he'd never marry me, he wouldn't say it out loud and humiliate me like that.

"Forgive me for being an insensitive ass," he whispered against my lips, his forehead pressed to mine. "Please don't take what I said to heart. I didn't mean it that way and I would never intentionally say something so thoughtless."

My heart and my brain warred with each other internally as I struggled to come to terms with what he was and wasn't saying.

"I have to know something," I whispered, clearing my throat.

"Anything."

"Is this just a fling for you? Something that has no future? Because if so, I should know. I'm pretty chill with dating, but we live and work together, and I've uprooted my whole life to move to Limaj. It's not fair for you to let me think there might be a future for us when this is nothing but live-in sex until something better comes along."

"*Bloody hell.*" His British accent rarely showed itself after so many years in the U.S., but it came out in all its glory with that exclamation. He shifted in the booth so he was almost facing me, to the extent the close space allowed, and gripped me by the shoulders. "Not a week ago I told you we were together exclusively—does that sound like nothing but a sex thing?"

"It sounds like a good thing where you're almost as sure as you can be that you have a willing partner in your bed every night who's not sleeping with other people and potentially bringing diseases and such home."

"We use condoms," he protested. "That's not an issue."

"Sandor, I'm not good at this dating stuff either. You have to say the words. You have to be clear about your intentions, whatever they may be at this stage in the relationship. Because I'm too old, and have been burned enough times, to allow anyone to play with my heart."

For a moment I thought he was angry, but then I realized he was upset. Probably at himself, but I couldn't be sure, because he wasn't saying anything. He was just watching me, something he did a lot, I noted.

"I've thought of no one but you for weeks," he said, slowly bringing one of my hands to his lips, kissing the back of my palm so sweetly it nearly made me squirm in my seat. "I told the construction crew that your suite was to be done last, because even though I didn't have the nerve to say it to you directly, I can't even fathom the idea of you not being beside me every night when we go to bed." He turned my hand over and brought the heel of my palm to his mouth and gently nibbled the soft flesh there. "On the nights you have something to do or you're up late talking to Casey, I can't sleep until you're beside me." His lips moved to my wrist, and he pressed more light kisses on the inside, trailing them up the inside of my arm. "I get a little tongue-tied every time I look into your eyes because there's so much I want to say, but it feels like it's too soon and I'm woefully inept at expressing my feelings properly."

I blinked at him in surprise. This wasn't what I'd been expecting his response to be at all. I was getting a little misty-eyed again, but for a totally different reason this time, and I wasn't sure how to respond. He'd just said the sweetest things, made my insides get a little jiggly, and shown me a side of him I hadn't seen before. Damn this guy, he was such an anomaly.

"You never fail to surprise me," I said quietly. "I wish I wasn't so awkward with this stuff because I don't know if I'd ever be able to say something as sweetly eloquent as what you just said."

"You and me both," he whispered, kissing the side of my face. "If what I just said came out eloquently, it was pure luck. Believe me."

We both chuckled, our faces close together.

In my peripheral vision, I had the feeling we were being watched and turned my head just in time to see a photographer duck down behind a wall.

"What is it?" Sandor immediately followed where I was looking.

"The press," I said softly. "Someone was taking pictures."

"Shit." He made a face and pulled out his wallet, motioning for the waiter. "Let's get out of here."

"Is it going to be a problem?" I asked as he paid the bill and took my hand, leading me out to the car.

"What? Pictures of us having a romantic dinner?" He shook his head as he unlocked the door and opened it for me. "In fact, the only problem will be Erik and Casey not leaving us alone and wanting all the details of what we're doing and when and how many times."

I chuckled as he shut the door behind me and got into the driver's seat. "I just meant, you know, with you being a prince and all...is there certain behavior expected from you?"

He shrugged. "Yes and no. Should I be seen smoking a joint at a rock concert with my middle finger in the air? Probably not. Kissing the woman

I'm currently dating while we're out to dinner? That's never going to be a problem."

"Sandor?"

"Yes, love?"

"I'm sorry if I put you on the spot before. You know, after Veronique left us."

"It's fine. We needed to discuss our relationship, and it was a kick in the ass for both of us to say what was on our minds."

"Okay." I hoped he was right. Not about the need for us to have the talk we'd had so much as the pictures of us that would inevitably make the tabloids or something. I wondered what was being said about me behind closed doors. I had no doubt he and Erik had discussed our relationship, and though I didn't think Erik disliked me in any way, I honestly didn't know how this was supposed to work. Erik had married a commoner, of course, but maybe that meant that Sandor needed to marry someone with some status. Someone like Princess Veronique.

Ugh. The thought made me sick so I put it out of my mind. There would be plenty of time to second-guess myself and everything about this relationship. Tonight, I wanted to enjoy our first real date and the hockey game since there wouldn't be any hockey once we went back to Limaj.

25

S *andor*

I WAS FAIRLY certain I couldn't have screwed up our first date any worse than I had. I thought about that as we watched the Sidewinders take the ice. I cursed my royal upbringing and Veronique in ten different languages in my head, hoping I hadn't ruined everything with my girl.

My girl.

I hadn't used that phrase in a long, long time. Maybe fifteen years or more, since my early days at university, and it was strange. But it also felt right. Comfortable. Well, it had until Veronique had shown up and made me say something incredibly stupid. God, it had come out with such superiority, and I hadn't given a second thought to how my proclamation might make Lennox feel. It had been arrogant of me to respond like that, but it was habit. I always shot down women who ran in royal circles because they could be like vultures, hungry to feed on any vulnerability, always looking for their golden ticket to marriage to a royal.

Even before Anwar's deception and going into hiding, I'd decided I would never marry a woman like that. I wanted someone who cared about the man I was, not the title or money I brought to the table. Any woman I married could be granted the title of princess, but it was optional and would depend on Erik. Only he could make that happen, and of course, it was something both the woman and I would have to agree to. I didn't use my title anymore, being much more comfortable with a regular first and last name. Erik had been hinting that it might be better if Daniil, Elen and I all used our titles because the royal family needed to be much more public than we'd been over the last decade. I was still on the fence, though, and figured it would come up again at some point.

It was hard to explain my aversion to the royal life. I'd always been uncomfortable with it, which was why I'd made the decision at sixteen to train as an official Bodyguard to the Royal Family. My mother had been disappointed, but my father understood and had told me to do what felt right. My father was a distant cousin to the royal family in Sweden, and though he carried the title of prince, he'd never used it after marrying my mother. Like me, he'd been uninterested in life as a royal and had only taken on some light ambassador-type duties because it was expected of my mother and King Isak had wanted to keep a good relationship with Sweden. Accordingly, my father had been my biggest ally when I'd balked at the life of a titled prince.

In retrospect, my decision had been the best one for me at the time, but not so much anymore. The royal family had dwindled down to just a few of us—Erik, me, Daniil, Skye, and Elen. Erik's children were now part of that, but as far as adults went, it was just us. His father, my uncle Ben, was still alive of course, but he'd abdicated so he couldn't be anything but an ambassador of sorts.

It was a shame, I thought, because if he hadn't abdicated, perhaps none of the events that had followed would have happened at all. I didn't dwell on that very often, but for the first time in years, I longed for my father's counsel. I'd barely had time to mourn the loss of my parents and older brother because our lives had been thrown into chaos immediately after their deaths. Then I'd been tasked with protecting Casey and Luke so I hadn't had time to think about much of anything. Every so often it caught up to me. Like tonight. When I would have loved to ask my father for advice about Lennox.

My parents hadn't been snobs. They would have liked her. In fact, everyone that knew her liked her. Elen thought she was great, Erik and Casey would probably walk us down to a chapel on the Strip right now if they could, and Joe was incredibly happy we'd gotten together. He thought of Lennox like a daughter, so his approval meant a lot and I appreciated it.

"You look like a man with a lot on his mind," Erik said, coming up behind me. He'd invited us to join them in the owner's box, and after our run-in with the press, I'd decided to take him up on it. Lennox had seemed a little disappointed, but I'd at least had the good sense to explain to her why I thought it was a good idea. Mostly, it was because I wanted to avoid any run-ins with the Veronique's in my life since they were apparently going to make appearances at the ball on Saturday.

"Yeah, well, my first real date with the woman in my life has been less than memorable," I muttered. "Well, it's been memorable, but probably not in a good way." I told him about Veronique showing up at the restaurant and my gaffe in the conversation that followed.

He let out a low whistle. "Damn. That was an epic fail."

"Tell me about it."

"Well, you could eliminate the Veronique's of the world if you'd just make it official that you're off the market."

"I'm trying. I *told* Veronique she was my girlfriend."

"Yeah, but you know how that is. Until there's a ring…"

"It fucking pisses me off."

"Why do you think I tried to marry Casey as quickly as possible?" He laughed.

"Hey, Uncle Loco." Luke joined us. "Is it true Lennox is your girlfriend now? How come you never had a girlfriend before? She's really pretty and—"

I put my hand over his mouth, leaning over to whisper in his ear. "You gotta play it cool around girls, man. Chill." I wiggled my eyebrows to show him I was just kidding, but Lennox had heard him and I caught her chuckle from where she was watching the game.

"Oh. Sorry." He glanced at Lennox, who was still laughing, and he turned bright red.

Erik bent to whisper something to him and Luke smiled, though his ears were still a cute shade of pink.

"I miss you," Luke said to me, dropping his voice considerably.

"I miss you too, kiddo." I gave him a half-hug.

"I wish you weren't going back to Limaj already."

"We aren't going back for two more weeks," I reminded him. "And then you'll be coming for three weeks at Christmas."

"Yeah."

"And maybe we'll come back here during spring break," I said, catching Erik's eye meaningfully.

"And maybe," Erik joined in, "we'll have an English-speaking school set up in time for next year so you can live with me."

Luke nodded. "Yeah." He turned to the game and yelled just as Anton Petrov scored. "Woohoo! Go, Anton!" Luke was caught up in the moment, along with everyone else, as Anton celebrated his first official goal as a

Sidewinder. Sasha seemed a little subdued, but Casey was beside her, whispering in her ear.

I used the distraction as an opportunity to wrap my arms around Lennox from behind and rest my head on her shoulder. "Having fun?" I asked her.

"Of course. You?" She turned to me questioningly.

"Any time I'm with you and not working, I'm having fun," I responded.

She shook her head. "Uh-huh. Still trying to sweet talk me after the Veronique thing, huh?"

I made a face. "Let's not use her name, okay? It makes me nauseous."

"You and me both." We laughed together and I was glad we seemed to be back to normal. I didn't know what was next for us, but I was genuinely interested in finding out. Hopefully, there wouldn't be any similar episodes at the ball Saturday night.

JOE AND CHAINS, with some input from Ace, had put together half a dozen candidates interested in working for the royal family. Though we always had to double- and triple-check their backgrounds and history, all of them had been working for Joe for at least two years and had been vetted by him personally. But choosing three to bring back to Limaj was a daunting task. The older guys, though they had more experience, were probably not good fits because while none were currently married, they all had major ties to home. Elderly parents, children living with an ex, something that made them less likely to be happy seven thousand miles away.

The younger guys seemed much more untethered but I wasn't sure how I felt about them. I realized I was being over-the-top in how protective I was of the family, but that was the problem: They *were* my family. This wasn't just a job to me; this was my life and it would be hard for anyone on the outside looking in to understand the depth of my concern.

My top pick was a twenty-eight-year-old veteran named Jonas Germano. He'd done four years in the Marines before being accepted into the FBI Academy. He'd been about to graduate when equipment failure during a training exercise sent him off the top of a building and toppling two stories to the ground. He'd broken his back and both legs, but while the FBI had given up on him, Joe hadn't. He'd befriended him at a VA rehab facility and had eventually brought him on as part of his cyber security division. Jonas had worked his ass off and was now as fit and badass as any of the others, and I was looking forward to meeting him.

I had Lennox with me today because I knew from my own biases that a lot of men had a problem working with women in a protection or security capacity, so I needed to make sure anyone we brought on would be okay with that. I'd narrowed down the five candidates Chains had sent me on Tuesday to two, even though we really needed three. A good fit was going to have to trump convenience, even if it meant the team would work long hours and have very little time off.

One of the great things about Jonas was his experience with cyber security, something none of the rest of us had beyond Joe. We were all fairly adept at utilizing technology to do our jobs, but preventing cybercrime and protecting the privacy of the royal family as well as the security of the country was another matter altogether.

The other candidate had an interesting connection to us. He was the twin brother of the bass player of Casey's old band. I hadn't even known Tyler had a brother, much less a twin. Apparently, they'd had a falling out as teenagers and had lost touch. They'd reconnected a year or so ago, but I didn't know anything beyond that.

"I think Jonas and Marcus are great additions to our crew," Lennox told me two nights later as we crawled into bed.

"That's only two, though," I lamented, hands behind my head as I stared up at the ceiling. "And Marcus isn't joining us until the new year, so we're still going to be short-staffed."

"It's okay. At least we'll be overworked and exhausted together," she said, laying her head on my chest. My arms came down and wrapped around her, one hand closing around her ass and the other settling in her hair. We both seemed to be enamored with the other's hair; she loved when I set mine free of its usual ponytail and I felt the same when she took down hers.

"Very true."

"So, tell me what to expect on Saturday."

"What do you mean?"

"I'm assuming there will be Veroniques en masse and I need to know how to deal with all of that. At the end of the day, you're still royalty and the world will be watching, even if it's a small stage."

As much as I hated it, she was right. There would be a lot of scrutiny on anyone I dated, but I didn't know how to guide her because this was new territory for me. I'd fallen under the radar in college because I was essentially nothing but a bodyguard then. All of that had changed and I had to deal with this whether I wanted to or not.

"To be honest," I told her, "I think you'd be better served talking with Casey. She's had to learn to navigate these waters in a short time, so I think she'll have better advice than I will."

"But what do you want of me?" she asked quietly. "Do you want me to be a certain way?"

I shook my head. "I want you to be you. Obviously, be careful what you say, and to whom, about the royal family, but in general, we don't have anything to hide, do we?"

"Not at all."

"Then don't worry so much, okay?"

"Okay." She said it, but I could tell she didn't mean it. She was going to worry no matter what I said, and the truth was, so would I.

26

———————

L *ennox*

CASEY HAD BOOKED a suite at the Charleston on Saturday and we settled in around noon. She'd been talking about the dress she'd had made for me, but I'd forgotten about it until today. Now I was standing on a small dais as this wisp of a woman named Alexa laced me into a satin creation of royal blue. It was sleeveless, revealing my shoulders and elegant neck, though I tended to hate my arms when it came to things like this.

"Why are you making that face?" Casey demanded, standing there with her hands on her hips.

"I'm too muscular," I murmured. "I prefer to cover my arms. They make me look masculine."

"There is nothing masculine about you in this dress, sugar." Alexa spoke in a light Southern accent as she adjusted the ruffled bottom. It was tight-fitting through my hips and then opened in the front with an upside-down V surrounded by layers of ruffled fabric. Alexa said it was so the gun I would wear in my thigh holster would be more easily hidden, and she was right, but I'd never worn anything like this.

"You're beautiful," Casey said gently. "Sandor is going to lose his mind when he sees you."

I shrugged. This was so not my thing. I was in fantastic shape, but I was self-conscious about my arms when I was dressed up like this.

"I wish I had a body like yours," Sasha said. She was on the nearby settee, staring at me with a faint smile.

"Lots of hours at the gym," I told her.

"I'm trying," she said. "But it doesn't seem to help anything but my stress level."

"You're too young to have so much stress," I told her.

She sighed. "College is hard."

"Agreed," I said, "but worth it."

"That remains to be seen. I'm to the point now where I'm hoping my new stepfather can find me a billionaire prince that will whisk me away to his private island and feed me bonbons all day."

We all laughed, including Sasha.

"You'd be bored to tears," Casey said.

"Okay, your dress is perfect," Alexa told me. "Take it off, put on your robe and go get your hair done. Casey, you're up next."

I sat in chairs for the next few hours, alternately snacking on hors d'oeuvres Casey had brought in and checking my phone to see if anything was going on. Sandor had told me not to worry about security, other than keeping an eye on Casey and the girls, of course, but it wasn't in me to take time off. Work was pretty much all I did.

I had Sandor in my life now, but we were both workaholics so it hadn't changed much for me, except for the companionship. Since we worked together, professional and personal had mostly merged into the same thing. Except for tonight. Even though I would be armed and on alert should a crisis arise, this was something different.

"You look like someone kicked your puppy," Casey said, sinking into the chair beside me as the stylist did my hair.

"I don't want to embarrass him," I said quietly. "Or myself."

"You won't. The biggest thing to remember is that no one is better than you. You're just as worthy and important as someone born to royalty or someone extremely wealthy. Sandor is crazy about you, so everything else is just background noise. Trust me. Focus on your relationship, on who you are when you're with him, and forget about all the outside nonsense."

"She's right, you know." Elen came in, her makeup already done, to wait for her turn with the hairstylist. "I've never seen Sandor as enamored with someone as he is with you. I know he doesn't show it much, but it's there. And really, who cares what anyone else thinks?"

"I care," I answered. "I was already insulted by that Veronique woman and I don't want to be someone the people in his circles make fun of."

"Some are going to make fun of you no matter what," Elen said with a shrug. "But there are some who'll make fun of princesses and heiresses too. No one is safe in the world we live in."

"That's depressing," I said.

"It is what it is." Elen stared off at nothing, her pretty face thoughtful. "I lived under the radar all those years while Erik and Sandor were in hiding, and now that I'm back in the limelight again, it's hard readjusting."

"Did you miss your life?" I asked her. "I mean, your life as a princess?"

She shook her head. "Not really. I was a college student when it happened and after I finished college, I lived off the grid. I did a lot of things I never would have done otherwise...tended bar at a tiki bar in the South Pacific, taught children to read on a reservation in North Dakota, climbed mountains... The thing is, it was lonely. I knew where Sandor was, of course, and I had Uncle Ben in an emergency, but mostly I was alone."

"No boyfriends?"

Elen wrinkled her nose. "I had male friends and a handful of lovers over the years, but it was too complicated to get close to anyone, so I didn't. And now that I'm not hiding anymore, I don't know who to trust or how to be normal. I got used to being in hiding, watching everything I said and did, I forget that I don't have to anymore. It's been a lot harder than I thought." She took a sip of champagne. "But tonight I plan to find someone who might want to get horizontal. The prospects in Limaj are terrible."

"You think?" I asked, cocking my head. "I saw some cute guards around the palace and some of Erik's associates weren't bad."

"You mean the statesmen in Parliament?" She stuck out her tongue. "Not my thing. I need someone a little more...rugged."

Casey smiled. "Like Xander."

"Xander?" Elen let out a huff. "He's *obnoxious*. I wouldn't sleep with him if he was the last man on earth."

"He's nice," I said in surprise. "I've known him a few years and I've never known him to be obnoxious."

"Has he ever thrown you over his shoulder like a sack of potatoes?" Elen demanded.

I hid my smile. "Well, no, but I'm also a bodyguard, not a client, so to speak."

"Next time he tries something like that, I'm going to punch him. Right in the dick."

After a moment of startled silence, we all burst out laughing.

"Harsh," Casey chuckled. "But if it comes to that, I'll have your back."

We talked for a while longer and I was finally ready. It was late in the afternoon now, and almost time to get dressed, but I sat in my robe, nibbling some fruit as I perused the internet on my phone. I checked hockey scores and was about to click off when the word "Limaji" caught my eye in a headline:

Limaji prince off the market?

The article went on to talk about Sandor and the mystery woman he was seen dining with in Las Vegas. I cringed at the blurry picture taken of us at dinner, my face mostly hidden because his larger body had been blocking me in the booth.

Great.

I copied the link to the article and texted it to Sandor just as Alexa came in and told me to get dressed.

"They're not going to announce us or anything, are they?" I asked Casey as we took the private elevator down to the ballroom.

She shook her head. "No. This is Sasha's night—she's the only one who'll be announced."

"I think I'm going to be sick," Sasha whispered.

"You've got this, sweetheart." Casey hugged her. "And I'll just be a few feet away."

"Think about something you really like," I told her. "Like, your favorite place to shop or your favorite beach, something that makes you happy. And keep your focus on that as you walk in. You'll be smiling and mostly relaxed and no one will know it's because you're thinking about the hot cabana boy in Waikiki that gave you a surfing lesson once."

Sasha giggled. "Thanks. That's a good idea. Though I don't have any memories quite that fun."

We separated once we got to the mezzanine level where the ballroom was located. Erik was waiting for Casey, and Sasha was whisked off to an anteroom where she would wait to be announced. Elen, along with Casey's mother, Teal, and Erik's mother, Kari, all headed toward the ballroom, but I froze when I spotted Sandor, standing just off to the side.

His eyes were fixed on me as if no one else existed and I was a little starstruck myself since he was gorgeous in a black tuxedo with tails. He approached me with a purposeful stride, his blue eyes slightly narrowed as he reached for me. He took my hand and very slowly brought it to his lips, his eyes never leaving mine.

"You're absolutely stunning," he whispered, drawing me closer.

"Thank you." I swallowed. "You look pretty great yourself."

"I read the article," he said, holding me against him. "After tonight, you're not going to be anonymous anymore."

I swallowed. "Are you okay with that?"

"I'm fine with it, but you look really nervous."

"I'm a little nervous, but I'll be fine as long as you're with me."

"Then shall we join the festivities?"

"I guess." I took his arm and he leaned over to kiss the side of my face, something he did a lot, which I hadn't known I loved until he started to do it.

"Don't worry." He led me towards the entrance and I found myself a lot steadier on my feet than I'd expected. I drew from Sandor's strength, even though I'd never been that kind of woman. I'd always prided myself on my own strength, my ability to do everything the men I knew did, and more. Anything less would have been a weakness in my mind, but that wasn't the case with Sandor. He complemented me somehow, in ways I'd never thought about. His strength didn't mean mine was less, it simply added to it so that together we were untouchable.

I hadn't realized there would be photographers catching everyone as they came in and Sandor squeezed my arm just before we got through the door. "Smile and breathe," he said softly.

Somehow, I did exactly as he instructed and got through the doors without embarrassing myself. Jesus, how did celebrities do this shit? I was so much happier living in the shadows as a bodyguard.

But that won't be the case if you and Sandor get serious.

The thought was fleeting, but it was enough to give me pause.

"You okay?" Sandor gave me a funny look.

"Fine." I smiled up at him just as Veronique appeared, as if she'd dropped out of the sky.

"Sandor. Darling, you look so handsome in a tux. I've been waiting for you."

"Veronique." His voice was laced with impatience. "I don't know what you've been waiting for, but I'm completely devoted to the woman in my life, who happens to be standing right here. Try using those finishing-school manners you were taught and stop being an annoying dilettante whose behavior reeks of desperation." He turned, pulling me along with him as he strode toward the table Erik had reserved for our group.

"Holy shit," I whispered. "Did you seriously just talk to her that way?"

"I told you, I never wanted that life, and while I'll do my duty for my country and my king, I won't play by their rules. Never have, never will."

Part of me relished the look on Veronique's face after Sandor's response to her blatant flirtation, but another part of me was worried. Women like her wouldn't just go away and I had a feeling this wouldn't be the last time we crossed paths.

"Wow, Len, you look fantastic." I turned in surprise to see Dax smiling at me, a blonde on his arm who was gorgeous but looked decidedly uncomfortable.

"Thanks." I smiled.

"Hey, Sandor." He held out his hand and Sandor shook it.

"This is Lacy." Dax patted her hand.

We made small talk for a few minutes before Lacy excused herself to the ladies' room and Sandor went to get us drinks.

"You and Sandor, huh?" Dax was grinning like an idiot and I resisted the urge to roll my eyes.

"Yes. Be nice."

"I'm nice!" He laughed.

"Who's Lacy?"

"Showgirl. She's okay. Not really my type, but I needed a date and she wanted to come, so we're here."

"Why isn't she your type?"

He hesitated. "You know how sometimes you just know when someone is right or isn't? She just isn't. I'm not sure what I'm looking for, but it's not her."

"Well, if it's not her, don't lead her on. It's not fair to let her think she has a chance if she doesn't."

"No, I wouldn't do that." He paused. "You really do look gorgeous tonight. Sandor's a lucky man."

"I hope he thinks so."

"If he doesn't, he's an idiot."

27

———————

S*andor*

I'D BARELY MADE it to the bar before Veronique accosted me again.

"It's okay, I'm not angry," she said, motioning to the bartender to get her another of whatever she was drinking. "I understand you had to say that in front of her."

"Are you truly so narcissistic you can't recognize when someone genuinely has no interest in you?"

She blinked, staring at me in confusion. "But a man like you...can't possibly marry a woman like her. Your king already—"

"I'd be very careful of the next words that come out of your mouth," I rumbled, taking a swig of scotch before looking at her again.

"I was only pointing out that the royal bloodline is already diluted with your king's marriage to a commoner. The rest of you need to make sure it remains intact."

Why did there have to be rules about hitting a woman? I'd never wanted to before but right now I might have gotten a great deal of pleasure from smacking her. That was frowned upon, though, so I merely shook my head. "Veronique, I love her. I'm not in line to the throne and really not concerned with any bloodline except that of carrying on my father's name." I turned on my heel and headed back to Lennox, who was now talking to several of the Sidewinders.

I hadn't known guys from the team would be here, but not only were they here, they were surrounding Lennox. My gut told me Dax had feelings for her, but she denied having any for him and I wasn't so insecure that I didn't trust her word. She'd had plenty of opportunity to get involved with him before I came along since they'd been friends for a while, so that wasn't an issue. Of course, with Veronique constantly in my face, I wouldn't blame her if she was trying to make me a little jealous.

"Hey, babe." I slid my arm around her waist, making sure the three men around her understood she was mine.

"Thank you." She took the glass of champagne from me and motioned with her head. "Do you know Viggo Sjoberg and Jamie Teller?"

"I know who they are, of course." I held out my hand. "But we haven't met."

"Nice to meet you."

Now I felt like an idiot. Viggo and Jamie were married, an openly gay couple. Viggo still played for the Sidewinders and Jamie had just retired and taken a position as an assistant coach. I hadn't recognized them from across the room but now that I was standing here, I knew them.

"Mind if I steal her for a dance later?" Jamie asked me. He made an impatient motion with his head in his husband's direction. "He doesn't dance."

"Not at all," I replied. "I'm not much of a dancer myself, although I'll suck it up for Lennox."

"See, babe?" He turned to his husband. "You're supposed to suck it up for the person you love."

Viggo muttered, "Not a chance in hell," in Swedish, under his breath. Since my father was Swedish and I knew the language, I laughed.

"Whatever." Jamie laughed too, obviously not upset about his husband's attitude. "You can stand at the bar by yourself while I dance with a beautiful woman. No skin off my teeth."

We chatted for a while before they wandered off and Lennox slid her hand into mine.

"You look really hot in a tux," she whispered, her breath warm against my ear.

"Thank you." I ran my hand over the curve of her ass. "You already know what I think of your dress. I'm already looking forward to seeing you in nothing but those heels, though."

"Yeah?" She bit her lip. "Then I'm looking forward to showing you."

I dropped my head to kiss her when someone tugged at the tails of my jacket. "Uncle Loco, don't do that in public!" Luke's voice was low but filled with horror. I looked down at him with a grin.

"Someday you're going to want to kiss a pretty girl in public too. Trust me."

He made a face. "Really?"

"Oh, yeah. Unless you want to kiss boys. Which is okay too, but—"

"No, I like girls," Luke interrupted quickly. "You look pretty, Miss Lennox."

"Thank you." She smiled. "You look very handsome in your tuxedo as well."

"It feels weird." He tugged at the collar of his shirt. "I don't know why we have to get dressed up for stuff like this."

"Well, for one thing, girls like it," Sandor said. "For another, sometimes it's fun to get dressed up. Probably not at your age, but that's another thing you'll like when you get a little older. I prefer jeans and a T-shirt, but this is nice a few times a year."

"You and Lennox should go dance. Mom said it's fun but I don't know how."

"Perhaps when you move to Limaj we'll get you some dancing lessons. Everyone in the royal family has to take ballroom dancing."

Luke's eyes widened. "For real?"

"Yup."

"I may have to rethink this moving thing," he muttered, heading off toward Erik.

"He cracks me up," Lennox said, watching him go.

"Me too."

"Should we dance?" she asked quietly.

"We should." I paused. "Are you comfortable with a waltz or would you rather wait for something contemporary?"

"Contemporary, please."

"All right. Come, let's mingle."

I KEPT Lennox close to me because it didn't take long for a group of European princess-types to zero in on me. Most of them hesitated to approach when they saw me with Lennox, but I spotted Veronique whispering to them and silently cursed all of them for making my life difficult. As if I hadn't just lived through a decade of hell, ten long years worried that Anwar would come for Casey or Luke or someone else I cared about. I didn't regret the sacrifices I'd made, but I sure as fuck didn't appreciate this kind of bullshit. I was a protector by nature. I'd known this at a young age, and I'd taken steps to follow my calling. More than twenty years later, I still felt the need to protect those I cared about.

Tonight, this was all about Lennox. She didn't need my protection in general, but some of the women here could be incredibly cruel. My mother had taught me how to steer clear, but my mom was long gone and I was in an untenable situation because Erik needed me to be Prince Sandor for now. I had to make the Limaji royal family look good and while I'd prefer not putting on airs, I was happy to help him re-establish our place in the world. But not at Lennox's expense. Not that he would expect that, but I had to be a lot more cognizant of the things I said and did with regard to her.

"Your dance with Sasha is coming up," Lennox reminded me.

Shit. I'd forgotten about that.

The charity ball tonight made money from the tickets sold and then by charging a ridiculous amount of money to dance with the belle of the ball, which was Sasha. Erik and I had both purchased dances because Casey said that while Sasha had been excited about the opportunity, she wasn't all that keen to dance with rich old men who might get a little grabby. It had happened in previous years and though it was always handled swiftly, Sasha was a little sensitive right now. Her breakup with Anton had been a year ago but she still pined for him and hadn't been the same since, so we'd arranged for as many familiar faces as possible that we knew to fill her dance card.

"You should go sit with Casey," I told her.

She gave me a look. "I can take care of myself. I've got a gun strapped to my thigh, remember?"

I chuckled at the thought of her pulling a gun on Veronique. "I know you can protect yourself physically, but Veronique and her crew tend to use the force of their tongues much more viciously than anything else."

She shrugged. "Sticks and stones and all that." She leaned up to kiss me. "Go dance with Sasha. I'm going to powder my nose and I'll be right back."

I wanted to protest, but that would be silly. She would be fine. She could handle herself. And honestly, this might be a good test of her mettle. If we were going to be together long-term, she had to be able to take the kind of scrutiny she would get as the wife of a member of the royal family.

28

———

L*ennox*

SASHA LOOKED beautiful tonight in a stunning lavender gown that showed off her tanned skin and dark curls. She had a gorgeous figure and the four-inch heels on her feet made her closer to my height than her usual five-foot-two. I squeezed her arm encouragingly just before Sandor led her onto the dance floor, and then I made my escape. I'd had to pee for an hour but Sandor had been stuck to me like glue. It was kind of cute, but I had a feeling he was too afraid to leave my side. He probably thought Veronique would hurt my feelings again, and he might have been right, but the more I thought about it, the more annoyed I got. Women like Veronique meant less than nothing to me, and I'd be damned if I let her intimidate me.

Yes, she'd caught me off guard when we'd been at dinner, but that was before he'd told me he wanted to explore something more with me. That he couldn't sleep at night until I was beside him. Made it clear that I was his girlfriend. Those things changed how I viewed both our relationship and the world he came from. If he was willing to buck the system for me, I had to be willing to step up and take a few shots from stupid people who meant nothing to either of us.

I did my business and then washed my hands, lamenting my aching feet, even though the thought of parading in front of Sandor wearing nothing but my heels kind of turned me on. Hopefully, I'd be flat on my back sooner rather than later once we started that, but for now, I was having fun. I knew quite a few people here tonight, from the owners of the Charleston Hotel to friends of Casey's to some of the Sidewinders and guys I knew from the gym. Our entire security team was here as well, though most of them were working.

I dabbed some gloss on my lips just as Veronique and a petite brunette came in, snarky smiles on their faces.

If I didn't know better, I'd swear they were spoiling for a fight, and it was kind of funny. They probably had no idea who I was to the royal family, or that I was a highly skilled professional bodyguard with military and intelligence training. No, they probably thought I was just some random American girl Sandor was fucking. I'd have to dispel those notions sooner rather than later, but it might be fun to play along.

"Well, hello, Lenore." Veronique took her place beside me at the mirror while the brunette moved to my other side.

Oh, goody. These two morons thought they could surround me.

As if.

So I smiled. "Hi, Vera. And you know damn well it's Lennox."

"Lennox. What kind of name is that? Isn't that some type of cheap china?"

I smiled. I'd heard all of this before. "Actually, it's been around for nearly a hundred and thirty years and was the first American china to be used in the White House, so it's not all that cheap."

Veronique pressed her lips together. "It's still a silly name."

"Well, it's been lovely chatting with you." I picked up my purse and started to leave but Veronique moved in front of me, blocking my path. I arched a brow. "Really?"

"You have to know he's never going to marry someone like you," she said in a clipped voice. "His family is looking to rebuild the royal bloodline and a commoner like you isn't going to cut it."

"I probably know more about what his family is looking for than you do," I said with a smile. "I live in the palace, after all."

Veronique's eyes widened slightly but then she shrugged. "You're just keeping his bed warm until the right woman comes along and then he's going to dispose of you like yesterday's trash."

"I guess we'll see." I tried to move past her but she gripped my arm.

"Don't be stupid. He's going to humiliate you."

Jesus Christ, what was it with this woman? Did she really think she could get away with talking to people like this because she was tenth in line to the throne of a country no one outside of Europe had ever heard of?

"I suggest you let go of my arm," I said quietly. "I'm not afraid of you, nor am I intimidated by you and your little pixie bodyguard over there."

The brunette frowned but I was too close to laughing to worry about her.

"You have no idea who I am," Veronique hissed.

"Don't care either," I responded. "But right now, I'm going to go dance with my very handsome prince of a boyfriend."

The door to the restroom opened and Elen stepped inside, quickly taking in the scene and giving me a wink.

"Hello, ladies. Hello, Lennox, darling." She reached up to kiss my cheek. "How's it going, Veronique? Still dating... What was that prince's name? Rupert? Rudolph?"

"Roberto," Veronique said, all but gritting her teeth. "And no, we're no longer together."

"That's right. He married an Olympic skier, didn't he? American, I believe. Or Canadian?" She gave a little shrug as she looped her arm through mine.

"Aligning yourself with your brother's whore isn't going to help you establish yourself as part of the royal family."

"I'm already part of the royal family, and what makes her a whore?" Elen asked bluntly. "The fact that she's fucking someone you wish you were? Get over yourself. Lennox has more class in her little finger than you have in your entire body. Go find another sucker to chase after—it'll be a cold day in hell before my brother dates a woman like you." She tugged my arm and led me out of the room.

"Why'd you spoil my fun?" I asked her, laughing. "It was just getting good."

"Veronique's always been a bitch. She's two years younger than I am, and had just gotten to the Sorbonne when I was a junior, but she drove me crazy. She's a nutjob and has pretty much alienated all potential suitors in Europe because everyone knows how crazy she is. She's after Sandor now because he's just come back from the dead, so to speak, and she figures he hasn't had time to hear all the stories about her."

"So not everyone in royal circles is an asshole?"

Elen smiled. "Definitely not. I'll introduce you to some lovely friends I have and you'll see there are plenty of nice people. Veronique's not the only bitchy one, though. They're not all crazy like she is, but some of them are definitely biased against those who aren't royalty and who don't come from money. That's everywhere, though, and we can't be bothered to care about people like that."

I glanced at her. "Did Sandor send you after me to make sure I was okay?"

She smiled. "He did, but not just now. This morning he texted and asked me to keep an eye on you, in case he was busy and anyone tried to blindside you the way they did at the restaurant. He was looking out for you."

"He's pretty sweet."

"He's smitten, Lennox. I've never seen him like this."

"Well, to be fair, you two didn't see each other for a long time."

"No, but I know my brother, and we were in touch. We didn't see each other, but we talked and he was always a phone call away. Daniil was the one who was incommunicado. I understand why he did, while he was working behind the scenes to aid the rebellion, but it was hard. My brothers are all I have left."

"Hello, sweetheart." Sandor joined us and slid an arm around me.

"Hi. How was your dance?" I asked him.

"It was nice. Sasha's having a good time." He cocked his head. "What about you?"

"I'm having a lovely time. I was just chatting with Elen about the non-bitchy members of the royal elite in Europe."

"Veronique followed her into the bathroom," Elen told him. "But she held her own until I got there."

"I spent the time thinking about different ways I could break her arm," I said with as straight of a face as I could muster.

Elen laughed, nudging me. "I love her, Sandor. You should keep this one."

"I plan to," he responded.

Elen went to join other friends and Sandor pulled me onto the dance floor.

"Don't you have any other family?" I asked him. "I mean, I know you lost your parents and brother, but aren't there aunts and uncles or cousins from the other side of your family?"

He nodded. "Yes, my father has a sister and a brother, who both have children. When I was in hiding, it was much safer for them to think I was dead, and after being gone for eleven years, it's been hard to rebuild those relationships. To be honest, I just haven't had the time. I called and visited them once not long after Erik took power, to explain everything, but I've been busy and they live in Sweden, which is where my father was from."

I moved with him easily, as if I was a lot more comfortable dancing than I actually was. He was an excellent dancer, I noted, which surprised me since he was such a big guy.

"What about you?" he asked after a moment. "I know your mother is alive, but you've never mentioned her and I never thought to ask."

I shrugged. "She wanted a girlie-girl who would play dolls and want to paint each other's nails. Instead, she got a tomboy who joined the military. We don't see each other very often. She still lives in Florida. I have two half-sisters but she never really wanted us to be close, as if being a tomboy was contagious or something."

"How old are they?"

"Harlow is twenty-five and Vivian is twenty-one. I talk to Harlow pretty regularly, but Vivian wants nothing to do with me. It's okay. I do my thing and don't worry about it."

"I'm sorry. I can't imagine not having a relationship with my parents or siblings. I mean, obviously Daniil, Elen and I were out of touch because of circumstances, but growing up we were close. I miss my parents a lot, and my brother Vardan as well."

"That had to have been so hard," I said softly. "I can't imagine losing most of my family in one fell swoop like that. You must've been heartbroken."

"When it first happened, it was like a year-long adrenaline rush. We had no time to mourn because all of our lives were in danger. Later, after Erik and I went underground, I had to bury those feelings because it made me vulnerable." He paused. "I've buried a lot of feelings over the years. Partially because I'm a guy, but mostly because it was just too damn hard and I couldn't afford distractions. That's probably also a big part of the reason why I stayed single. I didn't have it in me to trust my heart to anyone."

"And now?" I asked. "Are you willing to trust your heart to someone?"

"I'm getting there," he said, his mouth gently covering mine, kissing me like we were the only two people in the room even though it only lasted for a few seconds. And damn, I never wanted it to end.

29

———————

S *andor*

THE BALL WENT until well after midnight. At two thirty, it was still going strong but Casey and Erik took their leave, heading back to the house with Xander and Joe. Lennox and I stayed a little longer, spending time with Daniil, Elen and a handful of friends. Chains had brought his wife, Emilie, and she and Elen were deep in conversation. Emilie was Swedish and since Elen was also proud of our Swedish heritage, they'd found a ton of things they had in common.

Lennox was chatting with Jamie, Daniil had just come off the dance floor with Sasha, and she went off in another direction as he sank into the chair beside me.

"Sweet girl," he said. "The men are falling all over themselves to get to her, but she's mostly oblivious."

"She's a good kid," I replied, glancing at him.

"What do you think? Is the brunette safe or do I avoid that group altogether?" he asked, referring to a group of women standing at the bar.

"I'd avoid them," I said automatically. "They were chatting with Veronique earlier."

He grimaced. "Well, that settles that then. I guess I won't be getting any tonight."

I glanced at him. "Are we ever going to talk about that?"

"You want to talk about my sex life?" He turned to me with guileless blue eyes that were just like my own.

I scowled. "Come on, don't do that. You were married to a man and I had no idea you were gay. That's not fair. I'm not some judgmental asshole you couldn't share with."

"I'm not gay," he said quietly. "I'm bi. And I didn't know I was bi until after you'd gone into hiding. Then some shit happened and I wound up exploring that side of myself. When I met Jesper, things snowballed out of control. I shouldn't have married him because even though I care about him and the kids, he's not the love of my life. But I was vulnerable and lonely and he was someone from home, from my life before Anwar took almost every-thing I cared about."

"So...Jesper was a one-off?"

Daniil gave a half-shrug. "I don't know. But there hasn't been another man since him and I'm not attracted to any I've met so far. Maybe that'll change going forward, I'm not trying to hide anything, but right now my interest has all been in women."

"Fair enough." I glanced over at Lennox.

"She's lovely," Daniil said after a moment. "I like her. Is it serious?"

"I think so. She's pretty great. It's hard, though. We barely spend any time together that isn't working or in the bedroom."

"You should remedy that."

"When?" I looked at him. "We're busy. It's not just me. She works as many hours as I do, and with the kind of work we do, it's not easy to just take a day off. When we're in Limaj, it's essentially twenty-four seven, though we sleep, of course."

"I can step in for a couple of days right now, while we're here in Vegas. Take her away, spend time as a couple. You have to. It's not right to treat her like a convenience—let her know how you feel. Because if it gets to the point of marriage, no matter how small your role is in the royal family, she has to be prepared for it."

"Oh, I think after today, she's prepared. Veronique made a nuisance of herself."

Daniil made a face. "She's a menace. Why doesn't her father rein her in? Yes, I know how sexist that sounds, but she's literally crazy and makes him look bad on a daily basis. Why not have a talk with her or threaten to cut off her funds if she doesn't knock it off?"

"Obviously, she's not *our* daughter," I laughed.

Daniil grinned. "Thank god."

Damn, I'd missed this. I hadn't spent a lot of time with Daniil prior to our self-imposed exile, simply because of our age difference and us being at university at different times and such, but there were always events. A family gathering, a holiday, something that brought us together multiple times a year. Daniil, Vardan and I would sit and drink, even when Daniil hadn't been old enough, and talk until late in the night. About life, love, women, everything. Sometimes our father would join us, and those were the moments I'd clung to when life had been at its darkest.

Now that I was living in the light again, I still craved this closeness with my brother and sister. Erik was another brother to me, and our relationship transcended cousins or best friends, but Daniil was still my actual brother.

"So, are you going to do it?"

"Do what?" I'd forgotten what we were talking about as I'd slid down memory lane.

"Take Lennox away for a few days. Take her to New York, to a Broadway show and such. Visit the 9/11 Memorial—do normal vacation-y things. It's important. Trust me. I didn't nurture my marriage at all, and though my feelings for Jesper might not have been what they should have been, it might have worked had I tried harder."

I hesitated but nodded. "That's a wonderful idea, and you're right—I should. Let me talk with Erik and Joe, make sure we can both be away."

"Also, have you shown her Gustafhaven?"

I chuckled at the nickname for our family home. It had been my parents' official residence until they'd given it to Vardan when he'd gotten engaged. They liked the ease of living at the palace and had a summer home in the south of France that they visited regularly. Giving Vardan the house we'd jokingly nicknamed Gustafhaven—after our last name and a fun play on words—had been a logical step. When he'd died, as next in line, I'd inherited it. Uncle Ben had done his best to assure it had been protected to the degree it could be during Anwar's reign, and though some of the valuables inside had been taken, almost everything was intact. Vardan's clothes were still in the closet of the master suite and there was a pile of wedding gifts that had never been touched in a corner of the guest room. He and his fiancée had been planning to marry in two months, but hadn't lived to do so.

"No," I said after a moment. "In fact, I've only been there once. The memories...the essence of our parents and Vardan was almost tangible. It freaked me out a little."

"I get it. I couldn't bring myself to go in, though I've driven past a few times."

We shared a knowing glance.

"Are you two reminiscing about things that make us sad?" Elen asked, dropping onto my lap.

I smiled at her. "We were. But it's okay. I was thinking of showing Gustafhaven to Lennox."

She smiled too. "Oh, that's a wonderful idea. Perhaps the two of you could fill it with little Gustafbabies and bring it back to life."

We all laughed. Everything growing up had been Gustaf-something. Gustafhaven—which had irked my father to no end, though he came around eventually—Gustafdinner, Gustafholidays, etc. And now Gustafbabies. For some strange reason, that didn't bother me in the least. In fact, it had a nice ring to it. Though I had no idea where Lennox stood on that subject. Did she even want kids? At this rate, even if we were to start trying immediately, I'd be forty before we had any kids, and part of me thought that was old.

"You're not too old," Elen said softly, kissing me on the cheek. "You're young and strong and healthy. And you'll be a great dad."

I shifted uncomfortably. I'd given up on kids and marriage a long time ago, but now that it seemed possible again, I honestly didn't know what to think or how to react.

"You've stunned him into silence," Daniil laughed. "Trust me, brother— being a father is great."

"I'm sure it is, but as you well know, the lifestyle we live isn't always conducive to parenting and family life. I'd hate to bring kids into the world while I'm working a hundred hours a week and never see them."

"At some point, something has to give, because that's not sustainable long-term."

"My feet are killing me." Lennox dropped into the chair next to mine with a grin.

"I can massage them for you later," I told her, leaning over for a kiss. My need to touch her seemed to be never-ending, because I kissed her all the damn time. Luckily, she appeared to like it.

"Sounds like a plan." She gave me a flirtatious wink that made me chuckle.

30

———————

L*ennox*

I SLEPT SOUNDLY THAT NIGHT, surprised to see it was almost noon before I stirred. Sandor was sitting up in bed with a cup of coffee, doing something on his laptop, and I frowned.

"Why did you let me sleep so late?"

"We went to bed late," he said. "And obviously you needed it."

I sighed. "I can't remember the last time I slept until noon."

"Me either. I've only been up about half an hour." He kissed the tip of my nose. "You want some coffee?"

"I can get it—" I began.

"I've got you." He got up and poured me a cup from a carafe on the bedside table, handing it to me as I sat up.

"Thank you."

"I have a proposition for you."

"Okay."

"Would you like to go to New York for a few days? Just the two of us?"

"I... How can we get away like that?"

"I spoke to Joe and Chains and everything is handled on this end. Things are a lot more mellow when we're in Vegas, so I thought the timing was good for us to spend some quality time together away from work."

"Are you sure?"

"About which thing?" he asked, sitting next to me. "That things are more mellow here or that the timing is good for us?"

"Both?" I took a sip of coffee. "I mean, you have to admit you're a control freak. You trust Joe and Chains to take care of the family so we can get away?"

He reached for one of my hands. "It's hard, for sure, but I can't be in charge of everyone, night and day, every day. Right now, Erik and I haven't even defined my place within his organization, so I can take some time off if I want to. I haven't taken a real vacation in nearly thirteen years. I went on vacation with Casey and her family, of course, but I was still on alert, protecting everyone, so it wasn't the same."

"Wow." I wound my fingers with his. "Then yes, let's go. I haven't been to New York in a long time and I'd love to spend time together not working."

"Bring those heels," he whispered. "I really liked seeing you in them."

"You'll be massaging my feet," I told him with a grin.

"Deal."

We left for New York two days later, on his uncle's private jet since his uncle and aunt had decided to come too. Though we wouldn't see each other on the trip, we would travel there and return home at the same time, which was convenient. I loved not having to go through regular terminals and wait in lines. I could get used to this part of living with royalty.

The limo dropped us off at our hotel first as Uncle Ben and Aunt Kari continued on to theirs. They were staying at the Waldorf Astoria but Sandor had booked us at the St. Regis. He said he liked the location better and he didn't want to be at the same hotel as his aunt and uncle because he wanted to avoid inadvertent opportunities to hang out. We needed alone time, he'd said, and I agreed with him.

"Welcome, Your Highness." The clerk at the desk addressed him formally, catching me off guard, but Sandor just smiled and handed him a black American Express card. I'd never seen him use a card before—he usually paid for everything cash—but it made sense that he'd need a card for a room at a place like this.

Our room was huge, with twelve-foot ceilings, chandeliers, and a fake fireplace with a marble mantel. Bathrobes hung in the bathroom, the fixtures all gleamed gold, and the room appeared to be stocked with every toiletry I could think of. This was extravagance I wasn't used to, but Sandor didn't even bat an eyelash, using the bathroom and then coming out and settling on the couch in the sitting room area.

"What would you like to do today?" he asked me. "It's not even three o'clock, so we have a couple of hours to kill before dinner. Our reservations are for seven."

"Do I have to get dressed up?" I asked him.

"Only if you want to. I'm a prince—no one is going to tell us what to wear."

"Well, yeah, but I want to look right. I don't want to wear jeans if every other woman in the place is in a dress and heels."

"It's a dress and heels kind of place," he said. "Is that okay? I plan to wear jeans and a sport coat, but not a suit."

"I don't...have anything like that with me," I admitted softly.

"Then let's go shopping. Bloomingdale's should have something for you."

"How about the big Macy's in Herald Square? I've never been and I read about it all the time."

"Sure."

I was a little freaked out because I rarely spent money on clothes and I'd never shopped at a Bloomingdale's in my life. At least I'd been to Macy's on occasion, so I felt more comfortable there. New York prices couldn't be that extravagant there, could they? I couldn't let him buy me clothes, but I also didn't want to embarrass him. Not to mention, I was thirty-two years old and maybe it was time I added something other than jeans and cargo pants to my wardrobe. I had a boyfriend now and there were no rules that said I couldn't be a tomboy most of the time and a girlie-girl some of the time.

We took a cab uptown and I felt like a little kid as we got out. The Macy's was huge, unlike anything I'd seen in the malls I'd been to over the years. It was a little overwhelming as we walked in and were immediately assaulted by case after case of designer handbags. It occurred to me I couldn't use my denim cross-body purse out to dinner tonight if I was wearing a dress and heels, so I headed for one of the counters, looking for something appropriate. Black? Small? Jesus, I sucked at being a girl.

"This one," Sandor said gently, pointing out a flat Michael Kors clutch that was big enough for my phone, credit cards, some lipstick and keys.

I tried to surreptitiously check the price but he just pushed my hand away. "You wouldn't be buying this stuff if not for me, so let me get it."

"Oh, no, really, I can't—" I began.

"Okay." He took a breath. "I guess it's time to have the talk."

I raised my eyebrows.

"My mother, Uncle Ben and their other brother, Uncle Isak, owned the rights to most of the oil in Limaj. Forty percent of the profits go to running the country, the rest is ours. When King Isak started making moves toward a more conservative, theocratic government, Uncle Ben and my parents moved all of our family holdings to the U.S. and the U.K., and put the bulk of our money into either Swiss bank accounts or investments. All of us kids had large trust funds. When my parents were killed, all of their oil holdings came to us kids. The way it was set up, Anwar couldn't keep them from us, and the money was funneled directly to our accounts.

"When I went into hiding, my share of the money went to Daniil and Elen, who of course, kept it for me, and invested it with their own. Now that I'm back, they've transferred my money to my own accounts and I'm... beyond wealthy. We're talking many, many millions. If it was up to me, we'd be over in the Prada and Gucci stores, buying you one in every color, but I know that would make you uncomfortable. This bag is maybe two hundred dollars. Truly, let me do this for you. I understand it will take some getting used to, and I'm not trying to make you feel bad, but it will make me happy to shop for you. I've never done it. I barely shop for myself. So please, do this for me and be gracious. Please."

I didn't know what to say but yes. I should've known he was that wealthy, but I hadn't, so it was mind-boggling. But money didn't change who he was and I already knew the man, which made his net worth a cool, but completely unimportant, bonus.

"Okay," I told him, "but then can we look at all the purses? I've never shopped without a budget before."

"Absolutely."

31

S*andor*

Shopping for Lennox was a new experience for both of us. She'd always had a budget and I'd never had a girlfriend serious enough to take shopping. She didn't try to act coy by looking at prices, but rather took her time to find something that was good quality and would last. We probably spent a little too much time with the purses, but then I got her into the clothing department and she tried on a handful of party dresses. One was the stereotypical little black dress. Short, formfitting and low-cut, showing off her incredible legs and slender physique. It was simple but stunning on her, and I couldn't wait for her to wear it tonight.

The second dress was pink. A pale, baby pink made from soft, shimmery material. It was longer, falling to mid-calf, but with a slit up one side. It was the perfect dress to go dancing in, something that moved as she did, and the color somehow softened her. She'd been on the fence about it, but I loved it and insisted she get it. We also found shoes to match, a pair in black and another in a slightly darker shade of pink. Even if she only wore them to bed, I loved her in heels and they worked with the dresses.

The whole thing probably made her a tiny bit uncomfortable, but she was a good sport even though we had to rush back to the hotel so she could change in time for our reservation.

When she came out of the bathroom in the black dress, with incredibly high black heels, her hair falling in gentle waves around her shoulders, we almost didn't leave. She seemed to get more beautiful as we spent more time together, and though that didn't make sense, I didn't question it. I was crazy about her and didn't want to overthink things. I did that with pretty much everything else and this little getaway was about discovering who we were together, beyond work and the royal family.

"Is it okay?" she asked softly.

"Okay?" My voice was a little hoarse as I drank her in with my eyes. "It's sensational. You're beautiful, Lennox." I shouldn't have kissed her because she'd just put on lipstick, but I didn't care. Our mouths moved together easily, and by the time I'd finished making love to her mouth, she was a little glassy-eyed.

"That's not fair," she whispered. "You got me all hot and bothered."

I just smiled. "Go fix your lipstick."

THE NEXT TWO days were two of the best of my entire life. It was a mini-vacation, stolen time with a woman I'd started to have strong feelings for, but it was much more. We had fun. Actual fun, talking and laughing in ways I never remembered enjoying with a woman. With anyone, really, not since childhood anyway. In the back of my mind, I'd wondered if we were as compatible as I'd thought we were, if we would have anything in common beyond work and sex.

It turned out that though we didn't have a ton in common, we had a mutual love of adventure. She was happy to wander through unfamiliar neighborhoods, window-shopping and taking fun pictures of the plethora of wonderful architecture all over the city. She talked me into going ice skating in Central Park and I got her to go to the top of the Empire State Building. She said she wasn't a fan of sushi, but agreed to go to a place I loved, since sushi was one of my favorite things, and tried everything. In the end, she wound up loving it, which made me happier than such a small thing should have.

When she dragged me to a place that had axe- and hatchet-throwing, and kicked my ass with her accuracy, I might have fallen a little in love with her right then and there. Where had I found such an incredible, diverse, and passionate woman? Not to mention beautiful and intelligent. I was in big trouble and when we passed Tiffany & Co. on our way to dinner on our last night, I pulled her inside, despite her protests.

"Come on," I said. "What woman doesn't love jewelry?"

"A woman who works as a bodyguard and can't wear much."

"You can wear it to bed, along with the heels."

She rolled her eyes, but went with me. I saw she was drawn to rose gold, which was trendy right now, and figured it would look great with that pink dress I'd bought her. She would balk if I tried to buy her something, so I made note of the bracelet and earrings she kept going back to, and would call as soon as I had a moment alone. There were very few times I used my title to my advantage, but this was one of them. They would deliver to the hotel if I asked it of them, and it would be waiting for us when we returned from dinner. I smiled, thinking about her wearing nothing but the bracelet, earrings and pink heels.

"Why are you smiling like you're imagining me naked?" she demanded as we walked back onto the street.

"Because I was?" I looped my arm around her neck, laughing down at her as she rolled her eyes. It was unseasonably chilly for October and we were both in hoodies and jeans. I had a baseball cap on my head, which helped to keep me anonymous, so I wasn't expecting a flashbulb to go off as a member of the press snapped pictures. I wanted to lash out, because I didn't want our incredible time in New York to end on a negative note, but this was part of the life. If we were going to be together, she had to deal with it. We weren't doing anything wrong and though the guy was annoying, he wasn't actually touching us or preventing us from going on our way.

"Shit." I felt her tense and squeezed her arm.

"It's okay," I said. "Just ignore him. They won't let him into the hotel."

We walked in silence the rest of the way and I resisted the urge to reach out and smack the guy. He followed us from about six feet away, snapping pictures and calling out to me even though I didn't acknowledge him. People on the street were giving him side-eye, one of many things I loved about New York; these people didn't take any shit. I wished I didn't have to, but an altercation with a paparazzo wouldn't benefit anyone.

"You think they've been watching us all week?" Lennox asked as we walked into the hotel.

"Probably?" I shrugged. "You're going to have to get used to it, love. Much as it pains me to say that."

"I know. I'll be okay. It's a little jarring, but I'm sure it won't faze me after a while."

"It won't. As long as they stay respectful, I ignore them."

"Good to know."

We changed for dinner, though we were keeping it more casual tonight. We'd had our fancy dinner on the first night and spent the next two stopping when we felt hungry. Tonight, we were going to Little Italy since she said she'd never been there. We could eat and then walk around and explore the little shops along the street. Hopefully, the gift I'd bought her would be delivered and I'd spend the rest of the night between her gorgeous legs, fucking her like a man on a mission. I didn't know what the mission was, other than to make us both feel good, but it was a good plan regardless.

After dinner, we splurged on cannoli from a store a few doors down from the restaurant, both of us vowing to hit the gym hard when we got home. We'd done a lot of walking, but not enough to combat a cannoli the size of my arm. It was delicious, though, and neither of us voiced regrets.

"I am officially a fan of vacations," she told me as we walked toward the subway. She'd wanted to experience New York like a native, so we'd taken the subway today and she'd loved it. Personally, I thought it was a hassle, but it was okay since it made her happy.

"Me too," I said. "Do you ski?"

She nodded. "I have. I mean, I grew up in Florida, then moved around a lot in the Marines, and there was certainly no skiing when I was in the Middle East. But I've done it a few times and it's fun. Why?"

"How about a ski weekend this winter? There's a great mountain for beginners in Zakopane, Poland. That's not far from Limaj."

"Sounds fun. I'm always up for something athletic."

I unlocked the door to our suite and turned on the lights. She padded into the bedroom and stopped, glancing over her shoulder at me. "What did you do?" she asked.

"Who, me?" I asked innocently.

"Sandor, you can't keep buying me things..."

"Why not?" I countered. "I have more money than I'll ever spend. It makes me happy to have someone to spend it on. Didn't we already discuss this?"

"Yes, but..." Her voice trailed off and she raised her hands in surrender. "Fine. If you want to spoil me, I'm not going to complain." She reached for the telltale blue shopping bag and opened it with interest. She pulled out the two boxes and slowly opened the first. She looked at me. "I should have known you were watching."

"Always."

"It's beautiful." She slid the bracelet on her wrist and then opened the second box. "And the earrings. What, no matching necklace?"

I laughed. "I can have it delivered before we leave tomorrow."

"I'm kidding."

"I'm not."

She walked over to me and wrapped her arms around my neck. "Thank you. You're very sweet and I love the fact that you pay attention and go out of your way to indulge me. I feel very special."

"You are special." I dragged my mouth to hers and pulled her in for a kiss. I'd thought this insane insatiability would wane after a few weeks, or at least a couple of months, but it hadn't. I wanted her now as much as I'd ever wanted anyone, despite the fact that we'd been making love at least twice a day every day since we'd been here. It wasn't enough, for whatever reason, and I was okay with that. Apparently, she was too, because she was already shimmying out of her jeans and toeing off her boots.

"Get undressed," she whispered, pulling away.

"Where are you going?" I demanded as she moved out of the room.

"Get undressed," she reiterated as she disappeared. "And stay in the living room."

32

L*ennox*

IT WAS weird having a living room in a hotel room but we had one, so I hurried into the bathroom and shed the rest of my clothes. I dug around in my toiletry bag and found a clip that I could use to fashion a loose, messy bun that would accentuate my gorgeous new earrings. Then I dug out the pink heels and slipped them on. I was going to take our lovemaking to the next level tonight and I hoped it would be significant to him, the way this whole trip had been to me.

I hadn't known what to expect from him in an environment that was one hundred percent enjoyment. He was usually a little gruff around the edges, alternating between tender and awkward when it came to romance, but he'd upped his game on this trip and I realized his awkwardness mostly came from a place of restraint. He worried about his heart, his duties, his image, and who knew what else, so he tried to walk a line that would allow him to do it all, and it wasn't always possible. But now that we were alone, I'd seen the man beneath the facade and I was hopelessly in love with him.

I didn't care about his money, his title, or the royal blood running through his veins, but he made me feel like a princess, and that had nothing to do with the monarchy. His touch, the thoughtful things he did without even trying, all made me a little giddy with pleasure. I'd tried so hard not to let myself feel the way I was feeling, but how could I not? What woman could resist this gorgeous, kind, considerate man?

I stepped out of the bathroom and slowly walked into the living room. Sandor was naked, just as I'd asked, stroking that glorious cock of his as he waited for me. When he saw me, his eyes narrowed a little and he smiled.

"Will you turn around for me?" he asked in a throaty whisper. "Just so I can appreciate the 360 view?"

"Of course." I did a little turn, giving him a view of my ass, before turning back to him. "I have a surprise for you, handsome."

"Yeah?" He continued stroking his already hard cock and my mouth watered a little.

I strolled over to him, moving my hips from side to side as I walked. When I got to him, I pushed him back onto the couch and crawled over him, straddling his lap. "I'm going to make part of your fantasy come true," I whispered, leaning in to kiss him. I took the lead, sliding my tongue between his lips and curling it with his. I was in no hurry, basking in the look in his eyes as he'd watched me walk across the room. No one had ever made me feel like he did, and I wanted to give him something no one else ever had.

His hands were all over me, touching and stroking and bringing me more pleasure than anyone had a right to. It was always like this, but it never got old. I settled on his lap, his erection pressed between us, mouths fused together like two people starved for each other. Each stroke of his tongue seemed to move straight between my legs and I feared I was embarrassingly wet. The more we kissed, the more I needed him, and I slowly raised my hips, reaching between us to grip his cock.

"I can't give you your whole fantasy, because of the implant and because that's not a conversation we're ready to have, but I can give you part of it." I paused, my eyes trained on his as I waited for his consent. Neither of us had ever had unprotected sex before, so I would make sure he was in, but I hoped he trusted me enough to do this for him. For both of us.

He didn't say a word, merely pulled my head back to his, kissing me again as he thrust up in my hand. I guided him to my entrance and moved my hand away, letting gravity take over as I slowly, almost painfully, slid down. He entered me a fraction of an inch at a time, and I had to pull away from his mouth long enough to watch his face. Those incredible blue eyes were trained on me, filled with passion and lust and...something I didn't quite recognize. Whatever it was, it was breathtaking, and he brought his hands up to frame my face.

"You're so fucking beautiful," he whispered.

I finally sank down all the way, letting him fill me to the hilt, our bodies joined as closely as humanly possible.

"This is better than anything I ever imagined," he said, sliding his hands down my back and letting them rest on my hips. "So wet...so tight... Jesus, I had no idea it would feel like this."

"Me either." It wasn't that different for me, especially not with today's thin condoms, but the emotion-charged air between us changed everything. He was moving slowly, taking his time, and I gave him an inviting smile. "Do it the way you fantasized about. Take me. Fuck me like you've always wanted to fuck someone—so hard I'll still feel it next week."

"Fuck yeah." He stood up, still holding me, without even pulling out. He carried me to the dining room table and lowered me to the ground, turning me away from him. He gently pushed my chest down onto the table and positioned himself behind me. Without a word, he thrust back in, so hard and deep I gasped. He stopped, one hand on my back. "You okay?"

"I'm fine. You just surprised me. Do it. All of it. Whatever you want."

He thrust in again and used one of his feet to move my legs further apart. He gripped my hips and started to pound into me. I'd never experienced anything like it. It bordered on painful, but every time it started to hurt, that magnificent cock of his hit the place deep inside of me that made my knees get weak. Everything became a collage of passion, pain and pleasure, like nothing I'd done before.

"Can I spank you?" He slowed down long enough to whisper in my ear, waiting for my response.

"Yes."

"You're sure?"

"Yes!"

His hand came down on one of my ass cheeks and the sting was followed by the warm caress of his hand.

"I'm going to do it harder," he said softly. "Just tell me when it's too much."

"It won't be too much." I already knew that. Nothing was too much with this man. He could have all of me. Everything. There was no limit to what I'd give him.

The next blow was definitely harder, but he'd grabbed my hair too, so the stinging in my scalp rivaled that of my ass, and another thrust against my G-spot had me all kinds of confused. My body shook with the ferocity of his lovemaking, the carnal way he was ravishing me, the sheer roughness of it all. But I loved it. I never dreamed I'd enjoy this kind of savageness in the bedroom, or maybe it was just the man, but it was incredible.

"God, yes, please, harder..." I was gasping, panting, straining for something, I just didn't know what.

The next smack made me cry out and Sandor froze, much to my chagrin.

"I'm fine," I hissed. "Don't stop! I'll tell you if it's too much."

"Jesus fuck, you're gorgeous." He continued his passionate assault, alternately smacking my ass, pulling my hair and fucking me within an inch of my life. I didn't know what this was, but my first orgasm caught me by surprise and I was shocked when he didn't join me.

"What's wrong?" I asked, trying to catch my breath.

"Nothing. I'm just not ready for this to end."

"Oh my god."

With my hair wrapped in his fist, that monster-sized cock practically splitting me in half, and the occasional slaps to my ass, everything morphed into a haze of gritty pleasure and erotic stimuli.

"Can you come again for me?" he whispered, his touch gentling against my hair as he lifted my torso and pressed his front to my back. He had one arm wrapped around my waist, holding me in place, and his fingers traveled down to the sweet spot between my legs. I looked up to see our reflection in the big decorative mirror and moaned at how sexy this was.

"Yeah, baby, that's what it looks like when I fuck you." He held me tighter, working his magic against my clit as he continued to pump in and out of me relentlessly.

"Please, harder..." I needed more of the savageness, the wildness that was so new to me.

"I knew you'd like it rough," he breathed. He punched into me again, hard and fast, until the world slid away and there was nothing but my orgasm, crashing over and over and over. My breath left me in a rush, my vision blurred, and the scream that escaped me was animalistic. I shook and writhed and exploded around him, but when he came, I felt every pulse, every jerk of his cock, and when his semen ran back out of me, dripping down my thigh, I nearly came again.

This was next-level sex and it was a good thing he was holding me, because I would have collapsed if he hadn't been.

We stood that way for a few minutes, our eyes finally locking in the mirror, and I whimpered. Now that it was over, I was sore, my ass was on fire and I was pretty sure I'd still feel it next week.

He pulled out slowly and then scooped me up in his arms, carrying me into the bathroom. I collapsed against his chest, closing my eyes and letting him hold me.

"Let me run a bath," he said softly. "You're going to be sore, so it'll feel good."

As always, he read me like a damn book.

"Oh, not yet," I cried, clinging to him.

"Easy, baby. I'm right here." He kissed the side of my face, my neck, the soft spot behind my ear.

"Was it what you wanted?" I finally asked, coming out of my passion-filled coma. "I mean, the fantasy?"

"Baby, this was so far beyond my fantasies, I can't even express how good it was." He set me down and turned me to face him. "You sure you're okay? I went at you like...a fucking animal. I'm almost embarrassed. Please say I didn't hurt you."

"Embarrassed?" I shook my head. "Babe. I came twice, and the second time, I came so hard I might have blacked out for a few seconds. That was awesome. And no, you didn't hurt me. Although I had no idea I liked it so...*rough*."

"I had a feeling, but I wasn't sure and you were clear about the spanking thing early on."

"But you also asked me if I'd let you find out what I liked, and I said I would."

"Uh-huh." He reached over and turned on the water to fill the bathtub.

"I don't think I can take it this hard every time," I said. "So maybe every couple of times?"

"I think going at it this hard is for special occasions." He glanced down at my ass. "I also don't like smacking you so hard. You're really red and I don't know what I'll do if it bruises."

"I'm fine," I said firmly. "You made fantasies I didn't even know I had come true on this trip, so I wanted to do this for you tonight. It can be special-occasion sex, for sure. But even if it bruises, we'll just know to go a little lighter next time. I'm not upset."

He pressed his lips to mine, as tenderly and sweetly as he ever had, and I sighed a little.

"I think I love you."

"I think I love you."

We spoke in unison and then neither of us moved, our eyes locked as I stood up a little straighter.

"You do?"

"You do?"

We did it again and this time burst out laughing.

"I guess that's that," he chuckled, pulling me close. "No need to say much else."

"No, I guess not."

We smiled at each other and he gave me a little nudge toward the bath. "Go on. Get in."

"You too. I know it's small for you, but I need you touching me. I don't think I'll be able to breathe if you stop."

"Thank god you said that," he whispered. "Because I was thinking the same damn thing."

33

———

S *andor*

WE LEFT THE NEXT MORNING—AFTER the matching rose gold necklace arrived from Tiffany & Co.—making Lennox simultaneously laugh and get a little teary.

"Would it be dumb if I wore them for the trip home?" she asked me.

"Not even a little. Why do you think I bought them for you? I want to see you wearing them, and not just in the bedroom."

"Well, I can't wear them when I'm working, so that's why I want to wear them now."

I watched her put them on, pleasure drifting through me. I hadn't planned on telling her I loved her, but the softened version, with "I think" at the beginning, had just slipped out. That she'd said it at the same time had been kind of freaky, but wonderful too. Everything about her, this thing between us, was pretty wonderful, so I was in a relaxed happy mood as we boarded the jet. But that faded as soon as I saw Uncle Ben's face.

"What is it?" I asked automatically.

He held up a hand. "Everything is okay, but there was an incident."

"What kind of incident?" I asked through ground teeth.

"Apparently, Omar danced with Sasha at the ball."

"What?!" My voice was so loud Aunt Kari jumped, but I didn't care. I was too damn pissed.

"How do we know?"

"Because he sent a picture to the tabloids, talking about the lovely step-daughter of the King of Limaj, and what a great wife she's going to make."

I used so many curse words, in so many languages, Aunt Kari bit her lip to keep from laughing. The situation wasn't funny, but my obnoxious combinations of English, Limaji, Swedish, French and Russian curse words would have been humorous under other circumstances.

"She was never alone," Uncle Ben said calmly. "She was never in any danger."

"But he got close enough to dance with her!" I yelled. I got up and started to pace. "That means he got past all of us. What the fuck is it with this guy, that he keeps eluding us? He can't be that much smarter than all of us."

"He's wily," Lennox said quietly. "Which makes him more dangerous than a regular enemy."

"He bought the ticket off a friend," Uncle Ben said. "Including the special dance. Nick's already planning to upgrade security for future dances, requiring ID that matches the ticket. Any changes have to be announced seven days in advance."

"That's great for the future, but it doesn't help us now."

"But Sasha's fine," Aunt Kari reminded me gently. "Everything is okay. Erik wouldn't let anyone tell you so it didn't ruin your holiday."

I sighed in frustration. I couldn't even blame what had happened on my absence, because it had happened right under my nose, and everyone else's, so we would have to deal with that when we got home. For now, I logged into my laptop and contacted Joe. There would be a meeting first thing in the morning.

LENNOX WAS up before me in the morning. I awoke when the door clicked behind her and I frowned, rolling over and grabbing my phone to send her a text, and finding one from her waiting for me.

Lennox: Going to meet up with a few of the guys at the gym. Meet us if you have time before the meeting.

It was only six o'clock, so I got out of bed and hurriedly dressed after sending her a text asking her to wait for me. I didn't want there to be a weird emotional distance between us, not after everything that had happened in New York, but last night had been a little strained since I'd been preoccupied with the Omar incident. I was focused on my job again, instead of her, but that didn't mean anything had to change between us. We weren't on vacation anymore, but I didn't want her tiptoeing around me either.

She was in the kitchen when I came in, protein drink in hand. She poured one for me and smiled. "Good morning. I thought I'd let you sleep."

I made a face. "You thought I needed space and I don't."

"You sure?"

"Not from you." I pulled her against me. "We're good, babe. I have to figure out how Omar keeps getting so close to us, but that has nothing to do with our personal relationship. It's work, like always, just with a more focused direction today."

She nodded. "Regardless, after eating the way we ate in New York, I need a solid workout."

"As do I."

We finished our drinks and headed out. To my surprise, the whole gang was at the gym, except Joe and the night guard, who were still at the house. Chains, Xander, Jonas, Axel, Daniil, Elen, and even Ace was there. I hadn't known he was in town so I reached out to give him a quick hug, that weird upper-body-shoulder-slap thing guys did to pretend we were cool or something. I'd never understood it, merely went along with the culture here in the U.S. We were a bit more affectionate in Europe, but not here so much.

"When did you get to town?" I asked him.

"Last night," he said. "Erik and I had a few things to talk about, so I flew in. I was in D.C. anyway."

"All right, let's get this show on the road," Lennox said, running in place as she warmed up. "Who's up for a five-mile run?"

"Me." Xander stretched out on the floor next to her. "Just give me a second to get loose."

"I'm in," Jonas said, nodding.

I hated running, though I did it as often as necessary to stay in shape, but it wasn't my preferred form of cardio.

"Let's go." Chains started off and the rest of us followed. Lennox and Xander were both runners and they took the lead without even trying. Ace fell back with me and the others were in the middle. I didn't have anything to prove but I saw the younger guys trying to keep up with Lennox, which was entertaining. She was fluid when she ran, her body moving easily, her long legs taking strides the guys struggled to keep up with even though they were taller than she was.

"The thing with Sasha bothers me," Ace said as we jogged at a more moderate pace.

"Yeah." I didn't want to get pissed off all over again.

"We need to catch this guy because he's not going away and I'm afraid things are just going to escalate."

"No shit. The question is how."

"I'm thinking."

"Well, I've been thinking about it for months, and so far, can't come up with anything. Every time we get close, he gets away. I think we have to set a trap and use someone as bait."

"But who?" Ace countered. "Sasha's too young and not experienced enough should something go wrong. I think Elen could handle it, but it's a huge risk we may not want to take."

"The perfect target would be Luke, but obviously we're not in any position to take a risk with him either." I shook my head. "Thus our dilemma."

"Let me think on it some more." Ace grinned as Lennox took the lead by a lot, her ponytail flying out behind her as she circled the indoor track.

Xander was second, and I was surprised to see Elen in third place, Jonas, Axel and Chains dropping further and further back. Jonas and Axel were bigger guys, not quite as tall as I was, but probably just as muscular, so they weren't built to run. They could fight, though. I'd seen video of both of them showing off their skills and they would be formidable against an enemy. On the track, though, they were never going to keep up with Lennox.

"I was thinking maybe I'd come to Limaj for a while," Ace said slowly. "See if I could get a feel for the vibe around the country, maybe check in with some of my eastern European assets."

"Couldn't hurt and you're always welcome, but doesn't the agency want you on assignment?"

He shrugged. "I'm taking a little vacation time."

That surprised me. "You? Really?"

"Not in the way you think," he said. "I just mean, the red tape and legal constraints are making it harder and harder to do my job. I've seen a lot of bad shit over the years, but lately, I feel like I can't take a piss without someone chiding me. The whole point of being a spy is to be...*covert*. If I have to check in over every little thing, it kind of defeats the purpose."

"You think they're edging you out?"

"I'm not sure," he said quietly. "But I've given almost twenty years to my country between the military and the CIA, so I'm not going out without a fight. I want my twenty and my pension."

"I don't blame you." I paused. "But you know you always have a job on our team if you want it."

"I know. I'm counting on it." He gave me a cheeky grin and followed my gaze, where I was watching Lennox lap us.

"You're a man in love," Ace said lightly, following my gaze.

"I am." I wasn't going to hide it. I knew better than most how short life was, so I planned to enjoy every minute of it, despite the looming danger.

"She seems great. I'm glad you two found each other."

"Me too."

34

L *ennox*

I WAS ALMOST glad to be back in Limaj because the vibe in Vegas had been weird after the whole thing with Omar and Sasha. Axel had stayed behind, assigned to be with Sasha all day now, including at school, which she'd resisted before. We couldn't be too careful anymore, especially with the bulk of the security team here in Limaj. Chains went to school with Luke most days, which had become a bone of contention between Luke and his parents, but at this point we weren't sure what else to do. Logan was still in Monte Carlo with Leni and the twins, and the rest of us were here, trying to find a new normal.

The first couple of days back, Sandor and I barely saw each other, each of us assigned to different places, different people, different security details. We tried to find an hour at night, before bed, to just be together, catch up on our day, find some semblance of intimacy amidst the chaos of our daily routine, but it wasn't easy. We were up at five to work out most days, followed by showers, breakfast, and security briefings. Our schedules kept us apart most of the time, though we occasionally met for dinner, and we rarely finished for the day before seven or eight. By the time we wound down, we were usually too tired to do anything but make love and pass out. Sometimes we even skipped the lovemaking, which was rare for us, but we'd been working crazy hours.

Sandor and Joe had upgraded an already intense security system, and the protocols we went through each day were grueling. It was beginning to wear on Casey too, and I mentioned it to Sandor at breakfast one morning after we'd been home about three weeks. It was Saturday and we weren't scheduled to be anywhere until eleven. Erik had announced he and Casey were sleeping in and staying sequestered in their room for the morning, so we got to do the same.

"I'm glad Erik and Casey are taking some time," I told him as we sipped coffee and ate eggs and bacon. "She's been looking a little tired lately. I think being away from her kids is wearing on her too."

"For sure. Luke hasn't been doing well in school this semester and Liz said the twins have been getting into trouble."

"Casey told me the twins were extremely upset they didn't get to go to the ball, so it's been hard all around."

"That's why Erik worked so hard to pass the education bill. He couldn't very well start building a state-of-the-art, private, English-speaking school without ensuring that the public Limaji schools were up and running."

"Of course. It looks like that's on track, though. From what I've read, a dozen new schools reopened this year, just a few weeks later than usual, so if they have a few less days off during the breaks, they should be able to end with the others."

"Yes. We put a focus on the more rural schools since the ones in the city have been okay. Half a dozen more are set to reopen after the Christmas break to ease the overcrowding in the schools that were still going, and that should help a great deal. We fast-tracked the recertification process for teachers who had licenses in the past, with salary incentives across the board, and teachers are coming out of the woodwork now."

"So many things most people never think about in the U.S.," she said. "Whether or not there are public schools. Whether or not there are enough teachers to work at said schools. I mean, there are occasional schools or districts that are short, but it's mostly situational, not a national crisis."

"I know. And schools are just the beginning. Did you know there are only a handful of car dealerships in the entire country right now? Maybe five?"

My mouth fell open. "Really?"

"Yup. The few people who can afford it have had to travel outside the country to buy a car, and then they get slammed on tariffs when they get back."

"I feel so bad for the people," I said quietly. "I can't imagine what they went through when Anwar was king."

"Why do you think Erik is so torn? He desperately wants to help everyone, even though it's putting a strain on his marriage, his relationship with his kids, everything. But there are several hundred thousand people struggling and he has the power to help them."

"It just seems like he needs more help, more people working with him."

"Yeah, the problem is finding people who aren't trying to stab him in the back in the process."

"That sucks. Why would anyone do that? Don't they care about their people, their country?"

"Where there's power and money at stake, people often turn a blind eye. That's why being part of the royal family is so important right now, to show unity, to remind them of who we are, who we've been, and who we can be again."

"That kind of pressure must be monumental."

He smiled. "Sometimes."

"Well, any way I can help, you know I'm here."

"I do." I reached for her hand. "So. Tomorrow. We're taking a day off. I put it on the schedule. Every other Sunday, you and I are off. It works out well because Sunday is the one day Erik can take off as well, so he can spend time with Casey and the kid or kids, and you and I will have time to ourselves."

"Cool." I gave him a smirk. "Can we catch up on sleep?"

"We can, but I have something I want to show you. Can you be ready to go around ten?"

"Sure."

Sandor glanced at the time. "I guess it's time for us to get to work."

"Yup." I got to my feet and reached for my gun, sliding it into the shoulder holster I wore beneath my light jacket. I put another in an ankle holster as Sandor did the same and we headed down to start our day.

"Are you going to tell me where we're going?" I asked him the next morning as we got dressed.

"I want to show you my childhood home," he said, pulling on a jacket since it had gotten really cold the last couple of weeks.

"I assumed you grew up in the palace," I said, frowning. "How did I not know this?"

"Well, we had a group of suites here, so any time there were celebrations, holidays and the like, we would come stay, and as adults we each got a private suite like this one. But no, when I was a child, we had our own home just a few minutes outside the city. My mother inherited it from her paternal grandmother and when Vardan got engaged, my parents passed it on to him. They asked the rest of us, of course, but I didn't need it since my job at the time was to be wherever Erik was. Daniil and Elen were still at university, so they didn't care. It's not like the palace or anything, but it was home. Vardan and his fiancée had just begun renovations when they were killed."

"I'm so sorry." I wrapped my arms around him, holding him tightly. He rarely showed any emotion about the deaths of his immediate family, but this time his voice had gotten a little hoarse. "I'd love to see it if you want to take me, but not if it's too painful."

"It's been more than a decade," he said quietly. "It's time. I checked it out last winter when we first got here and there are still unopened wedding gifts in one of the guest rooms. It's time to bury the past and move on, get rid of all that stuff and maybe finish renovations. I thought you might like to help me with that."

Our eyes met. "I'd love to."

We took one of the palace SUVs and navigated the roads leading out of the city. It wasn't far, just fifteen minutes or so, but he'd led me to believe it was a quaint little cottage or something, and the house we pulled up in front of was not that in any way, shape or form. It was a large, sprawling estate, with a gate at the front and a large, if not somewhat falling apart, courtyard.

Mold had taken over what had once been a stunning and ornate fountain, leaving it an ugly black color, starkly dark amidst the snow-covered grounds. The columns framing the front steps were dirty and worn, and the carved double doors that led into the house creaked on their hinges as Sandor unlocked them. When we stepped inside, it was even worse. A decade of abandonment had left everything dirty, worn or broken. Someone, most likely soldiers, had obviously been here at some point, pillaging for valuables. Ironically, many of the paintings and other decorations had been spared, merely gathering dust. The furnishings appeared okay, simply covered with sheets or tarps.

The walls and carpets were filthy, however, as uncaring looters had run roughshod across the floors. I could see what it had been once, though, and my heart broke a little for Sandor as he quietly took in his childhood home. He said he'd been here earlier this year, so he wasn't seeing it for the first time, but he'd probably been in a hurry and frustrated then. Today, he just looked sad, and I slid my hand into his.

"It can be cleaned up," I whispered. "The carpets and such are probably ruined, but we could have the floors refinished, new carpets brought in, repairs made. If the foundation of the house is solid, and I think it is, this is all fixable."

"Come, let me show you the rest." He led me through dark hallways and empty rooms, but the kitchen was a delight. Huge, filled with dirty but beautiful stone countertops, and the kind of island most women would kill for. I didn't cook much, but I appreciated a beautiful kitchen as much as any woman, and my little sigh must have been audible because he turned to me with a grin. "Yes? You like it?"

"Who wouldn't like it? It's gorgeous. We could do so much with this." I wrinkled my nose. "The appliances have to go, though."

He chuckled. "We'd have to gut most of the house cosmetically. At least downstairs. The upstairs fared better, except the master suite." He paused. "I guess Anwar thought that was where the best stuff would be hidden, so it's trashed. He's an idiot, though."

"Why? Where was the best stuff hidden?"

He chuckled and walked to the refrigerator, using his bulk to move it, eventually sliding it out of place. The more he moved it, the more visible a door became, and I realized it was a vault.

"Holy shit, there's a safe back there?"

"A safe room filled with actual safes. That's where all of our valuables were. It wasn't a lot, thank goodness, because my parents took most of them when they moved out of the house. They'd left some things, though, and Vardan had added more, so as soon as he was killed, Uncle Ben sent some loyal soldiers to get everything and bring them to us. Anwar still got some valuables that were in the bedroom, but it was all jewelry, things Vardan had bought for his fiancée and more sentimental stuff, like the Rolex she'd bought him."

He pushed the refrigerator back into place and we went through the room, into a formal dining room. It was magnificent, despite the cracked mirror on the wall and the handful of broken chairs surrounding a long table. This setup would seat twenty-two, ten on each side of the table plus the seats on each end.

"Twenty-two," I said thoughtfully. "Your parents must have loved to entertain."

"Well, there were six of us, plus Uncle Ben's family was another four, Uncle Isak's family was another six, plus seats for grandparents since they were alive when we were little."

"That's so lovely. I never had anything like that."

"No?"

"My mother got divorced too often to count on anyone at the holidays, and she's not the sentimental type." I looked around. "That mirror needs to go, but the chairs could be repaired and recovered, maybe refinish the table, and you'd have your childhood memories brought back to life."

He looked around. "Yeah, maybe. But what if I didn't want to bring those memories back? What if I wanted to create new ones?"

"That could work too. There's so much we can do here with a little time, effort and money. Some things we could do ourselves, even though we don't have much time, but I think it would be fun."

"Me too." He met my eyes and smiled. Then he got a look of mischief in his eyes. "Wanna see the bedrooms?"

I laughed. "I'm not getting naked on anything that might have bedbugs."

He blanched. "Jesus, no. Okay, thanks for ruining that little fantasy."

"I'll make it up to you." I grinned.

We went upstairs and as he'd said, the master suite was a disaster. It could be fixed, and the glory beneath the rubble was still visible in the ornate tray ceilings and the raised dais that housed a massive four-poster bed.

"Was Vardan tall like you?"

Sandor smiled. "An inch taller."

"Wow. Daniil is what? Six-four?"

He nodded. "And Elen is tall too, five-ten. My father was six-five and my mother was five-nine, so us kids are all pretty big. Anwar was always jealous. He was only five-ten."

I laughed. "Asshole."

"You got that right."

It wasn't until we got to the guest room with the wrapped wedding gifts that both of us sobered. It was jarring because they were still so pretty. As if time, soldiers, looters, and even dust hadn't touched them. A few had been strewn around the room, but most sat in a neat little stack against one wall.

"Fuck." Sandor sank onto the edge of the bed and swiped at his eyes. "This part never gets easier."

I sat beside him. "What would you like to do with them? Should we just dispose of them? We could also open them and give the items away to people in need. Or..." I let my voice trail off as I ruminated another possibility that I wasn't sure how to present.

"What? Tell me." He looked genuinely interested.

"What if we had a...celebration?" I wrinkled my nose. "Like, a celebration of their lives? You guys didn't do that when they died, right?"

"No. The funerals happened quickly and they were cremated because there wasn't much left to bury after the explosion."

"So what about a celebration of their lives, like on a Sunday, after brunch. We gather your family, and anyone close to you like Jesper... Then you open the gifts like they're yours. Not to take anything away from them, but to celebrate what they would have done. In the U.S., we often do a gift-opening event the day after a wedding if the couple hasn't left for the honeymoon yet. Everyone gathers and there's food and mimosas and it's fun. We could do something like that, and maybe you, Daniil and Elen could open them and read the cards—I see cards attached to most of them—and then even split some of the items. Put them in your houses as a loving reminder of the brother and sister-in-law you lost."

"We."

"We what?"

"You and I. We. We could open them."

"Well, yeah, but I mean, you probably want your brother and sister—"

"I want you."

"Okay." I met his eyes questioningly. "But won't it be weird if—"

"No." He turned to me with a questioning look in his eyes. "You came up with a beautiful, loving idea and I want to do it, but I want to do it with you. Will you help me?"

35

———

S*andor*

We planned Lennox's thoughtful gift-opening brunch event for the Sunday before Christmas and I was looking forward to it. In the meantime, the kids had all arrived from Vegas and Monte Carlo, along with Jayson, Liz, and their new baby, Elijah. Nick and Skye had come with Luke and their girls, Madison and Megan, Uncle Ben and Aunt Kari were here, and Teal and her boyfriend, Matt, had arrived yesterday. The palace was full, every suite housing people we cared about, and it was a nice feeling. Casey and her staff had decorated for the holidays and gone all out, every wall, door, window, pillar and bannister touched by something red, green, silver or gold. It was beautiful and I'd opted to have a medium-sized tree delivered to my suite as well, so Lennox and I could enjoy some of the holiday festivities in private.

There was a lot of chaos, though. The kids were everywhere, exploring every inch of the palace, and we were busier than ever. Not just a dozen new people to keep track of and protect, but the sheer planning required for everything. Meals, shopping excursions, parties... It was exhausting. Tonight we were taking everyone to the tree-lighting ceremony in the town square in Hiskale, where Erik would be the one to flip the switch that would turn on the lights on the forty-foot tree. Staff had been decorating for several days and we would arrive at six o'clock to prepare. Erik would make a short speech, welcoming the holidays, and the tree would be lit at eight.

I'd been on site most of the day, securing the perimeter, checking every possible position for a sniper to set up. We couldn't check private residences or businesses, of course, but I couldn't control what I couldn't control, so I focused on the things that were accessible. Joe was with me, along with some trusted guards from the palace, and we hadn't had a break all day. He'd had to fill in when Ace had been unexpectedly called away, so we'd had to update the security roster at the last minute.

It was two o'clock now and I had to do another check of the tree itself, make sure nothing like an explosive had been slipped between the branches since a lot of people had access to it. It was cordoned off, so the general public couldn't get to it, but there were probably two dozen decorators and others from around town that could.

My phone buzzed and I saw a text from Lennox, asking specifically where I was. I frowned, but gave her my location. A minute later I heard my name and turned. Lennox, Casey, Sasha, Leni and the twins came bounding over to me. Lennox held out a box filled with something that smelled delicious.

"Lunch for you and the guys." She smiled.

"Thank you." I leaned down for a kiss and the twins and Leni started to giggle.

"Shush." Casey was laughing as she hushed them.

"What are you all up to?" I asked them.

"Shopping!" The ladies all spoke in unison and I laughed too.

"Better you than me," I told Lennox.

"It's fun." She shrugged. "I may or may not have done some shopping myself."

I feigned horror. "Jesus. Is there enough room in our suite for that?"

"You'll have to wait and see," she said with a cheeky smile.

"Looking forward to it." I kissed her once more before they took off. Logan was with them as well, keeping a slight distance to watch for anyone possibly following them or trying to approach from the rear, so I wasn't too worried about them. In general, we'd never been concerned about taking unplanned trips into the cities and towns. The people loved the royal family and usually the only issues were with people trying to get autographs and pictures. But with Omar on the loose, still trying to get to the family, we had to be vigilant in keeping an eye out for him. The children had been briefed, repeatedly, about what he looked like and who he was, so they were aware he was dangerous and to be avoided at all costs.

As it got later in the day, the temperature dropped by more than fifteen degrees and we all headed into a local café to retrieve heavier jackets that we'd left there earlier. Our family had known the owners for decades so we felt comfortable using it as an unofficial home base for the day, and they spoiled us with hot coffee, sweets, and a warm place to use the restroom.

I paused at the counter, smiling at the owner, Mr. Kreshi. He was in his seventies now, but as spry as ever, his blue eyes twinkling as he poured me a cup of his famous black and white cocoa—a fun mixture of two different flavors, one made with white chocolate and the other with dark. Instead of mixing them, he would pour them simultaneously, from two separate jugs, allowing them to swirl together. It was one of my favorite things, and I made a mental note to bring Lennox here on a day off.

"I need to show you something," I told him as I accepted the cup and took a sip.

"Of course."

I got out my phone and pulled up the picture of Omar. "This man. If you see him, even if you think you see him, I need you to contact me immediately."

He frowned, staring down at the picture. "I've seen him. He comes in for the cocoa sometimes. Usually on Sundays. He never speaks, pays cash, usually takes it to go."

"Good to know."

"But not every Sunday. Sometimes Saturday." He frowned. "Can you text me this photo? I'll show my wife and son, so they're aware also. I don't want to scare the waitresses, though."

"No problem. I appreciate it." I had his number programmed into my phone so I quickly texted it to him, took my cocoa and headed back outside.

"Hey." Joe fell into step next to me. "What's that?"

"You've never had the black and white cocoa from here? Oh, come on." We turned around, got him situated and were finally back out on the street ten minutes later.

"Almost better than sex." Joe grinned at me.

"My friend, if any food is better than sex, you're doing it wrong."

"I said almost."

We laughed.

"Erik and the family will be here soon," he said. "Crowds are already lining up on both sides of the street around the tree. How many men do you have coming from the Royal Guard?"

"Fifty." The Royal Guard consisted of active members of the military specially chosen to work at the palace and/or guard the king during public appearances. They wore special uniforms so they were easily recognizable and I'd spent weeks personally vetting every single one of them. The entire force would be here tonight, helping to protect Erik and the family, but I wasn't taking any chances. We had surveillance set up all around the perimeter, Chains was monitoring everything from Las Vegas, and the core group of us that were on site were wearing earpieces, allowing us to communicate constantly.

Lennox had just let me know that the family was en route, so I made my way to the café to wait for them. It was a five-minute drive from the palace to here, so they would arrive momentarily. Mr. Kreshi came out with a tray of plastic cups filled with his black and white cocoa and I smiled, hoping the kids would enjoy it the same way Erik and I had as children and even teenagers. Xander was inside, monitoring the new batch that had been made and assuring that it wasn't tainted between when Mr. Kreshi's wife made it and it was delivered to the family.

I waved as the big black SUV arrived and several of the Royal Guard surrounded the vehicle. Erik got out first, waving to everyone that began to cheer when they saw him. He reached in a hand for Casey, helping her out, and the kids followed. They all accepted the hot cocoa and then we began a slow walk towards the Christmas tree.

Luke fell into step beside me. "This is lame," he said, a scowl on his face.

"How come?" I asked. Luke wasn't usually like this and I'd been worried about him lately.

"Everything is such a big deal. We're not a normal family. Having divorced parents was way better than all of this. Maybe I'll just stay with Dad and Aunt Skye instead of moving here."

Ouch. I wondered if Erik knew he felt this way. "You think maybe you're not giving it a chance?" I asked lightly. "I mean, last year, you didn't want anything but to be with Erik. Now you're all grumpy. I think you miss your mom and aren't getting enough attention from your dad so you're being a brat."

Luke sighed. "Maybe."

"How about you give it a chance? Spend a little time getting to know Hiskale while you're here, try some of the cool foods—like the hot chocolate you haven't even touched—and learn a little about your new country. I mean, you are the Crown Prince."

"Ugh. That was my worst decision ever."

"Kiddo, you need to be talking to your parents about all this, not me."

"I don't want to hurt Dad's feelings, you know? I just...want to be normal again."

Sometimes it got confusing, hearing him call both Nick and Erik Dad, but they were okay with it, so it wasn't my place to say anything.

"I know. And I promise, it will be. I mean, it's never going to be like your life in Vegas. That ship has sailed. You're the son of a king and you're someday going to rule this country. So you have to adjust to that new reality. But as far as family goes, everything is going to settle down. You'll go to school, come home and do homework, watch movies with the family, go on vacations. The important stuff is going to be a lot more normal once you get here for good. Six more months and you'll see how much better it'll be."

He swallowed. "I hope so, because this sucks."

I wanted to chide him but decided not to. I wasn't his father and it wasn't my job to parent him. I wanted to continue to be his cool uncle. "Promise me you'll give it all a chance and you'll talk to your parents instead of bottling it all up."

"I promise." He didn't sound happy about it, but he'd promised, so that was good. Parenting was hard, I thought. And yet, I'd started thinking about it. Especially now that I had someone as wonderful as Lennox in my life.

We weren't ready for marriage yet, but I wanted to get her something for Christmas that would be a promise of sorts. Jewelry was nice, but we weren't kids and a promise ring sounded dumb, even in my head. Diamonds probably weren't her thing, and something random like earrings wouldn't signify the message I wanted to portray since I'd already bought her some. It was two weeks before Christmas, and I had nothing except one inkling of an idea that was a little far-fetched. It was probably time to break down and talk to Erik. He was the king of an entire country, but he was also the king of romance. He'd give me a little shit, but it wouldn't be in a malicious way, so I needed to suck it up. We just needed to get through tonight.

"Oh, wow, the tree is huge." Luke's eyes lit up for the first time since he'd arrived in Limaj and I breathed a sigh of relief. The sweet young man I knew was still there, just buried under hormones and teenage angst. Hopefully, we'd see more of this guy while he was here for the holidays.

36

———

L *ennox*

Christmas was almost here and I didn't have anything for Sandor. I'd been racking my brain to come up with something, but what did you get a billionaire prince who essentially had everything?

"Something basic," Casey told me when I asked her. "Because even though he has all the money in the world, he doesn't have the time or the patience to shop. I used to order his socks and boxers for him in bulk. Like he told me the brand and size and I would order twenty-four at a time for him so he wouldn't have to worry about it."

"I'm not sure we're so comfortable that we're at the socks and underwear stage of gifts," I laughed.

She grinned back. "You know what I mean. Like, you might think that great leather jacket you saw is no big deal, but for a guy like him, it might be exactly what he needs. That was just an example, but you get the idea."

"Yeah." I hesitated. "Does he have a Rolex? He mentioned that Vardan's had been taken from his house after Anwar took power."

Casey frowned. "You know, I don't know. Let me talk to Erik and I'll let you know. He'd know that kind of thing."

"Thank you."

"In the meantime, do you want to finalize the details for Sunday's brunch?"

Sandor had asked me if I would do most of the planning for the event because he didn't have time, and he'd enlisted Casey and Edita to help me. We hadn't told anyone except Casey and Erik what the purpose was, making it a surprise for Elen and Daniil, and parts of it would be a surprise for Sandor too. Erik had thoughtfully gotten together a video photo collage of Vardan, Krystal, and Sandor's parents, and it would be played once everyone arrived. The lack of closure and inability to say goodbye had probably been hard on all of them so we hoped this would be cathartic. Not only so everyone could heal, but also to help them move on.

Today was Friday and the event would be on Sunday, so we only had two days to finish everything up. There wasn't a lot, especially since the palace chefs were handling the food, Erik had taken care of the slideshow, and I'd gotten Xander to go pick up the gifts from what I was now also calling Gustafhaven. It somehow fit the house, despite the fact it had been a joke, and now it seemed to stick.

"Mo-om." Jessie came flouncing in the room, a scowl on her face. "Joss said she's not dressing up on Sunday. Aren't we supposed to dress up? I don't want to be the only one."

"You won't be," Casey said patiently. "You do you and don't worry about your sister. If she doesn't want to dress up, she can wear whatever she wants. She'll be the one who feels funny when she sees everyone else dressed up."

"She's so grumpy," Jessie said with a sigh, sitting next to her mom. "I think she wants to stay in Monte Carlo with Dad. But I want to come here. I don't know how we would do that."

"I don't know either," Casey said, sliding an arm around her. "But let's not worry about it until we have to, okay? We'll talk about all that when you get here for the summer."

"I'm bored, Mom."

"Are you?" Casey stroked her hair. "We'll have to figure something out then." They started whispering so I left the room and went to my laptop to check the surveillance videos. We all took turns doing it throughout the day because it was better to have fresh eyes. Having just one person staring at screens for hours at a time led to both eyestrain and boredom, so we rotated every hour. Once I was done, I'd take some time to think about Sandor's Christmas gift some more.

I WORE the pink dress on Sunday. It was a little formal, but Elen said they were all dressing up, so it was perfect for the occasion. Sandor was wearing a navy-blue suit with a white shirt, but no tie, and I looked him up and down appreciatively when I came out of our walk-in closet.

"Oh wow." He turned and reached for me, wrapping one arm around my waist as he pulled me against him. "Buying you this dress is one of the best things I ever did." He leaned in to kiss me but I moved back, shaking my head.

"I don't have time to fix my makeup if you mess it up, so you're going to have to wait."

"Fine." He smiled good-naturedly. "Are you ready to go?"

"Yes."

With his hand at the small of my back, we made our way to the elevators and down to the main dining hall. We ran into Daniil on our way in and he smiled at me.

"You look beautiful today, Lennox."

"Thank you. You look handsome yourself."

We stepped inside, and while my breath caught a little at the simple beauty of the decorations, I heard Sandor's sharp intake of breath. He and Daniil were both focused on the easels all over the room, with pictures of their parents, Vardan, Krystal, Uncle Isak and Aunt Klara, and the other three cousins who'd perished in the explosion as well. Everything was subtle, because I knew Sandor wouldn't like anything over-the-top, but the pictures were striking and he turned to press his lips to my cheek.

"Thank you," he whispered. "This is beautiful."

"You're welcome."

We moved into the room to mingle as everyone arrived, and Sandor held on to my hand, making it abundantly clear we were together, a couple.

"I wanted to thank everyone for coming," Sandor finally said, after everyone had gotten a plate from the buffet. He hadn't wanted to use a microphone or anything, he just wanted to talk to his family and the people closest to him, like this was much more informal than it actually was. "But first, special thanks to Lennox, whose idea this was and who made it happen for our family. Thank you, sweetheart."

Sweetheart.

Oh boy, my insides instantly turned to goo. He'd never called me sweetheart before, not that I could remember, and now he'd done it in front of everyone. I was a little self-conscious, but everyone in the room looked happy. For Sandor, for me, for us. Which made me pretty happy too.

"So, you all know me, and I hate being the center of attention, but I just wanted to take a minute to explain why we're here. When my parents, my brother, and the others were killed that day, our country and our lives were immediately sent into turmoil. Erik and Casey were planning their wedding, and we didn't want to let what Anwar did ruin that for them, so we took the path of least resistance, planning a small tribute to our lost family members at the wedding, but as we all know, the wedding never happened. And accordingly, neither did a funeral or true memorial service. We glossed over it, focused on staying alive and trying to do what we could to thwart Anwar's attempts to ruin our family's legacy."

He paused, looking at me for a moment. "It wasn't until I met Lennox that I realized just how much not saying goodbye hurt me, hurt my brother and sister, probably hurt all of us. So today we're going to do that, but this isn't a funeral or a wake. This is a celebration. It can never be the celebration it was supposed to be, but it's going to be our way of saying goodbye, remembering Isak, Klara, Harold, Miriam, Vardan, Krystal, Rafael, Yolanda and Yusef. Let us raise our glasses to them." He lifted his flute of champagne and the rest of the room followed suit.

"All right. Now, let's eat, and when we finish, there's another surprise."

I sank into the chair beside him. We were sitting with Daniil, Elen, Erik, Casey, Nick and Skye. Sandor, Daniil, Elen, Erik and Skye were what was left of the cousins in the royal family and Sandor seemed relaxed, leaning back, one hand casually slung across the back of my chair as we talked and laughed. They were a great group and I was grateful to be part of them now. My life had changed so much in the last few months and it would probably change even more in the months to come. Sandor had been talking about renovating Gustafhaven and us moving there at some point. He hadn't used the L word again since New York, but that was okay. I was happy to be taking the emotional parts of our relationship slow since everything else had moved along at warp speed.

"So...will there be a wedding soon?" Skye asked.

I nearly choked on the sip of coffee I was about to take, glancing at Sandor in what had to be wide-eyed horror.

He just smiled, though, giving his cousin a wink. "Don't rush us, Skye. We're trying to rebuild a country here."

Undaunted, Skye raised her eyebrows. "What does one have to do with the other?"

"Oh, don't put him on the spot." Erik winked at me. "They'll get to everything when they're ready."

"Oh, you're no fun." Skye was gracious enough to let it go but Sandor didn't seem put out, reaching down to squeeze my leg under the table.

. . .

THE REST of the event went beautifully. There were tears and laughter as we opened Vardan and Krystal's wedding gifts, reading the cards from friends and family. Some of the things were generic—a sterling silver picture frame or an imported embroidered tapestry—but others were movingly personal. There was a framed photograph of Vardan on a horse, winning a polo championship in college, which Sandor said he would hang somewhere in Gustafhaven. There were other gifts with special meaning, from friends who'd obviously taken great care with their wedding gifts. Elen and Daniil took many of them, while Sandor only chose a few. It was emotional for him, and I watched him struggle throughout the morning and early afternoon. He still didn't like to let his emotions show, but he came close today, which made me happy.

As we walked back to our suite, he was more affectionate than usual at the palace, holding me close against his side until we were alone. Then he sank onto the couch, pulled me onto his lap and buried his head in my chest. He didn't say anything, but he was so quiet, clinging to me as if his life depended on it. I gently stroked his hair, pulling it free of the ponytail at the nape of his neck, letting my fingers run through the soft locks.

"I can't thank you enough for today," he whispered. When he lifted his head, the emotion in his eyes almost brought tears to mine. "It nearly gutted me, but I needed it, I needed to be able to say goodbye."

"Of course." I cupped his face with my hands, staring into those startling blue eyes I loved so much. "I'd do anything for you, Sandor. You've made my life so much better just by being in it, so if I can do that for you, even in small ways, I will."

"Small ways?" He shook his head. "This was huge, baby. I can honestly say no one's ever done anything so thoughtful for me. I love you, Lennox."

"I love you too." My voice was probably a little shaky, because those three words turned my heart inside out. It was so much more emotional than anything I could have imagined and when he kissed me, the passion was tempered by his soulful touch, the way he showed me his heart. Nothing had ever rocked my world like Sandor Gustaffson telling me he loved me, and though our bodies yearned for something more, our hearts kept our kisses lighter, almost chaste, as we let emotion override passion for the first time since we'd met.

"Ah, baby, you're beautiful." He kissed the tip of my nose. "I'd love nothing more than to spend the rest of the day making love to you, but we promised we'd take the kids snowmobiling."

"That's right." I moved off his lap. "That's okay. I'm dying to get out of these shoes and this dress. Jeans and a sweater sound heavenly. I also have to get through that stack of mail Chains sent me."

"What kind of mail?"

"I had my mail forwarded to the Westfield office address. Just random stuff, like reminders to renew my driver's license, the occasional bill. Almost everything is paid online now and I don't have a lot of bills, but you never know. And there was a stack this time, so Axel brought it when everyone got here."

"Tonight should be mellow," he said. "We'll spend a few hours outside the city with the kids and be back by dark, so we can designate tonight sit-by-the-fire-cuddle-and-get-some-work-done night."

"Sounds perfect." I pressed my lips to his. "You feel up to a little friendly competition?"

He arched a brow. "A challenge, milady?"

"Absolutely. How about—" I was cut off as Sandor's phone rang. He glanced down and frowned.

"It's Erik. Hold that thought." He picked it up on the second ring. "What's up? What... Are you sure? Yes, of course, I'll be right there." He practically jumped to his feet.

"What's wrong?" I asked, stepping out of my dress while we talked, instinct telling me something was wrong and I needed to change quickly.

"They can't find the kids. They're all gone."

37

———

S *andor*

I CHANGED into jeans and a Henley, because if there was a problem, I couldn't do anything in a suit. Lennox changed just as quickly, while I repeated what Erik had told me.

"Casey went looking for the kids, to tell them to get ready to go snowmobiling, and Luke, Leni, the twins, Maddie and Megan were gone. Sasha said last she saw them they were going to play video games, but they've checked everywhere and they're not in the palace."

"Did they check surveillance at the exits?"

"Joe's doing that now."

We both stuffed weapons into our shoulder holsters, pulled on hoodies and ran out, skipping the elevator and taking the stairs down to the ground floor. We raced to the communications center and found Joe shaking his head.

"They left out the back entrance." He pointed to a monitor where he'd pulled up the video. "Xander's heading down to talk to the guard at the back gate but the last glimpse I had of them was them walking through the gardens on the south side of the property."

"What the fuck did they think they were doing?" I demanded. I grabbed my phone and called Luke, but it went right to voicemail.

Erik burst into the room, his eyes wide. "Did you find them?"

"Not yet. Call Leni," I told him. "She's attached to you, so she'll probably answer."

Erik did as I asked, but when her phone went to voicemail as well, he gave me a look. "Do you think…"

"Don't say it," I snapped. "Let's not panic. They could still be on the grounds. The woods out back are pretty dense, so they may have been playing around and gotten separated, lost…"

"I've got men searching," Joe said. "So far, there's no sign of them."

"*Fuck.*"

"I think they went to town." Casey came out from behind Erik. "They've been complaining about feeling cooped up, like they're prisoners here."

"It's Sunday afternoon," Erik said. "The Christmas markets are in full force in the center of Hiskale, not to mention the shops. Everything is open because it's the last weekend before Christmas."

"We need to split up and scour the area," I said automatically. "And no, you can't join us."

"The fuck I can't." Erik narrowed his eyes. "I'm just as skilled as you are at—"

"It's not about skill, it's about safety. I can't protect you if I'm searching for them, and you're a target, no matter how much you try to pretend you're not."

"Fuck."

Erik and I glared at each other until Casey put her hand on his arm. "He's right."

"What if they took the SUV?" Joe suggested. "They can ride with Jonas while they search. With the windows up, no one will know who's inside. That way they can be nearby when you find them."

"All right." I blew out a breath. "I'm taking Lennox, Xander, Logan, Axel and—" I cut off as my phone rang and Mr. Kreshi's number appeared on the screen. "Mr. Kreshi, what can I do for you?" I was probably a little abrupt, but I didn't have time for anything else.

"The man." He was whispering. "He's here. The man in the picture."

"Jesus fucking Christ. Thank you." I disconnected and started to run. "Omar is in the café on the square."

WE TOOK one of the palace SUVs and I broke all kinds of laws as we sped into town. I parked around the corner from the café and we separated. We each went in a different direction so both the front and back of the café would be covered and Axel would be at the wheel of the SUV in case we needed to chase him that way. I was desperate to catch Omar, but even more so now that I was worried about the kids. If Omar had somehow grabbed them... I couldn't even think about it.

I pulled up the hood of my sweatshirt and kept my head down as I walked on the sidewalk to the café. I didn't want him to run if he was still there, and there was no way to know. It was busy, people bustling about, but I didn't see anyone that could be him as I scanned the room. I spotted Mr. Kreshi and hurried to his side.

"He left," he said quietly. "About five minutes ago. He went north. He was on his phone and seemed agitated about something. I'm sorry."

"Thank you, my friend. Call me if you see him again."

I went outside in frustration, letting everyone know what was going on since we had our earpieces in.

"I'm heading toward the Christmas market," Lennox said in my ear. "Casey thought they might go that way so I'll start with the southernmost edge and go north."

"I'll take the SUV," Axel responded, "and drive to the north end and head south. We can try to hit them on both sides."

"I'll be on foot a few minutes behind Lennox," Xander said. "On the opposite side of the street."

"I'm going to take the east side of the street and check every shop," I added.

"I'll do the west side," Logan chimed in.

"Everyone stay in touch," I said, moving down the street.

The local stores were mobbed with last-minute shoppers. The economy had perked up so people were spending and from what I heard in snippets of conversation, we had tourists. I heard English, French and German, which would've been a great thing had I not been scared shitless.

How had this happened? Had the kids been lured away? Didn't any of the guards question where they were going? Did we really have traitors on staff? It was mind-boggling to me and I struggled to make sense of it, but I had to focus. This wasn't the time to freak out.

Part of me felt guilty because I'd been in a love-induced haze for weeks now, my focus shifting back and forth from my security duties to Lennox, and mostly on her. I'd never done that before and it bothered me that something like this had happened on my watch.

"You need backup?" A voice spoke behind me and I stared at Erik.

"You can't be here."

"The fuck I can't." He had on a hoodie I'd never seen before—with the

Sidewinders logo on it—and a baseball cap on his head. He didn't look at all like a king and if it hadn't been so serious, I would have laughed.

"Where's Casey?" I asked automatically.

"Still in the SUV. Jonas is circling the adjacent block and will be nearby if we need him."

"Let's go then." We picked up the pace and I threw some money at a street vendor selling sweatshirts, yanking off my own and putting the new one on instead. I dropped mine in the trash since I didn't want to carry it, and we took a sharp left, going down a side street. We came out on the other side and walked down and around to the back of the café, just in case Omar was somehow casing the joint or had sensed we were coming. Or, of course, if a traitor had told him.

"You armed?" I asked Erik.

He smirked. "Seriously? Of course I'm fucking armed."

"I'd prefer we take him alive, but at this point, I just want him gone."

"I hear that."

"Listen to me." I turned to him. "I understand why you're here, but you have to think about everything. If something goes wrong, you need to bail and get to safety. You understand?"

Erik gave me a look. "You didn't leave a dead man on the side of a mountain twelve years ago, so that dead man is *never* going to leave your side when the chips are down. Now shut the fuck up and let's find either Omar or the kids."

38

L*ennox*

I SCANNED the street and each booth as I passed them. It didn't appear the kids had been kidnapped or we probably would have heard from the kidnappers by now. At least that was the hope. None of this made any sense. As something of an outsider, despite my growing closeness to Sandor and the rest of the family, it felt like more than politics was going on here.

Anwar had killed his family to take power and he'd been king for eleven years before Erik had outed him as the murderer he was and taken his place on the throne. Though there were still some Anwar supporters, Erik had over a ninety-percent approval rating in the country, so he was popular, and Omar was technically a nobody. Because he was Skye's ex-husband, my gut told me this was more about her than the royal family. He might have been in league with Anwar, but his end game had always been something else.

I had no basis for this, but my gut had never steered me wrong and I wished I'd told Sandor about the nagging doubts regarding Omar's intentions. It was too late now, but I needed to assert myself more when it came to him. I wasn't the timid type, but he was very much an alpha male and while he didn't intimidate me, I hadn't been comfortable telling him I thought he was on the wrong track. He'd changed me a little, I realized. Not in a bad way, because he was one of the kindest, biggest-hearted men I'd ever known. But our relationship had helped me explore my more feminine side and somehow that had carried over to our professional relationship, with me blindly following his orders, and that wasn't who I was. Not professionally anyway. We had to talk about this going forward.

Despite my deep thoughts, I was still focused on the task at hand and I caught sight of two blond heads pressed close together. I hurried in that direction, my heart in my throat as I recognized them.

"Jessie! Joss!" I reached them in record time and they threw their arms around me, both speaking at once.

"—Luke said it was better if—"

"—and then there was a man—"

"—Maddie and Megan went the other way—"

"Okay, wait, stop." I wrapped my arms around them, speaking to the rest of the team. "Twins found. They're okay. I'm trying to find out more info." I leaned down. "Where are the other kids?"

"We don't know." Jessie's eyes were filled with tears. "We were buying hot chocolate and Megan said she was cold and wanted to go home. Luke tried to get a taxi but they wouldn't stop for us because we're kids."

"Why didn't you just call us?" I demanded in frustration.

"We didn't bring our phones," Joss whispered.

"You can track us with the GPS on our phones, so Luke said it was better if we left them home so no one could find us and we could have fun for a little while." Jessie's lower lip was starting to quiver.

I wanted to shake both of them, but instead, I said, "So how did you get separated?"

"There was a man and Luke was afraid he was following us, so we split up. Luke took Leni, Maddy and Megan went back toward the big Christmas tree, and we came here because there are a lot of people. We were going to find someone to let us use their phone."

I took each of their hands. "You stay with me, no matter what, okay?"

"Okay."

We walked a little further as my earpiece blew up with the guys talking to me, asking questions I couldn't answer.

"I don't know," I responded. "They said they separated on purpose because a man was following them."

"Axel, where are you?" one of the voices in my ear asked.

"I'm waiting at the top end of Floria Street," he replied.

"Keep your eyes peeled for Luke and Leni—they went in that direction."

"I'm on it."

Xander caught up to us. "I'll get them to the SUV," he said. "You keep looking."

I nodded and did a quick check to make sure Luke and Leni weren't nearby before continuing along the row of stalls. The whole area wasn't that big, but the pretty Christmas-themed booths were on both sides of the street, filled with cheerful lights, brightly colored merchandise, and delicious-smelling food. It was packed tonight, too, people filling the booths, the sidewalk, and the street. The street itself had been blocked off on all sides, so no cars could get in, but that just made it busier.

I was determined to find them. I didn't know what was going on, and Sandor had gone radio silent, but my gut was telling me the rest of the kids were close. I just needed to zero in on their location, and it felt like I was getting closer. I often had a sixth sense about this kind of thing, and I kept turning in circles so I didn't miss them.

"Lennox!" I knew Luke's voice and whirled around, spotting him as he swung his fist at a man grabbing for him.

"I need backup!" I yelled to my colleagues. "By the Belgian waffles and the booth with the ten-foot snowman!" I jumped over a bench and threw myself at the man trying to wrestle Luke into a car that was pulled onto the sidewalk on the edge of the street. "Run!" I yelled to him. I saw the man reaching for a gun and kicked it out of his hand, following with a punch to the throat that left him gasping for air. Asshole was lucky I didn't kill him.

"I'm here!" Logan came bounding over to me, looking down at the man on the ground. "We need to interrogate him. Axel, where are you?"

"I'll be there in a minute, but I've got kids in the car."

"I'll be there in thirty seconds—don't lose him." Sandor's voice in my ear soothed me the way the others hadn't. I wasn't worried about taking care of myself, but not knowing where the kids were had been nerve-wracking. I'd jumped into action when I saw this guy trying to grab Luke, but now that it was over, I was terrified because we'd come way too close to being too late.

Sandor pulled right up onto the street, ignoring the police that started yelling at him to move. He showed some kind of badge and they backed off. Then Erik got out of the SUV and there was chaos. Sandor handcuffed the man I'd taken down and threw him in the back while Erik grabbed Luke and Leni. We piled into the SUV with Leni on Erik's lap and headed for the palace. Logan had found Maddie and Megan just before joining me, so everyone was safe, but the air was charged with electricity as the adrenaline started to dissipate.

It was eerily quiet as we drove. Luke had tried to talk to his father twice and Erik had silenced him with a glare. Leni was just sniffling against his chest, and Megan and Madison didn't say a word. Casey was in the other SUV with the twins and I figured a lot of the same was happening over there. Sandor was driving, and Xander was in the far back with our prisoner, so I'd wound up in the passenger seat.

When I glanced at Sandor, he seemed strangely stoic, and I wondered what had happened with Omar. I tried to ask but he just shook his head, so I didn't say anything else, waiting to see how this was going to play out. We were going to have to debrief the kids, which wouldn't be easy, and that was probably on everyone's mind.

We were still quiet when we pulled up to the palace, and I followed Casey and Erik up the stairs toward their suites. Sandor fell in behind us and Joe met us at the top of the stairs.

"Where's the prisoner?" he asked.

"They're taking him to one of the security briefing rooms," Sandor said. "They'll hold him there until I can interrogate him."

Joe nodded and we all gathered in Erik and Casey's sitting room.

"Do you want to tell me what you did?" Erik faced Luke with his hands on his hips.

"We just wanted to go to the Christmas market," Luke said, looking down.

"Why didn't you ask?"

"We did!" Luke's head snapped up and he glared at his father with intensity in his green eyes. "We asked a bunch of times and it's always the same answer! You're too busy or it's not safe or there's no one to go with us or whatever. It sucks."

"So you left the palace by yourself and dragged your sisters with you?" Erik demanded.

"He didn't drag us," Leni whispered. "We wanted to go."

"Whose idea was it to leave your phones behind?"

"Mine." Luke stared at his father defiantly. "We just wanted to be kids for a little while and see some of the city without all the pomp and circumstance."

"You're the Crown Prince of Limaj—pomp and circumstance is your new reality."

"Well it sucks."

"How many times are you going to use that word?" Erik snapped. "It doesn't make you sound cool. You just sound like a spoiled brat."

"Erik." Casey went to stand beside him. "He did something wrong, but this isn't the time for that conversation. We have to talk about what they saw and who the man was that tried to grab him. Later, we'll talk about the rest of it."

Erik blew out a breath. It looked like he was counting to ten.

"It was fine until we stopped at that café," Joss said. "We wanted more of that black and white hot chocolate and Mr. Kreshi was really nice. He gave us all some and asked us where we were going. We told him we were going shopping at the market and he told us to have fun."

"Sonofabitch." Sandor looked furious. "Either he betrayed us or Omar was watching—it's fucking Sunday."

"Then I saw someone following us," Luke said. "I thought we should split up, that way they couldn't get all of us. I told the girls to try to find someone who'd let them use their phone, but no one spoke English and then that guy drove up and tried to grab me. I told Leni to run but she screamed and then Lennox came. That's everything that happened."

"You think old man Kreshi told Omar?" Erik asked Sandor.

Sandor tapped his foot impatiently. "I'm going to talk to him but my gut says no. This was a crime of convenience. He told me Omar hangs out there on Sundays and the kids walked right in."

"I'm sorry," Luke whispered sadly.

"I know, buddy." Sandor put his hand on Luke's head. "I know."

SANDOR DIDN'T COME to bed that night. I was up until three or four, sitting with Joe as we watched Sandor and Erik interrogate the man we'd caught, but they weren't speaking English and I wasn't proficient enough in Limaji to understand. Joe translated some of it, but the man wasn't telling them anything important and I figured I needed a few hours' sleep in order to be ready for the day.

I slept from about four to seven and then took a quick shower before heading down to the security briefing. Today's was going to be a doozy, of that I was sure, so I got an espresso instead of regular coffee and was the first one there. Sandor didn't even look up as I approached.

"Hey." I spoke softly, wondering what was wrong with him.

"Morning." He still didn't look up.

What the fuck?

"Babe?" I kept my voice soft but my tone was insistent and he finally met my gaze, though the only thing in his eyes was irritation.

"We'll talk later," was all he said. And then he went back to whatever he was doing.

Well, if he was going to be an asshole this morning, I'd see his asshole and raise him a bitch. He'd been acting weird since last night, as if it was somehow my fault, and that was bullshit. The kids had snuck out, plain and simple, and when it came to kids, where there was a will, there was a way. I'd been pretty sneaky as a teen myself, so I had no doubt they'd made a plan and seen it through.

Erik joined us for this morning's briefing and sank into the chair next to mine, giving me a tired but genuine smile.

"I wanted to say thank you," he said. "I didn't get a chance last night, but Luke told me how you tackled that guy and took him down even though he had a gun."

"It's my job," I said quietly. "And my pleasure to work for your family. There was no way I was letting him take Luke, no matter what I had to do."

"And you have no idea how much I appreciate that." He squeezed my arm and I felt a little better. At least he wasn't being a jerk.

39

S*andor*

Security briefings were usually less than an hour. Today, we went past lunch and into the afternoon because we had so much to talk about. The kids hadn't even really come up with a sneaky plan. They'd simply known the guards' schedule, and ours, and they'd left during the shift change. When the guard at the back door went to lunch, his replacement signed in and promptly left his post to use the restroom. The kids had seen an opportunity and slipped out, telling the guard at the back gate they were playing hide-and-seek. Then they climbed the fence, went through the trees that lined the street, and were on their way to the Christmas market within five minutes. It had been ridiculously easy and that pissed me off even more.

The kids were all grounded and pouting in their rooms, we'd lost Omar once again, and there was no rhyme or reason to any of it.

"While I don't condone what they did," Erik said that afternoon, "the kids aren't prisoners here. Yes, they have to follow protocol, but we have to be more cognizant of their needs. Going forward, we have to give them the tools they need should they ever find themselves on their own again. They need to learn their way around, learn the language, and, though it pains me to say it, we may need to put trackers in their shoes, backpacks, places they won't know about. We can't go through this again."

"Agreed." Joe nodded.

"On the flip side, we need to plan more activities. If they're going to be living here full-time, I want the palace to be their home, not their prison."

"That's all well and good," I said, "but until we find Omar, we have to be diligent."

"I had a thought about Omar." Lennox spoke up for the first time all day, and I glanced at her in surprise.

"Yes?" I asked her.

"You once mentioned luring him out. I think this is about Skye and she's the person to use for that."

"That's ridiculous," I snapped. I hadn't meant to be condescending, but the way her eyes narrowed told me my answer had pissed her off. Well, too bad. I was in charge here and she didn't know the players like I did.

"Maybe it's not," Erik said slowly. "She could be on to something. Omar has money and the intelligence we've gathered says he has a nice life in Paris. He's so far removed from the throne, though he does have some royal blood, that that can't be his goal. The only reason he has to continually go after us has to be personal. And I think it's the fact that we took Skye from him, so to speak, when we helped her leave him."

It made sense but now I was even more pissed that Lennox had thought of it instead of me, reinforcing the idea that I was too caught up in my feelings for her to be effective at my job.

"Well, even if that's his motivation, we can't use Skye as bait. She's not trained for that kind of thing."

"I could help her get ready," Lennox said, meeting my gaze squarely. "And we'd all be nearby."

"Every time we've gotten close to him, he's gotten away, and I'm not willing to risk that with her."

"I think that should be *her* choice," Lennox said firmly.

"She's right."

I fucking hated when Erik went against me, but I couldn't say that and right now I was annoyed with everyone, so I wasn't going to get into a pissing contest about this.

"Then we can discuss it, but not today. We have to focus on getting the guards we have working here properly trained, and running drills to test them."

"Fine." Erik got to his feet. "You and Joe can set that up, but I'm beat and it's almost Christmas. I need to talk with Luke because he's pouting, and spend a little time with Leni as well. Let's table most of the plans regarding Omar until after Christmas."

Everyone dispersed but Lennox stayed behind, waiting until the room cleared before approaching me.

"Did you seriously call my idea ridiculous in front of everyone?" she asked me.

"I did." I looked up. I was spoiling for a fight and while I didn't want it to be with her, she wasn't going to let this go so I was most likely going to say something I regretted.

"Why would you do that?" she demanded. "Especially since you know I'm probably right. Whatever is going on has to be about more than hating Erik."

"We don't know that, and you need to stop taking everything so personally. When we're working, I'm the boss and it's my prerogative to do my job in whatever way I see fit."

"What the hell does that mean?"

"Just what I said." I drummed my fingers on the desk. "And starting now, we can't be so familiar with Erik and Casey. It's either 'sir' or 'Your Majesty' for Erik, and 'ma'am' or 'Your Highness' for Casey. I'm going to put out a memo."

"Really." She gave me a funny look.

"Why do you question every fucking thing I say?" I demanded, getting more and more irritated by the minute.

"Because you're being a dick?" She faced off with me, her posture as rigid as mine. "So you want to fight? Is that what this is? You're pissed and embarrassed that the kids got out so you're going to take it out on me?"

Fuck. She knew me too well.

"Look, we're both tired and on edge. Let's talk later, okay? I don't want to fight like this."

"Fine." She turned and walked out. I had a feeling she would have slammed the door if she'd been able to.

I DIDN'T GET up to our suite until late, and after not sleeping at all the night before, I was tired. Lennox was still up, though, sitting on the couch doing something on her laptop. She looked up when I came in and gave me a small smile.

"Hey."

"Hi." I pulled off my hoodie and removed my gun and holster.

"I'm sorry about earlier." She got up and came over to me, putting a hand on my arm. "I don't want to fight with you."

"I don't either." I reached out and gently pushed her hair behind one ear. She was so damn beautiful, I often couldn't think of anything else when we were alone like this. It was a huge distraction. Too much of a distraction. I loved her, but how could I risk everything I'd spent the last twelve years protecting? She didn't just distract me, she completely overwhelmed me. The depth of my feelings for her was detrimental to everything I believed in, and what had happened yesterday only proved that I couldn't have it all. I couldn't protect the people I loved and love Lennox too. At least not the way she deserved to be loved.

"Can we just go to bed and forget all about yesterday for a few hours?" she asked softly, moving closer to me.

Dammit. I couldn't do this. One touch and I'd be lost all over again.

"Listen, we need to talk."

She froze, furrowing her brow slightly as she looked up at me. "About?"

"Us. This. Everything."

"Okay." She didn't move, waiting for me to say what I needed to say.

"I don't think..." The words caught in my throat and I straightened a little, strengthening my resolve. It was better this way and the sooner I did it, the better off everyone would be.

"You don't think..." she prompted.

"I can't be with you and do this job the way I need to do it," I said finally. "You distract me, shift my focus, and I can't live like this. I need to help Erik get this country running and that means making sure his family is safe. Twenty-four seven. Knowing you're waiting in bed for me, that you're waiting for me period, makes me want to finish work early, get back to you. Which isn't safe for any of us."

"So it's *my* fault the kids snuck out?" She took a step back, her eyes flashing.

"No, of course not. It's mine. That's the whole point. If I hadn't been so focused on you, I would've noticed that Luke was getting antsy, would've probably noticed him trying to gather the kids and get into mischief."

"You mean, you might have noticed them sneaking out if you weren't spending the morning in bed with me." Her eyes blazed with fire and though I wanted to back off, I couldn't. It would be better to end it now than drag it out.

"Precisely." I didn't flinch, even as she set her jaw and glared at me.

"You're full of shit, Sandor. This isn't about me—this is about *you*. You can't stand the idea of letting go of your control, the power you have as Erik's right-hand man. He's been giving you the freedom to be with me and you're afraid he's not going to need you anymore so you're dumping me."

"Maybe." I shrugged. "But whatever it is, I can't be the man you want me to be."

"I don't want you to be anything but what you are," she said quietly. "I've never complained about the fact that we only spend an hour a day together outside of sex. I never asked for trips to New York or dinner dates or anything else. That was all you."

"I know, and now I see it was a mistake."

"So what we have has been a mistake?" She wrinkled her nose slightly. "Everything we've shared has been a fucking mistake?" Her voice rose an octave.

"It's not that it wasn't good," I continued, trying to think of how to say what I wanted to say without being mean. "It just isn't for me. This is why I don't do relationships. I'm sorry if I've led you on. I never meant to."

"You told me you loved me."

"I told you I thought I loved you. I guess I was wrong." I couldn't focus on that one intimate moment just before hell broke loose.

She opened her mouth but nothing came out. She just stared at me with an icy-hot glare. If I lit a match, the anger seeping out of her probably would have caught fire. It was plain as day she wanted to hit me and I wanted to let her, but that wouldn't accomplish anything.

"I'll sleep in one of the guard barracks," I said finally. "You can take the bed until the guests are gone and then we'll get your suite ready. It'll be easier if we're not tempted by sharing a room."

"You think I'll be tempted to have sex with a man who just spewed the biggest bunch of bullshit I've ever heard? Think again, buddy. I'm not one of those women. If we're done, we're fucking done. And yeah, go sleep in the fucking barracks. I'll be out of your hair in the morning."

I hesitated, unsure if it was better to leave her now, while she was furious, or to try and soothe her a little. We still had to work together, after all. Unless she left.

Jesus.

I didn't want her to leave. I just needed to not be in love with her anymore.

I didn't know if that was possible, but I had to try. There was too much at stake and that man trying to grab Luke had scared me like nothing else ever had. How could I just go back to making love to the woman in my life as if nothing had happened, when she was the reason I'd lost my focus on Luke in the first place?

"I thought you were leaving?" She spoke coldly, her eyes lethal slits as she stared at me.

"I am. Just getting my things." I grabbed clean clothes and an extra blanket from the closet and then quietly slipped from the room. I paused outside the door, listening, though I wasn't sure for what. Would she cry? Throw things? Break something?

I waited for a few minutes, but there was nothing but eerie silence.

40

———

L*ennox*

I KNOCKED LIGHTLY on the door to Erik's office and peeked my head in. "Your Majesty, do you have a minute?"

He frowned at me. "*Your Majesty?* Did we have a falling out or something?"

I managed a smile, but shook my head. "Sandor said we have to be more formal from now on. No more first names."

Erik raised his eyebrows. "He does realize I'm the king, not him, doesn't he?"

I shrugged. "No idea, sir."

"Okay, what did he do?"

"Sir?"

"If you call me sir or Your Majesty one more time in private, I'm going to make you change Levi's diapers."

I smiled. "Well, even though you're Sandor's boss, he's mine, and he told us no more first names."

"Sandor and I are going to have a talk," he said. "But anyway, come on in and sit down. And shut the door. My office, my rules. It's Erik."

I shut the door and sat down. "Well, Erik, I need a favor."

"Anything."

"I'd like a few days off so I can spend Christmas with my mother in Florida, but there are no flights. Is there any way you can fly me there on the jet?"

"I can't do it personally, but of course, just tell me when. I'll have the pilot take you and bring you back."

"Thank you. That's very generous." I took a breath. "But there's one more thing."

"Short of selling my children into slavery, anything I can do for you, I'm in your debt. Always."

"I'd like to switch places with Logan and take over security duties for the kids in Monte Carlo."

His eyes narrowed and then he shook his head. "Jesus fucking Christ. What did he do? And don't say nothing."

I sighed. "It's no big deal, really. I just think this will be easier going forward. Less distracting for both of us."

"But you can't be together if you live in another country full-time."

"No. We can't." I'd hoped I wouldn't have to spell this out for him.

"Just tell me what happened. I understand it's probably none of my business, but if you're asking to leave your post here, it impacts my family and Casey isn't going to be happy."

"He said it wasn't working out. That's all. And short-term, it would be easier on me if I'm not around him every day. I'll be fine by the time summer comes, but if the twins decide to stay in Monte Carlo, I can stay or come back. Whatever you need. I need a little distance for a few months. That's all."

He met my eyes. "I'm going to kick his ass."

"Oh, no, please, don't get involved. You can't force someone to love you, you know? And it's obvious he doesn't. Not really. I'll be fine. I'm not one of those women who falls apart when a guy breaks up with her. I've been through a lot worse. It's the initial awkwardness I'd like to avoid. But this is between me and him, so please don't say anything."

"Oh, I've got a lot to say and it's not just between you and him. We had a conversation about his intentions when you first got together because I knew if he screwed up it would impact my family—and now it has."

"I can stay," I said quickly. "Really. Forget I said anything. I can—"

"Lennox, stop." He held up a hand. "You're *part* of our family now. Yes, Sandor is my closest friend as well as my cousin, but that doesn't negate the importance of my other relationships. One of those is with you. Casey is going to be upset and, frankly, so am I. But making you suffer through the early stages of a breakup would be selfish. So. Tell me your travel dates for Florida, as well as which airport, so my pilot can file the flight plan. Just take what you need for the trip and I'll have someone pack up your things and have them ready to move to Monte Carlo by the time you get back.

"In the meantime, is there anything I can do?"

"The trip to Florida is plenty. Thank you." I got to my feet. "I'll talk to Casey myself and make sure she understands why I'm leaving."

"She's going to kick his ass too," he called after me.

I smiled as I closed the door behind me.

One problem solved. At least a dozen more to go, but it was a start. As long as I kept moving, I'd be okay.

THE FLIGHT to Fort Lauderdale was long but I'd brought my laptop and that stack of mail I had yet to go through. I'd rummaged through it before I left, tossing out the junk mail, so all I had now were things I needed to take care of. Somehow, I had a fifty-two cent balance at Macy's, so I'd pay that, along with the thirty-dollar late fee, and then close the account. I took care of a few things and then opened something from my gynecologist's office. I scanned the letter and then froze.

Oh fuck no.

Dear Lennox:

Our records indicate that you missed your appointment to replace your birth control implant. Please note, less than one woman in one hundred gets pregnant during the three-year suggested period. However, you are now beyond three years, so be warned that your chances of becoming pregnant will increase the longer you go without a replacement.

If you'd like to schedule your appointment...

I closed the letter and took a deep breath. How the fuck had I forgotten about this? I hadn't given my yearly gynecological appointment a second thought when I'd moved to Limaj. I opened my calendar and scanned back. It was supposed to be in September. And I'd passed the three-year point for the implant back in November. It was now December and I'd been having sex almost daily with a virile man without any protection for over a month now. A sexy, virile man who'd just dumped me.

Holy fucking shit. What had I done?

FORT LAUDERDALE WAS hot even in December and I rented a convertible. I could afford it and I needed a little luxury right now because my heart was in a bad place. I'd be okay, because I was tougher than that, but what Sandor had done, the way he'd treated me, still hurt like hell. The idea of possibly telling him I was pregnant made me a little nauseated, so I tried not to think about it. I'd deal with all of that when I got to Monte Carlo. For now, I had more than enough to deal with in my mother. I hadn't told her I was coming, so it was a crapshoot as to the kind of reception I would get.

Since we weren't close, I don't know what had driven me to want to see her, but where else could I go? I no longer had an apartment in Las Vegas and couldn't fathom staying in Limaj through the holidays after what had happened with Sandor. So here I was.

I pulled up to the building she lived in and looked around to make sure I had it right. I hadn't been to this place and it was pretty swanky, right off Las Olas Boulevard and close to the intracoastal waterway. These were million-dollar homes and while my mom had done well with each divorce, I didn't think she'd done that well. Or maybe she had. What the hell did I know?

I left my suitcase in the car, just in case I didn't get much of a reception, put money in the meter for my parking spot, and went to the front of the building. The address I had for her said it was apartment 407, but her name wasn't on the directory. Impulsively, I pushed the button anyway. Only one way to find out if I'd wasted both my time and Erik's money since he'd flown me here.

"Yes, hello?" Well, that was my mom's voice.

"Mom, it's Lennox."

There was silence and then the buzzer sounded, indicating she was letting me in. I walked inside a fancy lobby and went to the elevator. When I got off on the fourth floor she was right there waiting, a weird look on her face.

"Hi, honey." She reached for me, hugging me awkwardly.

"Hey, Mom. Surprise." I cocked my head. "What's going on? Why do you look like you've seen a ghost?"

"Don't be silly. I just... I wasn't expecting you."

"I wanted to surprise you, but if it's inconvenient..." I let my voice trail off because I wasn't in any mood to be an inconvenience to anyone ever again. Especially not my mother. This had probably been a bad idea, but—

"Come on in. There's someone I want you to meet." She tugged me by the hand and we went into a beautifully furnished condo. It was decorated for the holidays and there were people inside, talking and laughing. Everyone turned as we entered and a tall, older man of about sixty turned with a curious smile.

"Who's this, Michelle?" he asked, holding out his hand.

"This is my oldest daughter, Lennox. Honey, this is Brad...my fiancé."

"I..." I didn't want to embarrass either of them since they had company, so I just smiled and shook his hand. "Nice to meet you."

"I've heard so much about you," he said warmly, his blue eyes twinkling. "Welcome to our home."

"Thank you. I apologize for barging in, but I didn't know Mom was... involved with anyone."

He chuckled. "We've kept things kind of private, but no worries. Come, meet our friends."

There were half a dozen people in the room, and a few more arrived within the hour, so I didn't have time to talk to my mother until much later. I also had no idea if I was staying here, and my mom hadn't said anything, so I got on my phone and started looking for a hotel. It was Christmas Eve, so choices might be limited, but I was hoping to find something on the beach. This might be my last vacation in a long time. Being a single mom probably wouldn't be that much fun. Christ, I needed to not think about those kinds of possibilities.

"You're more than welcome to stay here," Brad said, peering over my shoulder.

I turned and met his gaze. "Are you sure? Mom didn't even tell me she had a boyfriend, much less a fiancé, so I don't want to put you guys out. I thought it would be her and my sisters."

"I'm sorry, Lennox." Mom looked contrite, something I didn't see from her very often. "You moved halfway across the world so it's hard to talk, and I know how you get whenever I'm dating someone new. I figured I'd break it to you slowly."

"Mom, you're a grown woman. You don't owe me any explanations."

"Well, maybe I do." Mom sat on the couch and patted the spot beside her.

"I'll just be in the kitchen," Brad said, moving away.

"It's okay, Mom. I'm sorry you thought you couldn't talk to me."

"I know I usually have terrible taste in men, but Brad is wonderful. Handsome and rich and so great to me. Really. He's gotten Vivian back on the right path and—"

"Wait, what?"

"We haven't talked in a while," Mom said softly. "And that's my fault. I know it is. I should have worked harder but I didn't know how to handle a strong, independent woman like you. You're everything I could never be, Lennox, and I'm so very proud of you. I don't understand it, being in the military and special ops and all that stuff you did, but no one has ever been prouder than me."

"It's true." Brad came back in, wiping his hands on a dish towel. "She talks about her daughter with the Bronze Star all the time."

I grimaced. "Geez, Mom, why would you tell people about that? What I did to get it was horrible and..."

"I'm retired Army," Brad said quietly. "I found the medal when she moved in. I was helping her unpack..."

"I know how much you hate all that," Mom said quickly. "But he asked and, well, I'm proud of you, dammit."

"It's okay." What else could I say? No one but my mother and my dead commanding officer knew about my Bronze Star.

"And now you're working for some royal family I never heard of before... I just never know what to say or what not to say." Mom gave me a little shrug. "I was planning to call tomorrow, on Christmas, to see how you're doing, see if maybe I could come to visit. I miss you and I wanted to tell you about Brad in person."

"I'm moving to Monte Carlo," I said abruptly. "Going to guard the three daughters until summer. And then I don't know where I'm going or if I'll even be working for them anymore. It's kind of a long story."

"Does it have to do with a handsome prince and a trip to New York?"

I met her eyes sadly and let out a sigh. I didn't want to talk about the military, but I really didn't want to talk about Sandor. I just wanted to sleep. It had been a long day for me even though I'd dozed on the flight. And I was so damn sad right now.

"You look tired," she said, obviously reading the look on my face. "We can talk about all that tomorrow."

"Why don't you go get your things?" Brad suggested, getting to his feet. "And move your rental car into the garage. I'll give you the key fob. There are visitor spots..." He gave me instructions and I operated on autopilot. I moved the car, got my bag, settled into their guest room and then my body took over and I was asleep.

41

S *andor*

Though it wasn't a surprise, getting back to my suite to get clean clothes on Christmas Eve was jarring. Lennox had emptied the closet and the bathroom, and all that was left was one suitcase and two boxes in the corner of the closet, which would be moved to Monte Carlo with her when she came back from her impromptu trip to Florida. I didn't understand why she was going to visit her mother, since she'd made it sound like they weren't close, but I figured it was an excuse to get away from me. Which made sense since I'd been an asshole.

I shed my clothes and left them on the floor, stepping into the shower wearily. It had been a really long few days and I was tired, both physically and emotionally. Breaking up with Lennox had been harder than I'd anticipated and I felt fucking empty inside. It was weird because I'd been completely unemotional when I'd told her we needed to step back and reassess, making it sound like she was nothing to me. The look in her eyes had been one of utter disbelief, followed by fury.

Hell hath no fury like a woman scorned. Or something like that. If she could have gotten away with it, she probably would've had me in one of those headlocks. And I would have deserved it.

I let the water run over me, dreading the festivities tonight. What the hell was I going to do on Christmas Eve now that I'd dumped Lennox? I hadn't bought gifts for anyone except Lennox and that was sitting in a drawer now. I hadn't even thought to buy something for Luke this year, but what did you get a kid who literally had everything? It was the same for everyone else, except some of the guys, but we'd agreed not to get each other anything. Which left me somewhat bereft. The holidays weren't about gifts, but it added to the fun. Now it was just another day, another celebration that I would muddle through without really engaging.

I got out of the shower and toweled off, trying to rationalize how I was feeling and failing miserably. I missed her and hated myself for being such a jerk. I'd thought it would be easier if I pissed her off, but underneath her tough exterior, she'd been hurt. I'd seen it in her eyes, the pain reflected there cutting me deeper than any knife. But I'd let it go because my sense of duty always took precedence. *Always.*

I found black slacks and a red button-down shirt, absently pulling them on along with dress socks. I didn't bother tying my hair back in its usual ponytail, letting it fall free tonight. Lennox liked it long, I thought with an internal sigh. Damn, it was a good thing she'd asked to move to Monte Carlo, because I was having a hard enough time not thinking about her now, much less if I had to see her every day.

I slid my feet into my shoes and stuffed my phone in my pocket before heading down to Erik and Casey's. They had everyone gathering in their private living area tonight. It would be an informal get-together, friends and family mingling without worrying about the press or cameras. Tomorrow there would be more formal events with Erik giving a televised speech and he and Casey visiting a cancer ward in the hospital in Hiskale. That was why they'd wanted something private tonight.

I'd just gotten to their floor when Erik stopped me in the hallway.

"You and I need to talk," he said.

"Okay." I followed him to his office, going in behind him and watching as he poured two fingers of whiskey for each of us.

"Have a seat," he said.

"Okay." I had a feeling I knew what was coming but I didn't know what else to do, so I sat down.

"You want to tell me what happened with you and Lennox?"

"Not really." I met his gaze squarely.

"What the hell is wrong with you?" he demanded. "Why would you break things off with her? I know you're in love with that girl."

"You don't know any such thing," I said tightly. This was the last thing I needed. It was bad enough that Casey wasn't speaking to me, but I didn't need a lecture from my best friend when everything I did was essentially for him.

"Bullshit." He perched on the edge of his desk. "Talk to me, man. What is it? What happened?"

"You know damn well what happened!" I snapped. "Luke almost got kidnapped on my watch. I was so busy with the new woman in my life, I wasn't paying enough attention to him. He needed us and we were too damn busy with women, the holidays, and look what nearly happened."

"What the hell are you talking about?" Erik demanded. "We were too busy with Lennox and Casey? You mean, my wife and the woman you love? *Those* women?"

"You know what I mean," I ground out through clenched teeth. "We can't afford to be distracted. We've sacrificed too much to let something happen now, and it sure as hell isn't going to be because of me."

"This isn't on you!" Erik yelled, throwing up his hands in frustration. "This was about a stupid preteen doing a stupid preteen thing. It has nothing to do with a lapse in security or distractions or anything else—he was a kid who did a dumb thing and dragged his sisters into it with him. That's all. The idea that you broke up with Lennox because..." His voice trailed off and he muttered something under his breath I didn't quite catch, but it didn't matter.

"It's my job to prevent that shit from happening," I said, though it sounded lame even to me.

"Do you not remember being a teenager?" Erik demanded. "Do you remember the time we snuck off to freakin' Monte Carlo and got into a casino and charged over ten thousand dollars on my father's account? When we weren't even old enough to get in there?"

I grimaced. I did remember. We'd been fifteen and seventeen and subsequently had been grounded for a month. It was the only time we'd ever been grounded. Of course, it was also the only time we'd ever been caught, but that was another story.

"Or how about the beach in Dubai?" He wiggled his eyebrows. "And the girl with the bikini top that came off?"

"Okay, stop." I didn't want to hear it. This trip down memory lane wasn't making me feel any better.

"Don't you see? This isn't about anything you did or didn't do—it's about Luke being a kid and testing the waters. This is more about Casey and me not being very good parents right now because we both know he was looking for attention in a warped, twelve-year-old way."

"Yeah and maybe if I'd been spending time with him instead of Lennox, he wouldn't have felt that way."

"Sandor." He came and stood in front of me, his eyes searching out mine. "Listen to me. Your days of ultimate sacrifice are over. Do you understand? I will banish you from the country before I let you do this to yourself anymore. It's time for you to have your own life, a family, that beautiful woman who loves you... Our security is solid. We're going to deal with Omar, even though it's taking time and we've taken a break on that over Christmas. We're bringing the kids here full-time starting in June and Casey and I are working on a plan to be more present for them, even if more of it falls on her than me. I'm handling the country, the presidency, and my family. It's time for you to handle yours. Lennox. That family I know you want so badly. Bad things are going to happen, but your days of sacrifice are officially a thing of the past. We have to live in the present."

"But—" I started to protest but Erik was shaking his head.

"No. There are no buts. We're here, doing the best we can, but the sacrifice is in what we did, the past. Going forward, it's time to live in the now, especially you."

"Fuck." My head dropped, my chin hitting my chest as I let out a long, weary breath. I didn't even know how to start being my own man, because I'd always been Erik's sidekick, partner in crime, other half. Maybe it was a bit of an unhealthy relationship, but once upon a time, we hadn't had a choice. Now? Fuck, I didn't know what *now* meant.

I'd fucked up big-time and there was a chance it was too late. I didn't know how I would fix this or if that was even possible but I felt like the world's biggest creep. How could I have chosen what amounted to a job over the woman I loved, the woman who made me feel things I hadn't thought I'd ever feel? Why had my knee-jerk reaction been to let her go instead of fighting to have both?

"Erik, I don't know who the fuck I am if I'm not protecting you and the family."

"Then we'll figure it out together. Believe me, I've had plenty of those moments, but having Casey at my side keeps me grounded. She's the biggest part of me and I get my strength from what we have together. You'll have that too, with Lennox, if you let yourself. So consider yourself fired until further notice."

"Uncle Loco?" Luke's voice was tiny but Erik and I both whirled around.

"Hey, bud." I cleared my throat.

"Is it true? Is it my fault you broke up with Lennox?"

Erik and I exchanged a quick glance and then Erik nodded. "Indirectly, but yes. What you and your sisters did was dangerous and it scared us. Uncle Sandor was scared and blamed himself, thinking he was too distracted by his upcoming engagement and that it was his fault that you could have gotten hurt, or kidnapped, or worse." That wasn't the exact truth, but close enough since I'd thought about asking Lennox to marry me.

Luke's eyes filled with tears. "I'm so sorry, Uncle Loco!" He threw himself in my arms and I hugged him tightly.

"It's okay, kiddo. Really. I'm going to fix things with Lennox." Hopefully. "What you did was wrong, but I'm a grown man and I shouldn't have blamed her for something that wasn't her fault."

"I'll talk to her." Luke lifted his head and wiped his nose with the back of his hand, making both Erik and me grimace, but we opted to let it go. "I'll tell her what happened and how I was being dumb and—"

"Okay, hang on." I smiled. "Thanks for the offer, and you can apologize to her once I get her back here, but I have to be the one to make up with her. I'm the one who screwed up with her, not you."

"Are you sure? 'Cause I really like Lennox. I want her to be my aunt."

I smiled. I wanted that too.

"The jet is landing in an hour," Erik told me. "Once he's had time to refuel, he's taking you to Fort Lauderdale. You should be at the airport ready to go."

"Yes, okay." I turned and practically ran back to my suite. *Our* suite.

I was such an idiot. I hadn't had such a hollow feeling in the pit of my stomach since the night I'd almost left Erik to die on the side of that mountain. The story, as we all knew it, was that I'd refused to leave him even though it meant certain death for both of us. The truth was that I'd started to leave, gotten halfway back up the mountain when I heard the gunshots and then doubled back, unable to stand the sound of my friend being murdered. In the end, some higher power must have intervened, because I used the grenades I had left in my backpack to distract his attackers and carried him out of there.

Initially, I'd been planning to do what he asked of me and leave him there to die while I dedicated my life to protecting his woman and son. Instead, something had pulled me back, both to him and to this life. Somehow, I'd known that letting him die would be the end of all things Limaji and I hadn't wanted that. Not for him, not for his unborn child, and not for myself. We had a thousand years of royal blood running through our veins and it hadn't been right to let that go. In fact, I'd never let it go and continued to fight for Erik, for our family, for our people, no matter what it cost me.

For the guy who hadn't even wanted to be a prince, it made no fucking sense. And Erik was right, dammit. It was time to let go because this wasn't getting me anywhere. My need for complete control had started to crumble with Lennox, and that had freaked me out more than anything else.

My entire being had been focused on protecting Casey and Luke, and now Erik and the rest of his family as well. But that wasn't my reality anymore. The truth was that they didn't need me now. Yes, of course Erik needed and wanted me on the team helping rebuild the country in whatever capacity was most useful—something we still hadn't nailed down—but shit happened. Shit would always happen. It was part of life. Especially this life. But it couldn't control us.

It was that fucking simple and I'd ruined the best thing to ever happen to me because I'd been too damn stubborn to see it. Now I had to win her back and I wasn't sure how. The beautiful piece of jewelry I'd bought her for Christmas wasn't right. It was beautiful and had we not broken up, she would have loved it. However, for this, to make up with her, I needed something perfect. And I knew just where to find it. I turned and sprinted back down the stairs towards Erik's office.

42

L*ennox*

CHRISTMAS DAY SHOULD HAVE BEEN great. Harlow showed up less than an hour after I texted her, telling her I was in town, and there was a lot of laughing, hugging and squealing. I hadn't seen her in almost five years, though we exchanged texts and emails fairly regularly, and it was so good to hug her. Vivian was coming for dinner, and I was looking forward to seeing her, even though we weren't close.

"So tell me everything," Harlow said, following me onto the back patio. I'd just poured a third cup of coffee and was staring out at the intracoastal.

"Oh, you know how it is. Girl meets hot guy. Hot guy turns out to be a billionaire prince. Hot guy decides his job is more important than girl. Girl finds out her birth control implant is no longer working. Same shit, different day."

Harlow's eyes rounded. "You're pregnant?"

"I have no idea. I don't feel anything, but it could be as recent as a week. I forgot all about my appointment to replace the implant."

"Are you late?"

I frowned. "I don't get a period with the implant so no way to know. Although I'm assuming I would get it if it stopped working? I don't know. I have to call my doctor's office tomorrow, see if they're open. If they are, I might need to fly out to Vegas to handle this."

"Unless you're already pregnant."

"Yeah. That."

"Are you going to tell him?"

"Well, of course. I couldn't do that to anyone, least of all him. But probably not until after the baby is born because otherwise, he'll want to marry me out of some sense of duty and that shit isn't happening. Fuck that."

"You have to do what's right for you, but I think you should tell him. We definitely need to take a test, though. Like soon."

"We?"

"Well, yeah. That's what sisters are for. I think. I mean, I'm not sure since we didn't really grow up together but that's what sisters do in my head."

"How's Viv?"

She shrugged. "You'll see. She's a pain in the ass. She dropped out of school again."

"Mom said Brad has been getting her back on track."

"Yeah, he paid off the debt she ran up and helped her get a job. He told her he'll pay for it if she goes back to school next year, but she has to keep a 3.0 average and no more partying. I laughed at that, but she seems to like him, so we'll see."

I leaned back, letting the ocean breeze blow through my hair. I was a little sick and a lot sad and mostly overwhelmed, but being here felt right. My mother, in spite of her faults, wasn't a bad person. Brad seemed good for her. I loved Harlow to death and we were together for the first time in years. Everything should have been good. Except for missing Sandor. The baby thing didn't even stress me out that much because I could handle whatever life threw at me. Except missing Sandor. I was having a hell of a time handling that.

"Why don't you get cleaned up?" My mother came out on the patio. "We're going to have some people coming by and I'd like to get some pictures with my girls." She raised a finger when I started to protest. "I love you just the way you are, Lennox, but you know damn well you don't want our first family photos in years to be with you in a ratty old tank top and with your hair up in a messy bun. Go clean up, put on a pretty blouse. That's all I ask."

She was right. If we were taking family photos, I couldn't be dressed like I just rolled out of bed. "All right. I'll jump in the shower."

I WAS ready in less than half an hour since I took the time to dry and curl my hair. I put on a layer of mascara and some lip gloss, but that was the extent of my primping. I'd brought a black denim miniskirt that was both cute and comfortable, and a tank top that had sequins on it since I'd known my mother would want pictures. I slid my feet into black, low-heeled sandals and walked out into the living room.

"Much better." Mom smiled. "Are you hungry?"

I shrugged. "Not really."

"The broken heart diet," Harlow sighed. "Been there, done that. But come on, how about we share a bagel? Just put something in your stomach to soak up that gallon of coffee you've had."

"Yes, Mom," I teased.

Harlow put a bagel in the toaster oven and I poured myself another cup of coffee. Was this the fifth? Sixth? I was drinking way too much caffeine but I had to get through today and the guests that were apparently coming in and out all day.

"I'm sorry there aren't any gifts for you," Mom said, standing beside me. "If I'd known you were coming…"

"It's fine." I smiled. "I don't need anything. Really."

"Maybe we can go shopping tomorrow? You could probably use something practical like new slippers since it gets cold over there, or mascara? Something you don't have much time to shop for?"

I wanted to say no, I didn't need anything, but she was trying really hard to be accepting of my lifestyle and the fact that I wasn't girlie like she was, so that would be bitchy of me. Besides, she was probably right about the slippers—it did get cold in Europe, whether I was in Limaj or Monte Carlo, and I didn't have any.

"Okay. That sounds fun. Can Harlow come too?"

"Like you could keep me away." Harlow giggled.

The buzzer sounded and I straightened my spine a little. I could and would put on a happy face for my mother and Brad's friends. It was just a couple of days and then I'd go back to stoic, professional Lennox for the rest of my life. Unless I was pregnant. I couldn't be stoic or unemotional if I had a baby.

A baby.

Jesus Christ, what fresh hell had I brought on my life? I wasn't ready for a baby.

Was I?

Shit.

I heard voices in the hall but I grabbed half the bagel as it came out of the toaster oven and started to butter it. I turned to ask Harlow if she wanted butter or cream cheese but she'd disappeared, so I figured she knew whoever had arrived. I left her half of the bagel alone and put mine on a plate. I turned, plate in one hand, the bagel in the other as I raised it to my lips to take the first bite, and froze.

Sandor?

Sandor?!

What the hell was Sandor doing in my mother's boyfriend's kitchen in Fort Lauderdale on Christmas Day? How did he even know how to find me? I probably looked ridiculous, standing there with the bagel halfway to my mouth, but I couldn't seem to move.

"Merry Christmas." His deep voice gave me chills and I blinked. He looked incredible in tan slacks, a light blue button-down shirt with a few buttons open at his throat and the sleeves rolled up to his elbows. His hair was down, wavy and a little tousled, about as sexy as I'd ever seen him, his aquamarine eyes trained on me.

"M-merry Christmas." I abruptly put down the plate and the bagel. "What are you doing here?"

"It's Christmas. My girl and I had a fight. I came to apologize."

"Y-you did?" Oh no. I was going to cry. What the fuck was wrong with me?

"I did." He took a step forward. "I was an absolute idiot, Lennox. I'm so sorry."

"I... You are?"

Wow, I was quite verbose today.

He smiled. "I had my priorities mixed up and Erik set me straight. I flew all night so I could tell you."

"You did?"

Okay, I really needed to stop this. I swallowed and finally found my voice. "I mean, yes, you did, but I'm *really* mad at you."

"I know." He reached out a hand. One of those big, strong hands I loved so much. He brushed his knuckles across my cheek, sending a tingling sensation zinging through my body. How did he always do this to me?

Then he dropped to one knee and pulled something out of his pocket. "But I plan to spend the rest of my life making it up to you. If you'll have me."

I stared at him in absolute shock.

This couldn't be happening.

Everything I'd ever dreamed of and a few things I'd never allowed myself to consider were all coming true in the form of a big blond billionaire prince that I loved more than life itself. So why did I feel so weird?

"Lennox? Will you marry me?" He was looking up at me with those beautiful blue eyes and I desperately wanted to say yes but I felt really strange, a little clammy and kind of hot, as if I was having a hot flash. But I was too young for that. Right?

"Honey?" He looked a little concerned now.

Suddenly my world started to swim and I ran from the room, making it to the toilet just in time to empty my stomach. I clenched the sides, hoping I wouldn't pass out, and eventually, as I sat there on my knees, the queasy feeling started to pass.

A warm body moved behind me, Sandor's strong arms closing around me, holding me up.

"Baby, are you okay?"

"I just...need a minute." I was mortified he'd seen me throw up. What had just happened? I never threw up.

Holy shit.

This couldn't be happening.

I closed my eyes.

"I think I'm pregnant," I whispered.

His arms tightened around me and he pulled me close, though my back was pressed against his front, just in case I needed to heave again.

"Really?" His lips were against my ear. "Is that a bad thing?"

"Isn't it?" I turned to him in confusion. "You're not mad?"

"Why would I be mad? Making a baby with the woman I love is my fantasy—remember?" He was smiling again.

"I..." I collapsed against his chest, all the fight draining out of me. I'd been hanging on by a thread, trying to prove how strong I was, but now that he was here, I didn't want to be strong. I just wanted him.

"I'm not mad." He pressed light kisses along my temple. "I'm thrilled. I want to marry you and have as many babies as you'll give me, before I'm too old to enjoy them. I want to renovate Gustafhaven and fill it with all the light and love we can bring to it. I want you, Lennox."

"I want you too," I whispered. "Okay, can you give me a minute to clean up? I feel gross."

"If we're going to spend the rest of our lives together, I don't think you need to hide from me when you're feeling gross."

I managed a tiny smile. "Okay."

He got to his feet and helped me up. I brushed my teeth, gargled with mouthwash and fixed my hair a little. Then I turned and wrapped my arms around his neck. "What are you doing here, Mr. Gustaffson?"

He pulled me close. "I came to propose to my girl. You think she'll say yes?"

"Now that she's not about to puke her guts out anymore, you're going to have to try again. But probably not in the bathroom."

He laughed. "Deal."

"How did you know where I was?"

"Well, I do have some friends in the CIA. It wasn't that hard to get your mother's number, call her and get the address."

I laughed.

We walked back out to the living room where my mother rushed forward worriedly. "Sweetie, are you okay?"

"I guess my nerves got the best of me." I didn't dare mention a baby until we knew for sure. My mother would talk of nothing else if I did.

Then Sandor was on one knee again, holding out this amazing ring... Was that a sapphire? It was as blue as his eyes, set in platinum, and the most beautiful thing I'd ever seen.

"I didn't think a traditional diamond would be the right ring for my very untraditional girl," he said quietly. "And I hope you'll wear it for the rest of your life."

"Longer," I whispered, holding out my left hand, noting that it was shaking a little.

He got up, put the ring on my finger, yanked me against him, and then we were kissing like I hadn't just puked in the bathroom. Apparently, a little mouthwash was all it took for my man to stuff his tongue down my throat.

Mom, Harlow and Brad started clapping and we pulled apart grinning broadly.

"This is the best Christmas ever!" Mom burst into tears.

43

—————

S *andor*

CHRISTMAS TURNED out to be one of the best days I'd ever had in my life. Lennox's mother was sweet, if not a little overbearing, and Brad seemed like a good guy. Harlow was a doll, sweet and beautiful, and seemed to adore her older sister. We talked and laughed throughout the day, meeting a handful of Michelle and Brad's friends who came and went. Lennox's youngest sister, Vivian, showed up for dinner. She was a blonde who'd dyed her hair black, wore too much makeup, and was wearing a tiny little black minidress that was barely appropriate for a nightclub, much less Christmas dinner, but everyone seemed to tiptoe around her so I didn't say anything either.

All in all, we had a great day. Lennox had a feeling she'd thrown up because she'd had too much coffee on a mostly empty stomach combined with nerves and stress. It made sense, but I had to admit I would be over the moon if she was pregnant. I wanted babies with her so much I could taste it. More than one. Maybe four or five. I didn't know how she felt about that, but the urge to have a big family was suddenly overwhelming.

It was after midnight when we finally got to bed, and she curled against me since the full-size bed in the guest room was way too small for me, much less both of us. But it hadn't seemed prudent to leave, so I would suck it up for one night. If we stayed another day, though, we needed to get a hotel because I probably wouldn't relax at all in a bed this size.

"We need to find a drug store tomorrow," she was saying. "I need to know if I'm pregnant because it's kind of freaking me out."

"Is it?" I stroked her hair.

"My job isn't conducive to being pregnant, and think before you say something dumb."

I chuckled. "I understand that and would never tell you to stop working, but I very much want a family. Do you want one with me?"

"I do. But... I don't know how that would work. I couldn't just stop working to stay home and be a mom."

"I think we'll have to work out a new reality, a new plan for our future. I've been thinking about politics."

She smiled. "I see."

"Erik and I are talking about starting a Limaji intelligence agency, like the CIA, and I think I'd like to oversee that. It keeps my finger in the security game, but on a broader level, so that I'm not the one out there dodging bullets, so to speak. And I think you can continue your role as Casey's personal bodyguard, but in a more supervisory position. You could be in charge of maintaining the duty schedule for whoever's protecting her, and of course you could run point if there are outings or other things that require more than everyday protection. That way, you can work but also be home with me and the forty-two babies I want."

She chewed her lip. "I'm thirty-two, thirty-three in March. If you want forty-two, that has me popping them out well into my seventies. I'm not sure about that part."

"Triplets?" I suggested, laughing.

"Maybe." She sighed against my chest. "I couldn't believe the way you just kicked me to the curb. I was having a hard time with it."

"Yeah, well, Erik kicked my ass. You would've loved it."

"Did he? What did he say?"

"Essentially reminded me that a lifetime of sacrifice isn't necessary. Not even for the country and people we love so much. It's time for us to live again. Bad things happen and there's nothing you can do about it other than be diligent, and we are. We were. And then Luke came in and offered to talk to you, to make things right since he heard his dad say it was his fault."

"Oh, poor kid." She shook her head. "It's only been a few days, but I already missed our life together. I missed you so much it was hard to breathe. And then I saw the letter about my implant being expired and all I could think about was all the unprotected sex we've essentially been having."

"I love you," I whispered. "And I want to have all the unprotected sex, all the time."

"You don't really want a bunch of kids, do you?" she asked softly. "I mean, I want a couple...but you sound ready to start our own sports team."

I paused. I really did want a bunch, but I had to be realistic. Neither of us was young from the perspective of starting a family. Me more than her, since I would be turning forty in a few months, but we both had busy careers too. While I wanted to cut back some, it wouldn't be completely, and it didn't sound like Lennox would be either.

"Uh-oh." She turned onto her side to face me. "How many kids are we talking, Sandor?"

I grimaced. "Three?"

"I can do three. But we have to start right away."

"Well, we might have already gotten a head start."

"I'm not ready," she whispered. "I need time with just you, babe. Just us."

"If you're pregnant, we'll make it work. I promise. If not, I can go back to using condoms for a few months, or as much time as you need."

"I also don't want to be pregnant when we get married unless you want to elope tomorrow. I don't know how the country is going to feel about an illegitimate baby."

"They'll get over it. This is about what we want, not the people. I do think we need the big wedding, though. They didn't get it for their king and the people love the pomp and circumstance."

"Can't Daniil and Elen do that for them?"

"Neither of them are in relationships and we need something sooner rather than later. What do you think?"

"If I'm pregnant, that's not going to happen for at least a year. If not, yes, we can plan a big summer wedding."

"I fucking love you, Lennox Briggs." I flipped us over so I was on top of her. "And I need to show you right fucking now."

"Condom?" she whispered, biting her lip.

I dropped my forehead to hers with a sigh. "Oral it is."

WE GOT in her rented convertible the next day and headed to a drug store. We bought the tests but weren't going to use them until tonight, when we were alone at the hotel room I'd reserved. Last night in that bed had sucked and she wanted to stay a couple of more days, so we'd compromised by getting a hotel room. We checked in and dropped off our things, including the pregnancy tests. Then we got back in the car and she dropped me off while Harlow and her mother got in the convertible to go shopping. Brad and I were going golfing, something I hadn't done in years, but it sounded fun and I figured I should get to know the man who would be my father-in-law. Apparently, Michelle and Brad were getting married this spring, so we would be back in Fort Lauderdale in April for that.

It was a nice afternoon and I'd forgotten how much I loved to be outdoors doing something both physical and relaxing. Brad was a lot of fun and very down-to-earth. In some ways, he reminded me of my father, which was an interesting feeling, but it was in a good way.

We all met up for dinner and then Lennox and I took our leave. Though we'd been patient all day, now we were anxious to find out. She seemed nervous when she went into the bathroom but I would be okay no matter what the outcome was. It would be a bummer to go back to using condoms after these last months of not having to, but it wasn't a big deal to me. I'd used condoms my whole life until two months ago, and it had never been a deterrent.

I sensed Lennox wasn't ready for a baby yet, and while it was a little disappointing, it was okay. I loved her and though it felt like I was getting a little old for the parenting thing, she was only thirty-two. We had time.

She came out holding the piece of white plastic in her hand.

"Did you just pee on that and pick it up?" I teased, trying to make her laugh.

She rolled her eyes. "I peed on it, wiped it down and then picked it up. Cretin."

I pulled her onto my lap. "Whatever the result is, we're good. I don't want you to worry. Pregnant or not, we've got this. We're going to start renovating Gustafhaven whether you are or not. If you are, we'll work on the nursery first and plan a wedding for summer after next. If you're not, we'll start planning a June wedding now. Deal?"

"Deal." She rested her head on my chest. Finally, she lifted it again and handed the test to me. "You get to see first."

"Why can't we see together?"

"I want you to see first. I'm too nervous."

"Okay." I took it from her, pressed my lips to hers for a brief but sound kiss, and then looked down.

One line.

Not pregnant.

Damn.

"Summer wedding," I said softly.

"Oh." She practically wilted against me, her relief obvious.

"Do you still want to fly to Vegas to see your ob-gyn?"

"Is there a doctor who can remove the implant in Limaj?"

"I'm sure there is."

"Are you terribly disappointed?"

"Terribly? No. A little, obviously, but now we get to plan a big wedding and then I'm going to knock you up on the honeymoon."

"You know, you say you're not, but you really are a bit of a Neanderthal."

"I'll have to work on that." I kissed her. "In the meantime, I have another Christmas present for you."

"Sandor!" She made a face. "I don't have anything—"

"I don't care." I reached into my wallet and pulled out a few pieces of paper. "This is for you."

She looked confused. "What is this? It looks like a deed, but it's in Limaji and I'm not quite ready to read legal documents."

"It's the deed to the inn you loved."

"The inn?" Her eyes widened. "But we don't have time to run an inn."

I shrugged. "You wanted it. I wanted you to have it. Erik turned it over to me and I signed it over to you. The same rules we discussed before apply, about keeping the integrity of the building intact, but it's not going anywhere. And it's yours. For as long as you want it."

"Oh, Sandor." She kissed me deeply, running her fingers through my hair. "Thank you. This is amazing. I love it. Almost as much as I love you."

"I know." I grinned at her.

She cocked her head. "So...did you make any other purchases at the drug store?"

"I most certainly did." I reached around her for the box of condoms.

"I knew there was a reason I loved you."

"My big dick?"

She sputtered out a laugh. "Well, that's one reason."

"Let's see how much." I toppled us over onto the bed.

EPILOGUE

L *ennox*

RENOVATING a house was a lot of work, but renovating a prince's estate was over-fucking-whelming. Yes, we had contractors. Yes, we had money. But, oh my god, the time and the mess and the decisions. Paint colors for every room, appliances, rugs, carpeting, fixtures... It was like starting over. Parts of it were fun, but mostly it was drudgery. Especially since there weren't a lot of contractors and specialized construction workers available in Limaj in the winter.

Today was Sandor's fortieth birthday and I'd hoped to be able to have a family dinner in our newly renovated dining room as a surprise, but it hadn't happened, so Casey had helped me put together a dinner at the palace. We ate at the palace every night, of course, so it wasn't as special as I'd hoped, but I had a very special gift for him that I hoped would make up for it.

Life since we'd gotten engaged had been incredible. He was everything to me, for me, and with me. Together, it seemed like we could do anything. He was working covertly with Erik, Joe and Ace to create a Limaji intelligence agency and I was in charge of Casey's security. For now, I was still handling it myself, but I was training a local woman we'd found to take over when I was on my honeymoon and going forward when and if I got pregnant. Her name was Natalia and she was great. She'd been part of the Royal Guard but we'd stolen her and now she worked for us. She was only twenty-four but had a good head on her shoulders and was fascinated with the martial arts, so we worked out together regularly. She wasn't quite a black belt, but we were going to bring in someone who could train her until she could test for it.

In the meantime, I was planning a wedding, getting ready to be in my mother's wedding, and renovating a mansion. If I hadn't been happier than I'd ever been, I would have been exhausted.

I dressed for dinner in the pink dress Sandor loved so much. Erik had called him down to his office to keep him busy for a little while so I could get dressed up without him seeing me and then he would join us for dinner. It would be our inner circle, minus the kids since they weren't here, but it was the people we were closest to. Erik, Casey, Daniil, Elen, Jesper, Joe, Xander, Axel and Edita. Edita had been Casey's assistant for several months now and we all loved her. I thought Daniil had a crush on her, but they both denied there was anything between them.

I'd also flown in Sandor's aunt and uncle from Sweden, Lars and Claudia, so he would definitely be surprised about that.

I paced nervously as we waited for Erik and Sandor to arrive, and Casey grabbed my hand. "Would you relax? It's just dinner."

"I know, but it's my first time planning something special for him and I'm so bummed the house wasn't ready."

"He's going to love this, and when he sees your gift, not to mention his aunt and uncle, he's going to be overwhelmed."

"In a good way, I hope."

"Here they come!" Jesper whispered, hurrying back from where he'd been keeping watch.

Erik and Sandor turned the corner and we all yelled, "Surprise!"

Sandor actually jumped and then gave Erik a dirty look before coming over to kiss me.

"Happy birthday, babe," I whispered against his mouth.

"Thank you, you little minx. You know I hate surprises."

"But this is our family." I turned to motion with my head. "Your family."

His eyes widened when he saw his aunt and uncle, and there were a lot of hugs, tears and laughter as he greeted them.

DINNER WAS wonderful and Sandor was almost glowing with happiness. It was a rare sight, seeing him not just relaxed, but emotionally invested in someone other than me or Luke. And I loved knowing it was partly because of me. Our love brought out the best in both of us, everyone noticed, but all I saw was the man I loved so desperately. His demons were subsiding and he was both happy and fulfilled. He had his work but he had the family he'd never wanted to admit he missed.

"This is incredible," he whispered as dinner plates were taken away. "Thank you."

"You're welcome." I reached for a package and handed it to him. "And this is your gift."

"Baby, you're my gift." He kissed me again, something we still did far too often, but not nearly enough in my opinion.

"This is your *birthday* gift."

"This whole party, my aunt and uncle... There's nothing I need."

"It's not about something you need."

Everyone watched as he unwrapped the box. Other than me, only Casey and Erik knew what it was and Sandor looked at me in confusion. "Baby, what is..."

"It was Vardan's," I whispered. "Erik found it in a safe here at the palace and when I asked him for ideas for a birthday gift, he brought it up."

"It's..." He was at a loss for words, something I'd never seen before.

"Turn it over," I said softly.

He turned over Vardan's Rolex, the one Krystal had given him at their engagement party. The original engraving had been, "For my love, with all my heart, Krystal."

Now, it read, "For my love, with all my heart, Krystal and Lennox."

"Damn, baby." He actually swiped at his eyes and then pulled me into his lap, burying his face in my cleavage after he passed the watch to Daniil.

"Do you like it?" I whispered.

"*Do I like it?* It's fucking amazing. Just like you."

"It's kind of like all four of ours now," I said. "Vardan and Krystal's, and yours and mine. So we always keep them close to us."

"I love you." He kissed me with as much passion as he did when we were alone, oblivious to anyone in the room.

When we finally pulled apart, his eyes met mine. "You are my heart," he said softly. "My heart, my soul, my love. I'm so grateful I found you."

"I love you too," I whispered back.

Thank you for reading Sandor and Lennox's story! If you enjoyed it, I hope you'll consider leaving a review at the retailer of your choice. And turn the page for an excerpt from the next book in the series, XANDER.

EXCERPT FROM "XANDER" (ROYAL PROTECTORS BOOK 2, UNEDITED)

Chapter One
Xander

"Are you fucking kidding me?"

The beautiful woman in the bathtub looked like she wanted to stab me. I'd figured today's drill wouldn't go over well, but I hadn't been expecting to find her in the tub. Or fuming mad. Or completely unembarrassed by her naked body, which was on display for me amidst the bubbles skimming the top of the water.

"Let's not do this, okay?" I said amiably. "I have a job to do and—"

"Just get the fuck out and tell Sandor I was in the tub."

"I can't."

"The hell you can't."

"Dammit, Princess, are we going to do this dance every god damn time?" I asked, scowling.

"This is the third drill this week!" she yelled, throwing up her hands and giving me an unimpeded view of her breasts. Which were probably the most beautiful I'd ever seen. Too bad she hated me and I was about to piss her off even more.

"Take it up with your brother," I said, reaching for the big, fluffy towel on the warmer against the wall.

"Get out!" she hissed, glaring at me.

"You know I can't." I held out the towel and averted my eyes, offering her a modicum of modesty. But she only had about two more seconds before I did what I had to do.

"Xander, I'm not going anywhere."

With a resigned sigh, I dropped the towel, reached into the water and scooped her out. I wrapped the towel around her as best I could considering she was cursing a blue streak and swinging at me, and tossed her over my shoulder.

I could have grabbed her bathrobe but she was being a serious pain in my ass and I had a job to do. She knew this. As she'd said, this was the third drill this week and we both knew what was going to happen if she continued to resist doing what she would inevitably do anyway. I was bigger, stronger and extremely well-trained as a bodyguard. She was never going to get away from me, and why she continued this game every time we had a drill was beyond me. This was the first time I'd caught her in the tub, though, which I genuinely felt bad about.

Unfortunately, we were being timed and until Sandor and Joe, who ran security, were pleased with the results, we would continue to do unannounced drills.

"Put me down," she yelled in my ear.

"Why? So you can run away and continue doing everything in your power to avoid the drill?"

"God dammit, it's the middle of winter, I'm soaking wet and naked—put me the fuck down and let me get my clothes."

"That ship has sailed, Princess. Sorry." I took a side stairwell to the first floor, which was different than the ground floor, and headed to the newest hidden door that led to one of the palace tunnels. We'd been practicing every route, every exit, every possible option for escape the last few weeks, and though everyone was tired of it, no one more so than me.

"I'm going to fucking kill you in your sleep!" she growled when we got to the tunnel.

"I look forward to the challenge," I grunted.

Finally, as we rounded the corner and joined the others, I set her on her feet.

"You're late," Sandor said in a stern voice, though the tick in his cheek belied the fact that he was about to laugh since I'd had to throw Elen over my shoulder on more than one occasion.

His sister, otherwise known as Princess Elen Gustaffson or the biggest pain in my ass, whirled around, gripping the towel around her. "What the fuck, Sandor?! Are you kidding me with this shit?"

He sighed. "Elen, you know—"

"I've been working eighty-hour weeks trying to put the important elements of the new education bill into action," she snapped, her chest rising and falling with what appeared to be exertion. "I don't sleep, I haven't had a day off in months, and I found out this morning I've got walking pneumonia!" She turned to King Erik, her first cousin, and pointed her finger. "You have to choose. If you want me working as the Minister of Education, and doing it twenty-four-seven, enough with the drills."

Erik turned to her, his voice quiet as he said, "Once the drill is over, we'll take this up in private, in my office. Until then, you need to calm down."

"I'm standing here in a fucking towel. You calm down." She gripped it tighter around her. "And the drill is over for me. I'm going back upstairs." She turned on her heel, pushed past me and toward the exit.

I looked to Erik but he shook his head, indicating to let her go.

"She has walking pneumonia?" Sandor asked quietly. "And no one knew?"

There was a moment of guilty silence as the members of the royal family and the rest of the security team looked at each other. We were a close-knit group, even though I was nothing but a blue-collar kid from Michigan who'd lucked into the job of a lifetime working with this amazing family.

"Was she actually in the bath?" Sandor asked after a moment.

"I tried to get her to get out on her own and get her robe. She said she wasn't coming." I looked at Erik, whom I didn't have to address formally when we weren't in public. "You said I wasn't to take no for an answer."

He sighed. "Yeah, I know. But I didn't know she had pneumonia. Fuck. This is on me and Sandor. All right, the time tonight was really good aside from Xander and Elen, but that wasn't logistical—that was personal. I'll talk to her about this after she's had time to cool off. For everyone else, thank you for putting up with the constant interruptions to your schedules and time. We have to be prepared for anything and the only way to do it is to know the plan, escape routes and contingencies like the backs of our hands."

Everyone ambled back toward the stairs that would take us up to the palace, and I fell into step beside Sandor.

"You can't keep doing this to me, man," I told him. "I always look like the slacker and it's not fair. She was literally in the bathtub and I had to walk in on her naked. Yeah, in an emergency I wouldn't think twice, but this was the third drill in seven days and she was more pissed than I've ever seen her."

"I know." Sandor nodded, giving me an understanding smile. "Erik and I will talk to her. This isn't on you.

*****

Xander and Elen's story is coming soon! Sign up for my newsletter and you'll never miss a release or pre-order.

www.KatMizera.com